<u>INSPECTOR HADLEY</u>

THE HOLY GRAIL MURDERS

by

PETER CHILD

Benbow Publications

© Copyright 2011 by Peter Child

Peter Child has asserted his right under the Copyright, Designs and Patents Act, 1988 to be identified as the author of this work.

All rights reserved. No part of this publication may be reproduced, stored in a retrieval system, or transmitted in any form or by any means, electronic, mechanical photocopying, recording or otherwise without the prior permission of the copyright holder.

Published in 2011 by Benbow Publications

British Library
Cataloguing in Publication Data.

ISBN: 978-0-9558063-4-6

Printed by Lightning Source UK Ltd
Chapter House
Pitfield
Kiln Farm
Milton Keynes
MK11 3LW

First Edition

OTHER TITLES BY THE AUTHOR

ERIC THE ROMANTIC

ERIC AND THE DIVORCEE

<u>THE MICHEL RONAY SERIES:</u>

MARSEILLE TAXI
AUGUST IN GRAMBOIS
CHRISTMAS IN MARSEILLE
CATASTROPHE IN LE TOUQUET
RETURN TO MARSEILLE

<u>THE INSPECTOR HADLEY SERIES:</u>

THE TAVISTOCK SQUARE MURDERS
THE GOLD BULLION MURDERS
THE TOWER OF LONDON MURDERS
THE AMERICAN MURDERS
THE DIAMOND MURDERS
THE ROYAL RUSSIAN MURDERS
THE SATAN MURDERS
THE MEDICAL MURDERS
THE WESTMINSTER MURDERS
THE GIGOLO MURDERS

<u>NON-FICTION</u>

NOTES FOR GOOD DRIVERS
NOTES FOR COMPANY DRIVERS
VEHICLE PAINTER'S NOTES
VEHICLE FINE FINISHING
VEHICLE FABRICATIONS IN GRP

ACKNOWLEDGEMENTS

Once again, I wish to acknowledge the help and assistance given to me by Sue Gresham, who formatted and edited this book and Wendy Tobitt for the excellent cover presentation. Without these talented and patient ladies this book would not have been possible.

Peter Child

INTRODUCTION

One morning in May 1882, Inspector James Hadley left his comfortable home in Camden and hailed a Hansom cab to take him to Scotland Yard. No sooner had he arrived in his office than the Commissioner sent for him and Chief Inspector Bell, ordering an urgent inquiry into the recent hideous murder of an ex-army man living in Islington. He told the officers that the Bishop of London had received a letter from the victim informing him that a priceless religious relic had been discovered and requesting an urgent meeting. As Hadley and Sergeant Cooper begin the investigation, the victim's brother is found strangled at his lodgings in Whitechapel and from then on, the detectives play a dangerous game with the maniacal murderer, whilst trying to recover the mysterious priceless relic...

Characters and events portrayed in this book are fictional.

CHAPTER 1

It was a bright Monday morning in May when Inspector James Hadley left his home in Plender Street, Camden and hailed a passing Hansom cab to take him to Scotland Yard. The traffic was fairly light until the cab reached Trafalgar Square where a number of omnibuses were causing delays after a slight accident. It appeared that a horse had bolted and dragged a cab into the side of one of the omnibuses, badly damaging it. Other drivers and their conductors had stopped to assist fraught and distressed passengers. Hadley became impatient and glancing at his fob watch realised that he would not be in his office until after eight. He was always punctual and it did not suit him to be even a minute late so he decided to leave the cab and walked briskly across the Square to the top of Whitehall where he hailed another cab to take him the rest of the way to Scotland Yard. He had a feeling that something important was in the offing - his case book had been quite light since his investigation into the Gigolo murders.

Hadley arrived in his office as Big Ben finished striking eight o'clock and was greeted by his affable clerk, George.

'Good morning, sir.'

'Morning, George,' replied Hadley and a few minutes later Sergeant Cooper arrived.

'Morning, sir… George… I'm sorry I'm a bit late sir but…' began Cooper.

'No need to apologise, Sergeant,' interrupted Hadley with a smile 'these days things often happen in our busy capital that cause some delay.'

'There's too many people here if you ask me, sir,' said George 'they're flooding in from the country, as well as all the blimmin' foreigners, they're causing no end of problems in the streets… holding us all up they are.'

'You're possibly right, George,' said Hadley as he sat behind his desk.

'I expect you could to do with a nice pot of tea to start the day, sir,' said George.

'Yes, I could,' replied Hadley and the clerk hurried off to his adjacent office.

Hadley glanced casually through the files on his desk but nothing required his immediate action, Cooper made notes regarding a minor arrest he had made the previous day. The detectives remained silent until George appeared with the tea tray. He had just put Hadley's cup on his desk when Mr Brackley, the Commissioner's assistant, entered the office.

'Good morning Inspector Hadley.'

'Morning Mr Brackley.'

'The Commissioner would like to see you immediately, sir,' said Brackley with a slight nod.

'Very well, Mr Brackley, I'll come straight away,' replied Hadley, standing up and following the assistant out of the office. George looked at Cooper as he put his cup down and said 'I'll make him a fresh pot when he gets back, sir.'

'Yes, thank you, George, if you would,' said Cooper with a smile.

When Hadley knocked and entered the Commissioner's office, Chief Inspector Howard Bell was already seated in front of the great one.

'Morning, Hadley.'

'Good morning, sir... Chief Inspector,' replied Hadley as the Commissioner waved him to sit. They waited for a few moments whilst the Commissioner looked at the papers on his desk, then he raised his head and said 'what I am about to tell you must remain secret until I say otherwise, on no account disclose anything to anyone... is that clearly understood?'

'Yes, sir,' they murmured in chorus and waited for the great one to begin. The Commissioner cleared his throat and said 'early this morning, the body of a man named William Porter was discovered in lodgings in Islington. He had been hideously tortured before being strangled by his killer. Normally the investigating officer at Islington would be left to follow his own inquiries and arrest the person responsible for the murder, however, there is a most disturbing aspect to this case. The Bishop of London, Lord Stillwell, received a letter from Porter stating that he knew of the recent discovery of a priceless religious relic and he wanted to meet the Bishop in secret to discuss the matter.'

'Do we know what the relic is, sir?' asked Bell.

'No, Chief Inspector, we don't, but after their meeting the Bishop contacted me and informed me of his concerns but told me little else,' replied the Commissioner.

'Does the Bishop know that Porter has been murdered, sir?' asked Hadley.

'No, not yet, Inspector, I intend to inform him when he arrives here this afternoon and I want you both to be present at the meeting.'

'Very good, sir,' said Bell.

'The Bishop's appointment with me is at three o'clock. Meanwhile, Hadley, I want you to go to Islington and take over the inquiry from Inspector Barker, he has been informed by telegraph that you are coming, then go to the Marylebone where Doctor Evans has the victim... find out all you can and report back to me before the Bishop arrives,' said the Commissioner.

'Right, sir,' replied Hadley.

'And Chief Inspector, I want you to make this investigation your top priority, start making inquiries into Porter's background, keep everything under constant review and report any developments to me immediately.'

'Very good, sir,' said Bell with a nod.

'I cannot over emphasise the importance of this investigation and to add further weight to the matter, I must inform you that the Bishop has already spoken to his Grace the Archbishop of Canterbury about this priceless relic.'

'Good heavens,' whispered Bell.

'Go about your duties, gentlemen, as quick as you like!' said the Commissioner.

Twenty minutes later Hadley and Cooper were in a closed Police coach heading for Islington. Hadley explained to Cooper that they were taking over the inquiry into the murder of Porter at the Commissioner's request, but said no more, which left the Sergeant wondering.

'Is it something top secret, sir?'

'Yes it is, but I will be able to reveal all to you when the Commissioner gives his permission, which I think will be sooner rather than later, Sergeant,' replied Hadley with a smile.

'It sounds intriguing, sir.'

'It does indeed, now make careful notes of everything when we get to Islington.'

'Very good, sir.'

Inspector Barker welcomed the detectives to his drab, but tidy, office at the station and invited them to sit.

'I was a little surprised to receive the telegraph message from the Commissioner this morning informing me that you were taking over the inquiry into Porter's murder, do you know why that is, Hadley?' asked Barker anxiously.

'I'm sure it's no reflection on your competence, Inspector, I think it's just a new procedure that's been put in place for a murder where torture has been inflicted on the victim,' replied Hadley diplomatically, hoping that his answer would satisfy Barker.

'Well I'm relieved to hear it,' said Barker with a smile.

'So what do we know about this person?' asked Hadley.

'His name is William Porter, an ex-army man, lodging at 12 Gaskin Street, just up from 'The Angel' pub. His landlady, Mrs Dawkins, discovered his body first thing this morning and sent for us immediately. When we arrived she was in a dreadful state and I realised why when I saw the body,' replied Barker, hesitating for a moment.

'Go on,' said Hadley.

'Porter was naked and had been tied to a chair... he had a ligature around his neck, his eyes were bulging and his tongue was hanging out. Horrible sight I must say... but the worse thing was his skin... it had been flayed off his chest and was hanging down in strips, blood was everywhere... he must have been killed by a maniac.'

Cooper whispered 'good God.'

'Did the landlady see or hear anything?' asked Hadley.

'No she didn't, because after giving Porter his tea last night, she went out at about seven to a music hall and when she returned at eleven o'clock, she went straight to bed,' replied Barker.

'Then we know he was murdered between those times,' said Hadley.

'Yes.'

'Is there anybody else living at the address who might have seen or heard something?'

'No, Mrs Dawkins is a widow and Porter was her only lodger,' replied Barker.

'What did you find in his room?' asked Hadley.

'I haven't searched it yet because I haven't had the time... I was more concerned with getting the body to the Marylebone for Doctor Evans... then after I telegraphed the Yard to report the murder, I received the message back from the Commissioner saying that you'd be taking over the investigation,' replied Barker.

'Right.'

'I thought I best leave it all to you... seeing that you're in charge now,' said Barker.

'Quite so, well let's get to Gaskin Street and see what we can find,' said Hadley.

When the detectives arrived at the address the constable stationed outside the terraced house saluted and opened the door for them.

'When we've finished in Porter's room I'd like a quick word with Mrs Dawkins,' said Hadley as Barker led them along the corridor and up the narrow stairs to the landing.

'She's not here at the moment, she's gone to stay with her sister in Camden until we've finished our inquiries,' replied Barker as he opened the door to the room. They stood in the doorway for a moment surveying the dreadful scene before them.

The room had been ransacked and on the blood soaked carpet was a wooden chair, still hanging from the arms and legs were short ropes that had been cut to release the body. Hadley could smell the stench of sweat and blood as he entered the small room and glanced around at the disarray. Cooper followed him and they began searching for any clue that might give a lead to the killer's identity, Barker remained in the doorway.

On the small table next to the single bed, Hadley found a crumpled, bloodstained letter which he read aloud. *'Dear Billy, I'm glad to hear that you are settled at last. Jane and me look forward to seeing you next Sunday for lunch when you can tell us all about your good fortune, yours truly, your brother Edward.'*

'A useful lead, sir,' said Cooper.

'Yes, Sergeant, and at the top of the note we have his address in Whitechapel,' said Hadley placing the letter in his pocket.

'Will we be going there to inform him of the murder, sir?'

'No, we haven't time just now... I have to report to the Commissioner. When we get back to the Yard I'll telegraph Inspector Palmer at Whitechapel and ask him to relay the sad news, we'll talk to Edward later and find out what he knows about Porter's good fortune,' replied Hadley as he wondered if Edward knew about the religious relic.

'I could go to Whitechapel for you, sir,' said Cooper.

'You'll have to stay with me, Sergeant because I need you to help write up an urgent report,' replied Hadley.

'Very good, sir.'

The detectives searched the room carefully but found nothing of any relevance, which concerned Hadley.

'Whoever murdered Porter, were obviously looking for something and unfortunately we don't know if they found it or not,' said Hadley, thinking about the relic.

'They, sir?'

'Yes Sergeant, there must have been at least two assailants to overpower the victim before tying him to the chair,' replied Hadley.

'Possibly a gang of ruffians, sir?'

'Somehow I don't think so. When we get back to the station we'll send a telegraph to Jack Curtis at the Yard asking him to bring his photographic paraphernalia up here to record the scene,' said Hadley.

'Right, sir.'

'I don't think we can do any more here at the moment,' said Hadley

Returning to the Police station Hadley thanked Barker for his help and said goodbye to the relieved Inspector, whilst Cooper telegraphed Jack Curtis. The detectives climbed aboard the Police coach and Hadley ordered the driver to take them to the Marylebone Hospital as quickly as possible.

Doctor Edward Evans was the senior Metropolitan Police pathologist and had held the post for many years. He was always pleased to see Hadley and Cooper as he regarded them as intelligent officers with whom he could liaise without having to explain everything in laborious detail, which was a problem when dealing with their less enlightened colleagues from the Yard.

'Morning, Jim... Sergeant,' said Evans when the detectives entered his office in the hospital morgue.

'Morning, Doctor,' replied Hadley and Cooper in chorus.

'I suppose you've come to see the poor wretch who was brought in first thing,' said Evans as he stood up from his desk.

'You're absolutely right as usual,' said Hadley with a smile.

'I'm never wrong, Jim, and you should know that by now,' Evans said with a grin as he led the way out into the cold, white tiled dissecting room. He uncovered the body of Porter, which was laid out on a marble slab and the detectives looked down in horror at the tortured mess. Hadley remained silent but Cooper whispered 'good God Almighty.'

'My preliminary investigation showed that he probably died by strangulation but I cannot rule out shock from torture and blood loss as the cause, Jim,' said Evans.

'I can see why,' murmured Hadley.

'He would have suffered an excruciatingly painful death, Jim.'

'Why would anyone want to torture him this way, sir?'

'For information, Sergeant,' replied Hadley.

'Well, if that's the case, then to have endured so much pain before he died, this man certainly had something very important to hide from his killer,' said Evans.

'Have you seen this type of injury before, Doctor?'

'Only once, Jim, it was many years ago when I had just started working for the Met. The victim was a Chinese man living in Aldgate, he'd been flayed alive by a Triad gang for stealing opium from them, his body was stripped of skin just about all over... it was a terrible mess,' replied Evans.

'Blimmin'' foreigners,' mumbled Cooper.

'Were the killers caught and brought to justice?' asked Hadley.

'I don't think so, Jim, if I remember correctly, the main suspects escaped back to China.'

Hadley 'tut-tutted' before asking 'can you tell us anything else, Doctor?'

'Not really, Jim, I'm afraid you'll have to wait until I've

completed a full autopsy on our friend here,' replied Evans.

'Very well, but can you get an interim report to me as soon as possible?' asked Hadley.

'What's the hurry, Jim?'

'The Commissioner is taking a personal interest in this case, Doctor,' replied Hadley.

'Oh well, if the great one is involved then of course the answer must be 'yes', Jim, but what's it all about?'

'I'm afraid I can't tell you,' replied Hadley with a grin.

'Bloody hell… it must be serious then,' said Evans.

'Believe me, it is,' said Hadley.

The detectives hurried back to the Yard where Hadley wrote a note to Jack Palmer at Whitechapel Police station requesting he notified Edward Porter of his brother's murder.

George took it up to the telegraph office whilst Hadley and Cooper began writing the report for the Commissioner. As they finished compiling Cooper's notes Big Ben struck noon and when George arrived back Hadley asked him to type up the report as quickly as he could. The clerk had now become quite proficient on the new American typewriter and soon finished the task, in duplicate. Hadley read through it, signed the document and copy, placed them in folders and told George to take the top copy to the Commissioner's office and the duplicate to the Chief.

'Very good, sir,' said George as Hadley gave him the folders.

'And on your way down, please go to the canteen and get some sandwiches for lunch then make us a nice pot of tea,' said Hadley.

'Yes, sir… may I ask if you've had a moment to consider my request for an assistant?' asked George with a smile.

'I'm afraid it's out of the question George, the Chief Inspector tells me that we are stretched as never before with the Government's financial cut backs,' replied Hadley.

'That's a pity sir, if I may say so,' said George.

'You may. Now I think I'll have cheese and pickle today,' said Hadley and Cooper called out 'make that two please, George.' The clerk sighed and nodded.

It was just after two o'clock when Mr Jenkins, Chief Inspector Bell's clerk, entered and told Hadley that the Chief wished to see him. In the corridor outside his office Hadley met Jack Curtis carrying a folder 'I've got the photographs from Islington, sir... shall I put them on your desk?'

'Ah, well done, Jack you're just in time... I'm on my way to see the Chief so I'll take them now, thank you,' replied Hadley.

'Very good, sir.'

Chief Inspector Bell looked up from his paper strewn desk and nodded at Hadley before inviting him to sit in the creaking chair.

'I've read your report Hadley and it doesn't tell me much,' said Bell.

'Well at the moment there's not a lot to tell, sir.'

'I'm sure the Commissioner will be as frustrated as I am at the lack of any positive leads in this investigation,' said Bell.

'Possibly, sir... I have the photographs of the crime scene here and perhaps you would care to see them,' said Hadley.

'Of course, Inspector,' replied Bell and Hadley placed the folder on his desk.

Bell glanced at the sepia tint photographs and slowly shook his head at each one.

'The killer must be some kind of maniac and I'm surprised nobody saw or heard anything, Hadley.'

'I agree, sir, and I'm sure that there must have been at least two assailants.'

'Well the sooner we arrest these killers and get them into court for a quick trial before we hang them the better,' said Bell.

'Quite so, sir.'

'We are a civilised society and you know, Hadley, our system of fair justice is the envy of the world.'

'Indeed it is, sir.'

'Thank God we've been able to bring such enlightenment to our Empire,' said Bell as he leaned back in his chair and gazed at the ceiling.

'Have you been able to find out much about Porter's background, sir?' asked Hadley, which brought his Chief back to reality.

'Ah, yes... that's why I sent for you,' replied Bell before he shuffled some folders on his desk.

'Any information will be helpful, sir.'

'Of course, Inspector, here it is… you may like to read it before we see the Commissioner at three,' said Bell, as he handed the folder to Hadley there was a knock at the door and Cooper entered the office.

'I'm sorry to disturb you, sir, but this telegraph message just came in for Inspector Hadley and I think it is very important that he sees it,' said Cooper as he handed the buff envelope to Hadley.

'Read it out then, Hadley,' said Bell.

'Right, sir,' he replied as he took out the message and read *Inspector Hadley, following your request to advise Edward Porter of his brother's murder I went to the given address in Turner Street and after gaining access to the lodgings discovered the mutilated body of an un-identified man believed to be that of Edward Porter. Your attendance at the crime scene would be appreciated, yours Inspector Jack Palmer.'*

'Good God, Hadley… these maniacs must be caught!'

'Yes of course, sir… Sergeant.'

'Yes, sir?'

'Find Jack Curtis and take him with you to Whitechapel and tell Inspector Palmer that I am in a meeting with the Commissioner but will join him as soon as I'm free,' said Hadley.

'Very good, sir,' replied Cooper with a nod before he left the office.

'I think we'd better get upstairs, Hadley and report this latest unwelcome news to the Commissioner before the Bishop of London arrives,' said Bell.

CHAPTER 2

Chief Inspector Bell gave a succinct account to the Commissioner regarding the latest developments in the case and when Hadley handed Jack Palmer's message to him, reporting the discovery of the mutilated body in Whitechapel, the Commissioner's side whiskers bristled.

'This investigation is going to be difficult and we need fast progress to a successful conclusion, gentlemen,' said the great one.

'Yes of course, sir,' said Bell and Hadley nodded.

'I trust that Lord Stillwell will be able to throw some light on the matter which will assist our inquiries,' said the Commissioner.

'It would be helpful if his Lordship tells us everything he knows, sir and holds nothing back for any obscure reasons,' said Hadley.

'Indeed, Hadley, but we must be mindful of his position, he may be bound by religious confidences which make it quite impossible for him to speak freely. After all, we don't know what his Grace the Archbishop has said to him,' said the Commissioner.

'As you say, sir, this case is going to be difficult, so at the outset I would like to request the assistance of another officer,' said Hadley.

'Have you anyone in mind, Inspector?'

'Yes sir, Sergeant Talbot, he is very reliable and has been a great help to me in the past,' replied Hadley.

'Very well, please see to it Chief Inspector,' said the Commissioner.

'Yes, sir.'

'And I would also like your permission to tell my men what this investigation is all about, sir,' said Hadley. Bell glared open mouthed at Hadley, whilst the Commissioner's whiskers bristled once more, which was not a good sign.

'Let me be rightly understood, Inspector... I gave you an order to keep the details of this inquiry secret until I give my permission for you to confide in your men.'

'I believe that the time has now arrived, sir,' said Hadley.

'Inspector you go too far!' thundered the Commissioner as Bell looked on in horror.

'With all due respect, sir, I must request that you give me permission, it is simply a matter of operational necessity,' said Hadley.

Bell glared at Hadley and said angrily 'I've never heard such nonsense! The Commissioner has given us an order which must be obeyed at all times and never questioned!'

'Quite so, Chief Inspector,' said the Commissioner and there followed a few moments of shocked silence before Brackley entered, just as Big Ben struck three o'clock and announced 'Bishop Stillwell has arrived, sir.'

'Please show his Lordship in,' said the Commissioner as they all stood.

Bishop Stillwell strode into the office looking resplendent in his frock coat, clerical collar, silk top hat and gaiters. He was carrying a silver topped ebony cane which he tapped impatiently on the floor when he was standing in front of the Commissioner's desk.

'Good afternoon, my Lord.'

'Good afternoon, Commissioner.'

'May I present Chief Inspector Bell and Inspector Hadley,' the Commissioner waved his hand towards them. Stillwell looked hard at both officers before he said 'I thought our meeting was to be in private, Commissioner.'

'These two officers are leading the inquiry, sir and I'm afraid they must remain to hear what you have to say, but I can assure your Lordship that they have been sworn to secrecy,' replied the Commissioner.

'Oh very well then,' said Stillwell with a resigned sigh.

'Please be seated, sir,' said the Commissioner and Stillwell removed his top hat and sat down.

'I've brought the letter that I received from William Porter and after my first meeting with him, I showed it to his Grace the Archbishop.' Stillwell produced an envelope from his inside pocket and placed it on the edge of the Commissioner's desk.

'Thank you, sir, but before we discuss the matter any further, it is my duty to inform you that William Porter has been found murdered and…'

'Murdered!' interrupted Stillwell in surprise.

'I'm afraid so, sir,' said the Commissioner.

'May God preserve us,' whispered Stillwell.

'Initial reports indicate that he was tortured before he died.'

'It's the work of the very devil,' said the shocked Bishop.

'Possibly, my Lord... we believe that two assailants carried out the attack and it is obvious that they were looking for something,' said the Commissioner.

'Oh, dear God Almighty... I think that is probably true,' said Stillwell.

'Now, would you please relate everything you told me previously and leave nothing out, sir?' asked the great one. The Bishop gave a slight nod, cleared his throat and said 'two weeks ago I received this letter from William Porter, it is self explanatory but perhaps I should read it aloud for the benefit of your officers, Commissioner.'

'If you would, sir,' replied the great one as Stillwell picked up the envelope took out the letter then read *'Dear Bishop Stillwell, as an important man of the cloth, I thought you would be interested in something of great religious importance that has recently been discovered. It would be in our mutual interest to meet as soon as possible to discuss the matter and I look forward to hearing from your Lordship in due course, signed William Porter.'*

'Please say what happened next, sir,' said the Commissioner.

'My curiosity was aroused and so I wrote to Porter inviting him to come to Lambeth Palace immediately and he duly arrived the next day. Our meeting was quite brief but he said that he knew where this priceless relic was hidden and for a substantial sum of money he was prepared to tell me where it could be found.'

'May I ask what amount of money he demanded, sir?' asked the Commissioner and the Bishop hesitated before replying 'he wanted a hundred thousand pounds.' Bell gasped, Hadley looked surprised and the Commissioner sat open mouthed for an instant before asking 'did Porter say what this relic was, sir?'

'Yes, he told me at our second meeting, just over a week ago, Commissioner,' replied Stillwell.

'And what is it, sir?'

'I'm afraid I am not at liberty to say, Commissioner.'

'Why not?' asked the great one in a firm tone with his side whiskers bristling.

'After I told his Grace the Archbishop what the relic was, he gave me strict instructions to remain silent about it and I must obey his wishes,' replied Stillwell.

'I believe that what his Grace said to you about this relic is now redundant as Porter has been murdered and I have just received a report that his brother has also been found murdered in the same cruel fashion.'

'Oh, dear God Almighty,' said the Bishop.

'So I advise you most strongly to tell us everything you know, sir, so we may apprehend these maniacs before they claim your good self as their next victim!' said the Commissioner in an angry tone. The Bishop went pale as the colour drained from his face and his jaw dropped.

'May God preserve me,' whispered Stillwell.

'I'm sure he will in the long term, sir, but I know that the good Lord will possibly require some assistance from the Metropolitan Police in the matter of your immediate preservation,' said the Commissioner and Hadley wanted to cheer.

'Yes… yes, quite so, Commissioner,' stammered the Bishop.

'My officers need every single piece of information you have to lead them quickly to the killers and presumably you will also want them to discover where this relic is hidden,' said the Commissioner.

'Yes… of course… it is vital… absolutely vital,' he replied with wide eyed conviction.

'Well, sir, what is this relic?'

'May I speak to his Grace before answering that, Commissioner?' asked Stillwell. The great one stared at the frightened Bishop and replied in a menacing tone 'if you must, sir, but be advised that speed is of the essence and as I now consider your personal safety to be in jeopardy I would be failing in my duty if I did not protect you with armed officers from now on.'

'Oh dear God… this dreadful nightmare is all so unexpected,' whispered the Bishop.

'I can assure you that we face the unexpected daily, my Lord, but I must press you to reconsider your position and tell us everything you know to ensure my officers have some leads, however tenuous, to help track these killers down and recover your relic,' said the Commissioner firmly. The Bishop looked stunned and sat for a moment to compose himself.

'Very well, but before I say anything more, I must insist that you all, as English Christian gentlemen, give me your solemn undertaking that you will not disclose to anyone what I am about to tell you,' said Stillwell firmly.

'I'm afraid we cannot give such an undertaking because supporting officers may have to be told the background to the investigation, but I can assure you, my Lord, that we'll take every precaution to see that as much as possible remains confidential,' said the Commissioner. Stillwell looked decidedly unhappy but realised that he was in a difficult position and reluctantly gave way.

He sighed, cleared his throat and said 'when Porter came to meet me the second time it was to discover if the Church had agreed to his demand for a hundred thousand pounds for the relic.'

'And had it?' asked the Commissioner.

'Yes, his Grace had given his consent for the payment to be made,' replied Stillwell and the officers were taken aback and gasped.

'Good heavens... did you know what the relic was when you agreed to Porter's demand?' asked the Commissioner.

'No, we didn't,' replied Stillwell.

'On reflection didn't you think that was a trifle foolish, my Lord?'

'You may see it that way but Porter said quite categorically that if the Church of England didn't agree to his demand then he would take the information to the Vatican, where he was certain that the Pope would pay him handsomely for this priceless relic.'

'Blackmail,' whispered the Commissioner.

'Quite so. His Grace the Archbishop said that we could not allow that to happen under any circumstances,' replied Stillwell and the Commissioner looked stunned at the disclosure.

'I see,' said the great one slowly.

'And now, when I tell you what the relic is, you'll all agree that his Grace made the right decision,' said Stillwell.

'Please continue, my Lord.'

'It is the Holy Grail.'

'Good heavens,' whispered the Commissioner.

'Porter said that the Holy Grail existed because he had seen it and knew where it was hidden,' said Stillwell as the officers sat in stunned silence. The Commissioner glanced at Bell and Hadley, who were wide eyed with surprise, before he asked 'did Porter give you any indication where the Grail may be hidden, sir?'

'I'm afraid not, Commissioner,' replied Stillwell.

'May I ask, sir, did he say if anyone else knew of its whereabouts?' asked Hadley.

'No, Inspector, he told me absolutely nothing and only asked that the money be paid in cash and then he would disclose where it could be found,' replied Stillwell.

'Did you intend to trust him, my Lord?' asked the Commissioner.

'Yes I did, because he said that he would remain at Lambeth Palace as surety until the Grail was recovered and brought to me in secret,' replied Stillwell.

'Did he say how this was to be accomplished, sir?'

'Yes, he gave me an outline which I discussed with his Grace, and it was all agreed.'

'Please go on, sir,' said the Commissioner.

'Porter told me that he would come to Lambeth Palace this Wednesday and give me the final details of its hiding place. He suggested that two armed men, whom I could trust, should undertake the recovery of the Grail and that they would be away for at least four days and should have sufficient money for their travelling expenses,' said Stillwell.

'Did he give you any idea where this journey would take your men, sir?' asked Hadley.

'No, Inspector, but as he did not specify that they should carry passports then I believe it is likely that the Grail is in this country,' replied Stillwell.

'If that is the case it would be most helpful because in my experience foreign Police authorities leave much to be desired in such important matters,' said the Commissioner.

'Quite so, sir,' said Bell with a nod.

'Four days travelling would mean it's either in Scotland, Wales or the West Country,' said Hadley.

'I'm sure that is the case, Inspector. Now gentlemen, if I give you a brief history of the Grail, I believe it may be of help,' said Stillwell.

'If you would, my Lord,' said the Commissioner.

'As I'm sure you all know, the Grail is believed to have been used by our Saviour at the last supper and then Joseph of Arimathea used it to collect the blood of Christ at his crucifixion. It was not mentioned again until the Knights Templar returned from Jerusalem after the first crusade when it was rumoured that they had discovered the Grail and brought it back to France. There is no record of its whereabouts until 1312 when King Philip IV abolished the Templar's and raided their bank in Paris searching for gold and the Grail, but his men found nothing. At that time the Knights Templar had a fleet of ships at anchor in La Rochelle and it is rumoured that they sailed away to Scotland with all their gold and of course the Holy Grail. Robert the Bruce welcomed them and gave them sanctuary but nothing was ever heard of the Grail again. It is rumoured that it was taken back to France by a select band of Templar's after King Philip died, but as far as I know there is no written evidence to support this. So it may be that the Grail is still in Scotland, as I do believe, or it could be in France, which I doubt, but it appears that somehow William Porter knew where it is hidden.'

'And his killers knew that he had that information and used torture to try and discover its whereabouts,' said the Commissioner.

'It would seem so,' said Stillwell.

'If he has told them, then we have a race on our hands to find it before they do, sir,' said Bell.

'I don't think the killers know, sir,' said Hadley.

'What makes you so sure about that, Hadley?' asked Bell.

'Because his brother has been found tortured and killed in the same way, so it is reasonable to assume that the murderers are still searching for the information, sir.'

'I agree, Hadley, so we must follow up every line of inquiry, interview everyone who knew Porter or his brother to establish any link with the killers,' said the Commissioner.

'Very good, sir,' said Hadley.

'And if you need more resources I will sanction them, Hadley,' said the great one.

'Thank you, sir.'

'I'm sure that won't be necessary, sir, after all you have agreed to Sergeant Talbot assisting Hadley, and surely one officer is more than enough,' said Bell.

'Chief Inspector, I believe we have a major investigation before us which may well go to the very heart of what we know and believe in this Christian society of ours. Can you imagine what Mr Gladstone would have to say to Her Majesty and the country if we failed in our duty to apprehend the killers and find the Holy Grail through the lame excuse of lack of manpower?' thundered the Commissioner and Hadley watched Bell visibly shrink in his chair.

'No, sir, you're quite right as usual,' whispered Bell.

'I'm glad we can at least agree on that, Chief Inspector,' said the Commissioner and Hadley tried to hide a grin.

'Yes of course, sir,' said Bell sheepishly.

'Now Chief Inspector, select two armed officers to escort Bishop Stillwell at all times and instruct the Watch Office to organise a rota of armed men for his ongoing protection until we have apprehended these murderers,' said the Commissioner.

'Very good, sir.'

'Am I really in imminent danger, Commissioner?' asked Stillwell.

'I believe that you may be sir, and in my experience it is always better to take all necessary precautions at such critical times,' replied the great one.

'What about the personal safety of his Grace the Archbishop?' asked Stillwell.

'He must be informed of the murders of Porter and his brother then similarly protected by armed officers as your good self, my Lord,' replied the Commissioner.

'What a dreadful nightmare this has all become,' whispered Stillwell.

'Indeed it has, sir, now I presume that his Grace is in residence at Canterbury?' asked the Commissioner.

'Yes, he is at the moment, but he plans to travel to London tomorrow and join me at Lambeth for the meeting with Porter on Wednesday,' replied Stillwell.

'Then I will despatch armed officers down to Canterbury immediately to stay with his Grace and escort him to London should he still wish to come,' said the Commissioner.

'If you think it necessary,' said Stillwell.

'I do, sir… Chief Inspector.'

'Yes, sir?'

'Select two armed officers to go down to Canterbury Cathedral to guard his Grace.'

'Very good, sir.'

'Then send a telegraph message to the Police at Canterbury informing them of the situation and request armed officers to be in attendance at the Cathedral until our men arrive,' said the Commissioner.

'Yes, sir.'

'I think that's all we can do for the moment, my Lord, so if there is nothing more to discuss I can assure you of our close protection at all times until my officers apprehend the men responsible for these hideous murders,' said the great one.

'Thank you, Commissioner, for all your help,' said Stillwell.

'Chief Inspector, please go down and brief the armed officers now and have them join us here as quickly as possible to escort the Bishop.'

'Very good, sir,' said Bell and he hurriedly left the office. The Commissioner turned to Hadley and said 'get over to Whitechapel, Inspector and report back to me by the end of the day.'

'Yes, sir.'

'And make sure that you and your officers are armed at all times and when you find these killers don't hesitate to shoot them down if they resist arrest!'

'I won't sir.'

'Oh dear, oh dear, I'm surrounded by such unmitigated violence,' whispered Stillwell.

'Indeed you are, sir, now may I offer you some tea whilst we're waiting?' asked the Commissioner with a smile and the frightened Bishop nodded slowly.

Hadley hurried back to his office and told George that he was going to Whitechapel and that Sergeant Talbot would be joining them once again.

'Oh that'll be good, sir.'

'Yes, it will be… if he arrives before Sergeant Cooper and I get back, ask him to wait because it is very important that I speak to him before we go home tonight,' said Hadley.

'Yes, sir.'

Hadley made his way quickly down to the armoury and signed out two .45 calibre revolvers along with twenty four rounds of ammunition before climbing aboard a Police coach and ordering the driver to take him to 8 Turner Street in Whitechapel, as fast as he could.

CHAPTER 3

By the time the Police Coach reached Blackfriars, Hadley had loaded both revolvers, checked that the safety catches were on and placed them in separate pockets in his topcoat. He then opened the folder containing the notes on William Porter that Bell had prepared for him. Reading quickly as the coach rattled over the cobbles towards Whitechapel he made decisions on his first lines of inquiry. After visiting the crime scene he would go with Cooper to Porter's parents address in Mitre Square and inform them of the tragic loss of both sons. It was not something he relished, but a necessary part of his duties and he hoped that they may give him some leads to follow up. Porter had recently left the Army, after serving in Afghanistan and Hadley planned a visit to the Headquarters of the 4th Hussars to make further inquiries after he had reported to the Commissioner.

When the coach pulled up outside 8 Turner Street, Hadley caught a glimpse of Arthur Pilkington, a reporter he knew from 'The Times' newspaper. He was standing at the front of the crowd of onlookers and Hadley groaned inwardly. The last thing he needed at that moment was an inquisitive Press man asking awkward questions. If the Press discovered anything about the Holy Grail, Hadley knew that the pressure on him, as well as the Metropolitan Police, would be almost unbearable.

As Hadley stepped down from the Coach he heard Pilkington call out 'Inspector Hadley, any comment on the murder investigation so far, sir?'

'Not yet, Mr Pilkington, it's too early and I don't wish to speculate,' replied Hadley as he hurried passed the Constables at the door of the terraced house. In the parlour he found Cooper and Jack Palmer busy searching the ransacked room whilst Sergeant Morris gazed at the tortured, half naked corpse of Edward Porter, which was still tied to a bloodstained chair.

'Ah, you're here at last, Jim,' said Palmer brightly.

'Yes, Jack, the Commissioner kept me a little longer than I expected,' replied Hadley.

'Sometimes I think he likes the sound of his own voice,' said Palmer.

'Possibly, Jack. Now, Sergeant, has Curtis finished photographing the scene?' asked Hadley.

'Yes, sir, he's just gone back to the Yard to process his plates,' replied Cooper.

'Good, the Commissioner will want to see them along with my report,' said Hadley.

'Why is the Commissioner so interested in this case, Jim?' asked Palmer.

'It's because torture has been inflicted on the victim, Jack and he wants to know why,' replied Hadley.

'Mmm, I see,' muttered Palmer but Hadley knew that his old friend was not convinced.

'So, who found the body?' asked Hadley.

'His poor wife, she works at The London Hospital as a cleaner and came home at lunchtime to find her husband in this dreadful state,' replied Palmer.

'Where is she now?'

'She has been taken back to hospital, she's hysterical to the point of madness, poor woman,' replied Palmer.

'I'm not surprised,' said Hadley as he looked at the victim's blood soaked torso with the skin hanging down in strips.

'If you've seen enough, Jim, we'll get the body away to Doctor Evans now,' said Palmer.

'Yes of course, Jack.'

'Sergeant, tell the ambulance men to come in and remove the victim,' said Palmer

'Yes, sir,' replied Morris.

'Have you found anything significant, Jack?' asked Hadley.

'No, nothing I'm afraid, but whoever killed this man was obviously determined to find out something from him and only God knows what that might be,' replied Palmer and Hadley shivered slightly as he said 'I'm sure we'll find out in due course.'

'I hope you do, Jim. Are you officially taking over this investigation now?'

'Yes, on the orders of the Commissioner,' replied Hadley.

'Why is that?'

'Because as you already know, Jack, the victim's brother was discovered this morning murdered in the same cruel fashion, so the killings are obviously linked,' replied Hadley.

'Well, whoever did this must be mad beyond all reason, Jim,' said Palmer as he looked at the victim and slowly shook his head.

'That's what I'm really afraid of,' replied Hadley as the ambulance men arrived with Sergeant Morris.

The body was cut loose from the chair by the Sergeant before the attendants lowered it to the canvas stretcher. They covered it with a grey blanket and then carried it away to the ambulance.

'So what do you intend to do next, Jim?' asked Palmer.

'Break the terrible news to the parents that both their sons have been murdered and hope that they may be able to give me some leads,' replied Hadley.

'Dear God… rather you than me, Jim,' whispered Palmer.

'Yes, a Policeman's lot is not a happy one these days,' said Hadley with a sigh.

'Can I help you at all?'

'If you would, Jack.'

'Of course, you just have to ask.'

'Right, could you make inquiries and take statements from any of the neighbours who might have seen or heard anything this morning and send them to me at the Yard?' asked Hadley.

'Consider it done, Jim, and I will also speak to Mrs Porter when she has recovered sufficiently from her ordeal.'

'Thanks, Jack.'

Hadley and Cooper left the house, climbed into the waiting Police Coach and Hadley told the driver to take them to 16 Mitre Square, the home of the parents of the two murdered brothers.

On the short journey, Hadley gave Cooper a revolver and said 'this investigation will be dangerous, Sergeant and, on the direct orders of the Commissioner, we must be armed at all times.'

'Very good, sir.'

'And he added that should the killers resist arrest, we have his permission to shoot them down,' said Hadley firmly.

'I won't hesitate, sir.'

'I'm pleased to hear it, Sergeant. Now, I have asked for the assistance of Sergeant Talbot for this investigation and it has been agreed that he will join us immediately.'

'That is good news, sir as I've a feeling that we'll need all the help we can get before this case is closed,' replied Cooper as the

Coach turned into Mitre Square.

The door of number 16 was opened by an elderly man, who resembled the victims and Hadley asked 'Mr Porter?'

'Yes, and who wants him?' asked Porter in a suspicious tone.

'We're Police Officers, I'm Inspector Hadley and this is Sergeant Cooper, may we have a few words with you, sir?'

'What's it about?'

'It would be better if we spoke to you inside, sir,' replied Hadley.

'Blimey, it must be serious then,' said Porter as a woman's voice called out 'who is it, Charlie?'

'It's the Police, Ma,' he called back as held the door open for the detectives to enter.

'What do they want?' asked the woman as she appeared at the doorway to the front parlour. Hadley smiled and said 'Mrs Porter?'

'Yes… what do you want, sir?' she asked with a worried expression as she stepped back into the room and the detectives followed her.

'May we all sit down?' asked Hadley in a gentle tone.

'It's bad news isn't it?' asked Mrs Porter anxiously.

'Please sit down…'

'Tell us for God' sake!' she interrupted.

'I'm afraid it is bad news and there is no easy way to tell you…' began Hadley.

'It's one of my boys isn't it?' she interrupted and her eyes began to moisten.

'Yes, Mrs Porter…'

'What's happened?' she demanded and Hadley drew a deep breath, hesitated for a moment and replied 'this morning, your son William was found murdered at his lodgings in Islington.'

Mrs Porter let out a piercing scream and fell on to the sofa as her husband whispered 'good Gawd Almighty.' He sank down next to his sobbing wife and placed a comforting arm round her but she was inconsolable. Hadley dreaded telling them that Edward was also murdered but he knew he had to do it.

'And it is my sad duty to inform you that your other son, Edward, has also been found murdered,' said Hadley but he was sure that the distressed parents did not really fully comprehend the tragedy that had befallen them.

'Our Ted as well as Billy? Who could have done this to our boys? Who could have done this?' shouted Porter in wide-eyed disbelief.

'We don't know yet, sir, but rest assured that we will catch the killers,' replied Hadley.

'They've never done no harm to anyone, not anyone, as Gawd's my judge,' said Porter as the tears streamed down his face.

'I'm sure that is so, sir and I can tell you that the Police Commissioner himself has given me all the resources I need to apprehend the men responsible for these terrible crimes,' said Hadley.

'I bloody well hope they hang for this!' said Porter.

'I'm sure they will, sir.'

'Where have they taken them?' asked Porter.

'To the Marylebone Hospital, sir.'

'I want to see them... I want to see my boys!' screamed Mrs Porter between her sobs.

'Of course, madam and when I get back to Scotland Yard I will arrange for a liaison officer to accompany you in a Police Coach that will take you to the Marylebone immediately,' said Hadley. Mrs Porter nodded then sobbed uncontrollably.

'Where's Jane... Ted's missus?' asked Porter.

'She's been taken to The London Hospital,' replied Hadley.

'Is she hurt?'

'No, sir, but she found Edward and is understandably in a severe state of shock,' replied Hadley and Porter nodded. Hadley realised that it was pointless to stay and ask any questions so he said 'I am truly sorry to have brought you such dreadful news so Sergeant Cooper and I will leave you now, but we'll need to speak to you later.'

Porter nodded and said 'right' before getting up and showing the detectives out.

As the coach raced back to the Yard Hadley said 'it is quite unbelievable that those poor people have lost their two sons in one day to deranged, maniacal killers, Sergeant.'

'It is, sir, but I'm sure we'll bring them to justice and see them hang.'

'Please God make it so... but it won't assuage their grief,' whispered Hadley.

Once back at the Yard Hadley went immediately to see Chief Inspector Bell and report the latest events before requesting a liaison officer to be assigned to the case and accompany the Porter's to the Marylebone.

'Right, Hadley, leave all that with me and you telegraph Doctor Evans saying that they're on their way so he may be ready to receive them.'

'Very good, sir.'

'We don't usually allow people to see their loved ones until after the autopsy but I do feel that we have to make an exception in this case,' said Bell.

'I'm sure you're right, sir.'

'Of course I'm right, Hadley. Now make sure you have written reports for the Commissioner and me before we go to see him.'

'I will sir and accompanying them will be photographs of the crime scene,' said Hadley.

'That's good, because I know the Commissioner is keen on having pictorial evidence to hand when he is reading a report,' said Bell.

Hadley went to the telegraph office and sent a short message to Doctor Evans before returning to his office. Sergeant Talbot had just arrived and was talking to Cooper when Hadley entered.

'Ah, Sergeant Talbot, my heavy artillery!' said Hadley with a smile.

'Yes, sir, you can't beat an Army man I say... and I'm ready for anything,' replied Talbot with a grin.

'Good man... I'm glad to hear it.'

'Thank you for requesting me again, sir, I do find it exhilarating working for you compared with the usual run of the mill,' said Talbot.

'Well, Sergeant, I can promise you that this investigation will exhilarate you more than any case before,' said Hadley with a grin.

'That's wonderful, sir,' replied Talbot with his eyes shining in anticipation.

'Now I don't know what Cooper has managed to tell you about the case but just listen in if you would whilst we prepare the report for the Chief and the Commissioner,' said Hadley.

'Very good, sir.'

'George...'

'Yes, sir?'

'Make us a nice pot of tea whilst we write up this report ready for you to type as fast as you can,' said Hadley.

'Very good, sir,' came the reply accompanied with a sigh from the adjacent office.

The detectives had drunk their tea and just finished the report, which was given to George, when Jack Curtis arrived with the sepia tint photographs of the crime scene. Hadley thanked the cheerful man for his good work and he left the office with a broad smile. Hadley looked at the photos closely before handing them one by one to Cooper, and then Talbot, who exclaimed 'good God, sir, these killers must be lunatics!'

'I'm sure you're right, Sergeant and now you see what we're up against,' said Hadley.

'I certainly do, sir.'

'When you've finished looking at the photographs, please go down to the armoury and draw a revolver and a box of ammunition,' said Hadley.

'Right, sir.'

'The Commissioner has ordered us to be armed at all times and not to hesitate to shoot if necessary,' said Hadley.

'I can see why, sir,' said Talbot.

When George had finished typing the report in duplicate, Hadley read it through, signed both copies, attached the photographs to the Commissioner's copy and placed them in folders.

He stood up from his desk and said 'gentlemen, when I get back from seeing the Commissioner I will brief you on the case and after much careful thought I have decided to reveal everything I know to you.'

'That's good to hear, sir,' said Cooper brightly.

'Is there anything we can do whilst you're with the Commissioner, sir?' asked Talbot.

'Yes, Sergeant, both of you read the notes on Porter's background... they're in my folder, and prepare your selves for a late night, as we're off to pay a visit to the Hussars,' replied Hadley with a smile.

The Commissioner looked horrified when he saw the photographs of Porter's tortured body tied to the chair.

'Good God, Inspector, these fiends must be caught immediately before they have a chance to kill again,' said the Commissioner as his side whiskers bristled.

'Yes, of course, sir, we'll do our best,' replied Hadley.

'What do you make of it all, Chief Inspector?' asked the great one.

Bell looked confused for a moment then replied 'it's clearly the work of desperate mad men who are intent on finding where the Holy Grail is hidden, sir, and all we can do is follow every possible lead that links the Porter brothers to these deranged killers.'

'Well, I'm so glad I had the foresight to order round the clock protection for Bishop Stillwell and his Grace the Archbishop until these lunatics are caught,' said the Commissioner.

'Ah, yes, sir, I've always thought that your foresight is your greatest strength if I may say so,' said Bell with a smile as Hadley cringed in his seat.

'You may, Chief Inspector. So Hadley, now it's all down to you and your men,' said the Commissioner.

'Yes it is, sir.'

'What do you intend to do next?'

'Pay a visit tonight to the Headquarters of the 4th Hussars and see if any relevant leads come from that, then tomorrow, call on the distressed parents and interview them. Inspector Palmer is gathering statements from neighbours in Turner Street and he will be speaking to Mrs Porter when she has recovered sufficiently to be interviewed, sir,' replied Hadley.

'Well it's a start I suppose, Hadley.'

'I believe so, sir, and I must advise you that the Press are already on to it and I'm sure they sense something out of the ordinary.' The Commissioner rolled his eyes and said 'dear God, if they get hold of the real reason why these men have been murdered we will be under enormous pressure from all sides and there will be Hell to pay!'

'As usual there will be pages of un-substantiated rumours, accompanied by gory details, with every move we make under intense scrutiny, sir,' said Bell with a sigh.

'I couldn't have put it better myself, Chief Inspector,' said the Commissioner and Bell smiled then gave a little nod of appreciation.

After briefing the Commissioner on the details of the events of the day, Hadley left the Chief Inspector and the great one still discussing the ramifications of the case and returned to his office. There was a message on his desk from Jack Palmer stating that despite door to door inquiries none of the neighbours heard or saw anything untoward and Mrs Porter was still under medical care at the London.

Hadley told his Sergeants the news then asked George to join them before he sat at his desk and composed himself for a moment. He began by saying 'gentlemen, what I'm about to tell you must be kept absolutely secret and on no account discuss the details of this investigation with anyone else.'

'Very good, sir,' replied the Sergeants in chorus and George nodded.

'The Commissioner has given me a strict order not to tell you, but I regard you all as colleagues whom I can trust implicitly and I'm confident that you would never break that trust,' said Hadley.

'Certainly not, sir,' said Cooper and Talbot added loudly 'never, sir, never!'

'Not ever, sir,' said George quietly in an emotional tone.

'I'm pleased to hear it, gentlemen. Now, as you know the Porter brothers have been cruelly murdered, obviously by the same people. The Commissioner believes that because Lord Stillwell, the Bishop of London and his Grace the Archbishop of Canterbury are connected to William Porter, their lives are now in jeopardy from these deranged killers.'

'Good God,' whispered Talbot and George shook his head slowly whilst Cooper sat open mouthed for a moment before asking 'so what is the connection and why does the Commissioner think they're in mortal danger, sir?'

'Because Lord Stillwell contacted the Commissioner after receiving a letter from William Porter informing him that he knew of a priceless religious relic,' replied Hadley.

'May I ask what it is, sir?' asked Talbot.

'Yes, Sergeant, Porter told the Bishop at their subsequent meeting that it was the Holy Grail and he knew where it is hidden,' replied Hadley and they all gasped with surprise.

'The Holy Grail... I didn't know that it actually existed, sir,' said Cooper.

'Apparently it does and Porter wanted a hundred thousand pounds to reveal its hiding place,' said Hadley and the officers were struck dumb by the revelation.

'That's a King's ransom, sir,' said Cooper.

'Without a doubt,' said Hadley.

'No wonder the Commissioner wanted to keep it a secret,' said Talbot.

'Yes, and now you fully understand the reason for all the secrecy.'

'Oh we certainly do, sir,' said Cooper.

'These killers must also know of the Grail's existence and they will stop at nothing to find out where it is, they may believe that Porter has already told the Bishop,' said Hadley.

'And has he, sir?' asked Talbot.

'No, Porter was murdered before he was due to tell the Bishop this coming Wednesday,' replied Hadley.

'But he may have told his brother, sir,' said Talbot.

'I don't think so, because Edward's letter says that he is looking forward to seeing William this Sunday for lunch when he can tell him his good news,' said Hadley.

'It sounds like a dangerous race to arrest the murderers before they kill again and then recover the Holy Grail, sir,' said Cooper.

'You're quite right, Sergeant so we must be on our toes and make sure that we miss nothing.'

'Of course, sir,' said Talbot as Big Ben struck six o'clock.

'So I think we'll have a pot of tea to keep us going, then we'll pay a visit to the Hussars and afterwards we'll go to Whitechapel to make some inquiries there. So it will be a late night tonight, gentlemen,' said Hadley with a smile.

They had just finished their tea and were about to leave when Mr Jenkins, the Chief's assistant, arrived in the office.

'Inspector Hadley, I'm glad I caught you, sir,' said Jenkins.

'What is it?'

'The Chief Inspector has just received a message from the liaison officer, sir.'

'Go on, Mr Jenkins,' said Hadley fearing something untoward.

'Apparently when the officer called at Mr and Mrs Porter's address in Mitre Square to take them to the Marylebone, they had already been collected by another coach, sir.'

'Oh dear God... I fear the killers have got them,' whispered Hadley.

'The Chief Inspector has sent an urgent telegraph to all London stations requesting help in finding them, sir,' said Jenkins.

'Let's hope that when we find them they are still alive,' said Hadley.

CHAPTER 4

Major William Fielding was getting dressed in his Mess uniform when the detectives arrived at the gate of the barracks in Carriage Road in Hyde Park. Hadley spoke to the guard who immediately sent for the Duty Officer, Captain Anderson, who appeared to be a little concerned at the presence of the three detectives.

'What's this all about, Inspector?' asked Anderson in an anxious tone.

'May we come in and talk privately, Captain?' asked Hadley.

'I presume it is a serious matter?'

'Yes, it's very serious, Captain,' replied Hadley. Anderson nodded and said 'then please follow me, gentlemen.'

He led them into the building by the gate and to an office at the far end of an echoing corridor, where he invited them to sit as he sat behind a large desk.

'Now, Inspector, would you kindly explain the reason for your visit?' asked Anderson.

'Yes, Captain, we're making inquiries regarding a man named William Porter, who was in this Regiment until recently...' began Hadley.

'Ah, Porter, he was Major Fielding's batman... he left just a few weeks ago, is he in any trouble?' interrupted Anderson.

'Not any more, sir, he was found murdered this morning,' replied Hadley and he watched the colour drain from Anderson's face.

'My God.'

'So I'd be obliged if you would assist us in our inquiries, sir.'

'Yes... yes, of course, Inspector, but tell me, how did he die?'

'He was strangled, sir,' replied Hadley.

'Dear God... who would want to do such a thing?... and why?'

'That's what we intend to find out, sir, now tell us everything you know about William Porter,' said Hadley as Cooper took out his notebook.

'Well, from what I recall he was a quiet man, never got into any trouble, he was the Major's batman during the whole of our recent deployment in Afghanistan, Inspector.'

'Did he have any close friends in the Regiment, sir?'

'I don't think so, Inspector, but the Major would be the best person to ask, Porter was his batman for years and I know that he was very sad to lose him when he left the Regiment,' replied Anderson.

'That's understandable. Would you please advise Major Fielding that we're here and wish to see him, sir,' said Hadley.

'Oh, I can't possibly do that Inspector,' replied Anderson.

'Why not, sir?'

'The Major will be just getting ready for dinner in the Mess and...'

'Captain Anderson, we are conducting a fast moving murder investigation on the direct orders of the Commissioner and you would be well advised not to obstruct my inquiries,' interrupted Hadley firmly.

Anderson glared at Hadley and said 'then I'll ask the Major if he will see you but I cannot guarantee that he will do so, Inspector.'

'Then please tell the Major that if he refuses to see me I will report that fact to the Commissioner tonight and he will no doubt arrange a warrant for his arrest on suspicion of Police obstruction, sir,' said Hadley.

'My God, I do believe that you would arrest him!' exclaimed Anderson.

'Be in no doubt whatsoever, sir,' said Hadley in a firm tone.

'Right then, I'll find the Major and advise him of your intentions.'

'Thank you, sir.'

'Please be good enough to wait here,' said Anderson firmly as he strode from the office. After a few moments Cooper said 'I think this all could get a little difficult, sir.'

'It may well do, Sergeant, but we have our duties to perform and nobody is above the law, not even Army Major's,' replied Hadley with a smile.

'They only think they are, sir,' said Talbot with a grin.

'And with your experience in the Fusiliers you should know, Sergeant,' said Hadley.

'Oh, I do sir, believe me I do,' said Talbot with a nod.

Within a few minutes the door burst open and the Major swept in to the office and said loudly 'I'm Major Fielding and my Duty Officer here tells me that you Policemen have come to bloody well arrest me… is that true?'

The detectives stood up and the Sergeants waited for Hadley to speak. They were all taller than the Major and he was slightly taken aback by their presence. Fielding was a stocky man with grey hair, bushy side whiskers and piercing grey eyes. His appearance gave an impression of military efficiency coupled with ruthlessness.

Hadley said in measured tones 'good evening, sir, I'm Inspector Hadley… this is Sergeant Cooper and Sergeant Talbot, we're from Scotland Yard…'

'Well, what the devil do you want with me?' interrupted Fielding.

'I just wish to ask some questions about your batman…'

'My batman…what the devil's Browne been up to now?' asked Fielding angrily.

'I've no idea, sir, I'm making inquiries about William Porter, your previous man I believe, didn't Captain Anderson tell you?' asked Hadley.

'No, he didn't,' replied Fielding firmly before he glared at Anderson.

'Well sir, I suggest that we all sit down so that I may ask you some questions about Porter,' said Hadley. Fielding looked at him and asked 'is this going to take long, Inspector, because I'm expected in the Mess to make an important speech before dinner.'

'I assure that I won't keep you longer than necessary, Major,' replied Hadley as he sat down and waited for Fielding to take his seat behind the desk. Anderson stood to one side of the Major with his hands clasped behind his back.

'It is my duty to inform you that William Porter was found murdered this morning…'

'Good God Almighty, why wasn't I told Anderson?' interrupted Fielding as he glared once again at the Captain.

'Sir, I've only just been advised by Inspector Hadley and I thought it would be better coming from him,' replied Anderson.

'Well I suppose in the circumstances you're probably right,' said Fielding grudgingly.

'Can you tell me, sir when Porter…' began Hadley.

'How was he killed... shot was he?' interrupted Fielding.

'No, sir, he was strangled after being...' replied Hadley.

'Was it over a woman?'

'I can't answer that, sir, now...'

'Why not?'

'Major Fielding, in a murder investigation it is my duty to ask the questions so I would be obliged if you would stop interrupting me!' said Hadley firmly. The Major's jaw dropped, he was not used to being spoken to in such a forthright manner and said angrily 'Inspector, I believe that I cannot help you with your inquiries about Porter and this is all a waste of my valuable time. I'll have you know, sir, that I am about to give a welcoming speech in the Mess to General Sir Rodney Hughes-Bennett on behalf of the Regiment!'

'Major, if you will kindly co-operate this interview will be over quickly,' said Hadley and Fielding let out a sigh of exasperation then rolled his eyes.

'Then bloody well get on with it man!' he said angrily.

'Can you confirm that William Porter was your batman?' asked Hadley.

'You already know that,' replied Fielding testily.

'When did he leave the Regiment?'

'About two or three weeks ago, Anderson will give you the actual date of his discharge.'

'Do you know if he had any close friends in the Regiment?'

'No, he kept himself very much to himself.'

'Prior to him leaving did he have any visitors?'

'Not to my knowledge.'

'Has anybody made inquiries about him recently?'

'Not that I'm aware of, Inspector... do you happen to know anything Anderson?'

'No, sir,' replied the Captain.

'Well that answers that then, so is there anything else, Inspector?'

'Yes, sir, do you know if he was a particularly religious man?' asked Hadley and Fielding looked surprised before replying 'I don't think so.'

'Was he a Roman Catholic?'

'No, Inspector, and he never spoke to me about religion in all the time he served with me.'

'Why did he leave the army, sir?'

'I really don't know the reason and when I asked him, he just said that he had come to the end of his career and wanted to do something different, but I believe that our last posting to Afghanistan may have contributed to his decision,' replied Fielding.

'Why was that, sir?'

'This Regiment has lost many fine officers and men fighting the hill tribesmen in that God forsaken country and it's had an effect on all of us, Inspector and I believe that Porter felt it more than most... I know he certainly did not want to go back there.'

'And are you due to go back, sir?'

'Yes, we're being deployed to Kabul in September.'

'I see. Did he ever say what he wanted to do when he left the army, sir?'

'No, he didn't, he had no trade as such so I did offer him a position as a coachman with me for the time being,' replied Fielding.

'And did he accept your offer, sir?'

'No, he refused it, which surprised me a little.'

'Why was that, sir?'

'Well he'd been with me for many years and I thought he would be pleased to be in paid work with someone he knew well,' replied Fielding and Hadley nodded.

'You asked me if he was murdered over a woman... so do you know if he had any relationships that might have led to his violent death?'

'I'm not aware of any, Inspector, as I've already told you, he kept himself to himself.'

'Indeed you did, sir. Now I may wish to question you again as this investigation unfolds, so may I have your private address?'

'Whatever for, Inspector?'

'I think it would be helpful, sir, and better for us to talk in private if necessary,' replied Hadley and the Major rolled his eyes then replied 'my London home is at 26 Albany Street, just off Regents Park, Inspector.'

'Thank you, sir, I have no more questions at the moment,' said Hadley with a smile.

The Major left the office stony faced without saying anything further and after consulting the records Captain Anderson confirmed that Porter left the regiment on the 21st of April.

As the Police coach rattled over the cobbled streets towards Whitechapel the detectives discussed the case.

'I think that Major Fielding knows more about Porter than he told us,' said Hadley.

'Without any doubt, sir,' said Cooper.

'I'm not surprised that he turned down the job as coachman, sir, he'd probably had enough of him after all those years as his batman,' said Talbot.

'Yes, you're probably right, Sergeant.'

'Do you think the Major knows anything about the Grail, sir?' asked Cooper.

'No, Sergeant, it stands to reason that if he did he know about it he would have been more forthcoming, having just been told of Porter's murder,' replied Hadley.

'Fearing that he might be next on the killer's list, sir and asking for our protection,' said Talbot.

'Precisely so, Sergeant.'

Hadley looked out at the dreary streets of Whitechapel as the coach neared the Police station and they always brought back memories of him as a young constable on his beat around the foggy alleyways, trying to uphold the law in difficult circumstances. The poor had absolutely nothing, so the unemployed men resorted to theft of all kinds whilst the women turned to prostitution. Wealthy men would come down from their clubs in the West End to buy their selfish pleasure for a few shillings before returning to their wives and lives of luxury.

During this period Hadley first met Agnes Cartwright when he arrested her brute of a husband in a drunken affray outside the Kings Head pub. As a young constable he had been immediately attracted to the battered, pretty woman and their paths were to cross often until her husband was found drowned in the Thames after a drunken brawl. Hadley remained friends with Agnes after she had been duped by various men and had given up all hope of finding a reliable one. She now gave personal relief to preferred gentlemen for five shillings a time, two and sixpence on Mondays to encourage trade on her quiet night. Agnes had befriended Florrie Dean, a pretty blonde house maid, who had been caught half naked with the master of the house in the pantry amongst the pastries and had been instantly dismissed by the angry wife. Without any references she had no hope of employment so she had no alternative but to sell herself. Florrie offered a 'special service' for discerning gentlemen and soon had a number of satisfied clients who visited her regularly.

The two women frequented the Kings Head pub and were a constant source of valuable information for Hadley. Over a sixpenny gin they would tell him everything they knew that was going on in the area.

The coach pulled into Whitechapel Police station and the detectives entered the drab building and made their way up to Inspector Palmer's office.

'Any further developments, Jack?' asked Hadley as he sat opposite his friend.

'No, nothing, Jim other than an urgent telegraph from Bell requesting we keep a look out for Mr and Mrs Porter who have been collected from their home by a unknown coach,' replied Palmer.

'I fear that the killers have got them and now we'll be unlikely to find them alive,' said Hadley.

'It'll be like looking for a needle in a haystack round here, but already I've got some men carrying out house to house searches for them,' said Palmer gloomily.

'That's good, Jack. Now, I read your telegraph but did any of the neighbours in Turner Street notice anything unusual?'

'Nobody saw anything untoward and when I went to The London, the Doctor said that Mrs Porter was still heavily sedated,' replied Palmer.

'Poor woman,' said Hadley.

'Yes it must have been a terrible shock to find her husband in that state.'

'I wonder if she knows anything,' said Hadley.

'Well, we'll find out in due course, but the maniacs who killed Porter were obviously after something,' said Palmer.

'Yes I'm sure.'

'And do you know what it is, Jim?' asked Palmer with a knowing smile. Hadley hesitated for a moment then replied 'yes, Jack, I do, but on the strict orders of the Commissioner, I'm afraid I can't tell you.'

'Bloody hell... it must be something important!'

'Yes, it is.'

'So can you tell me anything, Jim?'

'Yes, it involves the Bishop of London and the Archbishop of Canterbury,' replied Hadley.

'My God... what have they been up to?'

'Nothing, but Porter had a meeting with the Bishop and now he and the Archbishop have an armed guard until we catch the killers,' replied Hadley.

'So these churchmen are implicated in something that Porter knew about?'

'Yes they are, Jack, but please don't press me any further and I promise I will tell you everything as soon as the Commissioner gives his permission.'

'Very well, Jim.'

'And I think it would be a good idea to give some protection to Mrs Jane Porter because our murderers may suspect that she knows something,' said Hadley.

'Right, I'll send two constables up to The London immediately.'

'Thanks, Jack, and when she's discharged from the hospital I think we should keep her in protective custody for the time being.'

'It makes sense, Jim.'

'It does, so please keep her here until I can make arrangements for her to stay at the Yard.'

'Right.'

'Now we're off to the Kings Head to see what we can find out from our ladies... care to join us for a swift pint at the end of a busy day?'

'I will, if you're buying, Jim,' replied Palmer with a grin.

'No I'm not, but Cooper is,' said Hadley and they all laughed, except Cooper.

The Kings Head was busy for a Monday night and the detectives had to push their way through the drinkers to the bar, where Vera and her girls were doing their best to serve everyone at once. She smiled when she saw Hadley and Cooper as she tidied up the scraggly hair that had fallen across her sweaty brow.

'Evening, gents… the usual is it?' Vera asked loudly above the sound of the general hubbub and the out of tune piano being played by an old chap struggling with the latest music hall favourite.

'Please Vera… and what are you having Jack?'

'I'll have a Guinness, thanks Jim.'

'And you Sergeant?'

'Just a pint of stout, sir,' replied Talbot with a nod. Vera quickly pulled the pumps and soon there were three pints of foaming stout on the wet counter followed by the Guinness, which she pulled slowly.

'That'll be two shillings and four pence please, sir,' said Vera as her hair fell back across her forehead.

'Pay the lady, Sergeant,' said Hadley to Cooper.

'I always do, sir,' replied Cooper with a grin as he fished in his pocket for the money.

'Vera, can you open the back room for us, it's too noisy in here to think,' said Hadley.

'Yes, guvnor, but it's a bit untidy,' she replied.

'That doesn't matter.'

'I'll get one of the girls to open up for you in a minute.'

'Thanks Vera… have the ladies been in yet?' asked Hadley.

'No, I expect they're still down at the Blind Beggar,' replied Vera as she took the money from Cooper.

'Well if they come in will you let them know I want to speak to them?' asked Hadley and she nodded as she rang up the till before serving another thirsty customer.

The back room was opened for the detectives and they sat round the table quietly sipping their drinks. Hadley had just started to tell Palmer about the interview with Fielding when the door opened and Agnes waltzed in with Florrie in tow.

'Blimey Jim, if the devil casts his net right now he'd get the blimmin'' lot of you in one go!' Agnes said with a grin.

'Evening, Agnes… Florrie, come and sit down and tell us

everything you know about the devil,' said Hadley with a smile and Florrie laughed.

'I know a lot about him... but it'll cost you a couple of gins,' said Agnes with a smile as she sat next to Hadley on the bench seat.

'I think we can run to that... Sergeant... if you would please,' said Hadley, Cooper nodded and left the room. Agnes looked at Talbot and said 'my Gawd, it's a long time since we've seen you, Sergeant.'

'It is and I must say that you both look lovelier than ever,' said Talbot with a smile.

'Blimey Jim, he's a sweetie... can't you get 'im transferred to you for always?'

'I'm afraid not, Agnes, he's only with me for a short while and because he's so good he's wanted by everyone else at the Yard,' replied Hadley with a grin and Talbot blushed.

'I'm not surprised,' said Agnes with a smile.

'I suppose he's helping you with that 'orrible murder in Turner Street?' said Florrie.

'Yes he is.'

'Do you know anything about that, Florrie?' asked Palmer.

'No guvnor, but everyone's talking about it... they say he had his blimmin'' skin torn off him by some maniacs... and I blame them Chinese I do,' she replied.

'Tell us about the Chinese,' said Hadley with interest.

'Well, according to Daisy Wells, a whole load more of 'em have moved in down at Limehouse and they're causing blimmin'' ructions they are and no mistake,' replied Florrie.

'Like what for instance?' Hadley asked.

'I hear that they've been skinnin' dead horses for meat and selling it in the market and some other blimmin'' foreigners said it was bad... there's been trouble I can tell you,' replied Florrie.

'Do you know about this, Jack?'

'No, Jim, it's the first I've heard of it,' replied Palmer.

'And I bet its one of them Chinese that done that poor fella in,' said Florrie.

'What makes you think that, Florrie?' asked Hadley.

'Because they're too blimmin'' handy with knives and when he wouldn't tell 'em what they wanted to know they just cut him up real bad,' she replied.

'And what did they want to know, Florrie?' asked Hadley anxiously.

'I dunno, guvnor, but the word is down the Lane that there's something valuable kicking about and them Chinese are after it.'

'Anything else you can tell us?' asked Hadley as Cooper returned with the gins.

'Oh blimey, guvnor, can I?'

'Go on then.'

'As Gawd's my witness, would you believe that some newspaper fella's have been asking questions? I mean to say, we don't never see them down here and Daisy says that they've been giving out money for any information about the dead fella in Turner Street,' said Florrie and Hadley sensed impending difficulties.

'And what are people saying to these newspaper men?'

'The word is that he's mixed up in something to do with his brother, I dunno what mind,' Florrie replied.

'I think we'll start making inquiries first thing tomorrow, gentlemen,' said Hadley and the Sergeants chorused 'right, sir.'

'Can I help, Jim?' asked Palmer.

'I'd be grateful if you could.'

'Right, I'll assign Sergeant Morris and two constables to assist you, Jim.'

'Thanks, Jack. Now ladies, the murdered man's parents live in Mitre Square and they have disappeared...'

'I bet them blimmin' Chinese have got them somewhere down Limehouse,' interrupted Florrie.

'What makes you so sure?' asked Hadley.

'I dunno, guvnor, it's just a feeling I've got,' she replied.

'Well if they are there, my men will find them, Jim,' said Palmer.

'I hope so, Jack... I think we'd better finish our drinks then get back to your office and stay for awhile to see what develops.'

'Oh that's a shame, Jim, I was just getting comfy,' said Agnes.

'There'll be many other times, Agnes,' said Hadley before he quickly finished his stout.

Nothing of any relevance was reported that night and the

detectives left Whitechapel Police station in the early hours and made their weary way home. On the journey to Camden, Hadley had an uneasy feeling of impending disaster and consequently had a restless night.

CHAPTER 5

Hadley arrived in his office just before eight the next morning and George told him that the Yard was already buzzing with rumours after the deployment of armed officers to guard the clergymen.

'It's to be expected in the circumstances, George,' said Hadley as the Sergeants entered and wished him good morning.

'Right, gentlemen, the first thing we have to do is follow up all the known associates of William Porter listed in the Chief's notes,' said Hadley.

'Very good, sir,' said Cooper.

'Should we work together sir, or separately?' asked Talbot.

'Separately... and each of you enlist a constable from the Watch Office to accompany you, it is vitally important that we cover as much ground as possible today,' replied Hadley.

'Yes, sir,' they chorused.

'Make lists of the people that you intend to visit... book out traps with drivers and get going as quick as you can,' said Hadley.

'Right, sir.'

'I'm going to see Inspector Palmer to find out if there's any news about Porter's parents.'

'What about the Chinese in Limehouse, sir?' asked Cooper.

'We'll leave them 'til later, Sergeant.'

'Very good, sir,' said Cooper as George appeared and asked Hadley if he wanted a pot of tea.

'I'm afraid there's no time for tea when the devil drives, George,' replied Hadley.

After the Sergeants had left the Yard, Hadley went up to brief Bell on his plans for the day and the possibility of Chinese involvement in the murders. The Chief Inspector looked up from his desk as Hadley entered the office and said 'I was just about to send for you... any news of Mr and Mrs Porter?'

'No, sir, not yet.'

'Dear God, I fear the worst.'

'So do I sir.'

'Well, I telegraphed all London stations last night as soon as the liaison officer reported to me that they were missing,' said

Bell.

'That's all you could have done, sir.'

'It seems so little in the circumstances... now, have you seen the papers this morning?'

'No, sir, I haven't.'

'Well it's a good job, because you might have been tempted to stay in bed and report in sick!' exclaimed Bell.

'Really, sir... is it that bad?'

'Bad does not begin to describe what 'The Times' reports on its front page, Hadley,' replied Bell.

'Ah, that'll be the work of my 'friend' Arthur Pilkington, sir,' said Hadley.

'Well he may be a friend of yours but he's no friend of the Metropolitan Police I can assure you!'

'I half expected it, sir after I saw him outside Porter's house in Whitechapel yesterday,' said Hadley.

'These bloody Press people are a nuisance, sticking their noses into everything and stirring up no end of trouble by making it up as they go along,' said Bell angrily.

'What does the report actually say, sir?'

Bell picked up the paper 'it says... *After the discovery of William Porter's mutilated body in Islington, his brother was found cruelly murdered in a similar fashion in Whitechapel. Inspector Hadley of Scotland Yard attended both scenes of crime but was unable to make any comment to the Press when asked by our reporter. It is obvious that the Police are baffled once again and mad killers are free to roam at will in London. As a precaution the Commissioner of the Metropolitan Police has placed armed officers with Lord Stillwell, the Bishop of London and His Grace The Archbishop of Canterbury, who is now in residence at Lambeth Palace after travelling up from Canterbury under Police armed guard, in case of attack by these murderous villains. This newspaper asks what are the links between William Porter and our illustrious clergy and possibly other important dignitaries, who may also be under threat? The Times now demands answers for its readers and understands that Sir George West, the Home Secretary, will be making a statement in the Commons in an attempt to restore the public's faith in the Metropolitan Police.'* do you hear that, Hadley? Restore the public's faith in the Metropolitan Police! My God… it just couldn't be any worse!'

'Oh dear,' said Hadley with a sigh.

'And you just wait 'til the Press discover that Mr and Mrs Porter are missing!' said Bell as Brackley entered the office and said in an anxious tone 'Chief Inspector, will you come to the Commissioner's office immediately, sir? And you too, Inspector Hadley.'

'Oh God' groaned Bell as he stood up. Hadley followed him out of the office and up the stairs.

On entering, the Commissioner waved them to sit without looking up from his paperwork. They waited patiently for him to speak and after some moments he gazed at each of them in turn and said 'the situation regarding the investigation into the Porter brothers' murders is becoming very serious indeed. If you have read the morning papers you will see that we are being accused by the Press of losing the public's faith in our abilities. So much so, that all Hell has been let loose and the Home Secretary will make a statement in the Commons this afternoon assuring Parliament and the country that the Metropolitan Police have the matter well in hand and arrests are imminent.'

Hadley groaned inwardly as Bell's face drained of colour before he said nervously 'I'm sure Hadley has suspects in mind and it is only a matter of time before we have the culprits behind bars, sir.'

'That may be so, Chief Inspector, but I am ordered by the Home Secretary to immediately place more resources behind this inquiry to ensure a quick end to this murderous mayhem,' said the Commissioner.

'Of course, sir.'

'What makes the situation worse is that the damned Press are reporting the fact that armed officers are guarding Lord Stillwell and the Archbishop, so questions are being raised as to why that is necessary and what is their connection to the Porter killings… believe me gentlemen, it couldn't be more serious!'

'I agree entirely, sir,' said Bell.

'Now, what I intend to do is assign two more Inspectors and four Sergeants to the investigation under your leadership Chief

Inspector.' Bell beamed and replied 'that's very good forward planning if I may say so, sir.'

'Will we work together or follow lines of inquiry separately, sir?' asked Hadley.

'Both, Inspector, I want the maximum effort to obtain the immediate arrest of the killers in this dire situation,' replied the Commissioner.

'I must report another unwelcome development to you, sir,' said Bell hesitantly.

'Well what is it?'

'Mr and Mrs Porter are now missing, sir,' said Bell and the great one's jaw dropped as Brackley knocked and entered the office.

'I'm so sorry to disturb you, sir, but there's a Major Fielding here and he is demanding to see you.'

'Who the devil is Major Fielding and what does he want, Brackley?'

'I think I can answer that, sir,' said Hadley.

'Well, Inspector?'

'I questioned the Major at the barracks last night because William Porter was his batman until he recently left the army, sir,' replied Hadley.

'Was he indeed... then show him in Brackley... he may have something important to tell us,' said the Commissioner and the assistant nodded.

Major Fielding strode into the office as if he were leading his men on parade then stood for a moment looking contemptuously at the officers.

'Good morning, Major, I'm the Commissioner... this is Chief Inspector Bell and Inspector Hadley, who I believe you know already.'

Fielding ignored the detectives and said firmly 'Commissioner, I have come here to demand immediate protection...'

'From whom, sir?' interrupted the Commissioner.

'I've no idea, but as you may already know, I was waylaid by your man Hadley here, asking questions about my batman, William Porter, which was damned inconvenient as I was about to give a welcoming speech to General Sir Rodney Hughes-Bennett in the Officers Mess...'

'Well I'm sorry about that, sir, but we have our duties to perform,' interrupted the Commissioner angrily.

Fielding ignored the comment and said 'further to that inconvenience, I read in my morning paper that Porter's brother was also found murdered and our leading clergy have had to be given armed protection because they are linked in some way to the Porter brothers!'

'I'm afraid that is so, sir.'

'Well, I now demand armed protection for myself and family as I was attacked last night by two men in the street outside my London home!' said Fielding and he held up his bandaged left hand.

'Goodness gracious me,' said the Commissioner as the officers gasped.

'I was injured in the fracas as you can see.'

'What can you tell us about the men who attacked you, sir?' asked Hadley.

'Not a great deal, they were waiting in a coach and set about me when I stepped down from a Hansom cab,' replied Fielding.

'What time was this, sir?' asked Hadley.

'I'd arrived back from dinner in the Mess, so it was about half past eleven,' he replied.

'Did they say anything to you, sir?' asked Bell.

'Yes, as they tried to force me into their coach, one of them kept asking 'did Porter tell you where it is?' but I was struggling fiercely so didn't reply... and I didn't know what he was talking about... but do you, Commissioner?'

The great one's side whiskers bristled and his face became flushed as the officers glanced at him anxiously waiting for his reply.

'Unfortunately I cannot comment on that, Major,' he replied.

'Why the devil not, sir?' asked Fielding angrily.

'Because it is...'

'Bloody hell, Commissioner, I demand to know!'

'Demand all you like, sir, but I cannot comment!'

'I'm attacked in the street by men attempting to kidnap me whilst asking if I know about Porter 'telling me where something was', a murdered man who was under my command until recently... who's somehow linked to Lord Stillwell and the

Archbishop... surely you have a duty to tell me what this is all about, Commissioner?'

'I'm sorry, sir, I cannot reveal anything to you but I will arrange for armed officers to guard you and your home immediately,' replied the Commissioner.

'Well at least that's some relief... my wife is in a terrible state of shock I can tell you,' said Fielding.

'I'm sure she is, sir.'

'And you'd also better organise some men to guard my country house, because we're going down there this weekend,' said Fielding.

'Where exactly is that, sir?'

'I live at The Manse, just outside the village of Kintbury, near Newbury in Berkshire, Commissioner.'

'Chief Inspector, please telegraph Newbury Police and arrange for armed officers to be in attendance at the Major's home.'

'Very good, sir.'

'Can you tell us anything else about these men, sir?' asked Hadley.

'Not really, the fracas only lasted a few moments before I struggled free after punching one of them and when they realised I was more than a match for them, they raced off in their coach.'

'That was very brave of you, sir,' said the Commissioner.

'Well, I am one of the Queen's Hussars you know and our acknowledged bravery always comes to the fore in adversity,' said Fielding smugly.

'Quite so, sir.'

'What did these attackers look like, sir?' asked Hadley.

'I don't know, it was dark and they wore their hats pulled well down,' replied Fielding.

'Did you notice if they were Orientals, sir?'

'Orientals?'

'Yes, sir.'

'What sort of Orientals?'

'Chinese, sir.'

'No, I don't think they were Chinese, they were too big and powerful... the one who questioned me about Porter had an accent, possibly Scottish, but I can't be sure,' replied Fielding.

'Thank you, sir.'

'I've reported the incident to my Commanding officer, Colonel Pickering, and of course I am safe from any attack whilst in the barracks, but I insist on a round the clock armed guard for me and my family, whilst at home, until these killers are caught,' said Fielding.

'Of course, sir, and I will see to it personally that you are well guarded at all times when you are away from your army quarters,' said the Commissioner.

'I'm pleased to hear it.'

Bell and Hadley were dismissed by the Commissioner to organise armed officers to accompany Major Fielding and to contact the Newbury Police requesting officers to guard The Manse at Kintbury.

As they descended the stairs Bell said 'God, what a mess this is, Hadley.'

'It is a desperate situation, sir and seems to get worse by the hour.'

'Without a doubt.'

'I'm glad that the Commissioner has assigned more help, sir.'

'Well that may be a problem in disguise because it could be that we lose direction and end up tripping over one another,' said Bell as they reached the landing outside his office.

'I suppose that's always a possibility, sir.'

'Now, while I go and organise men for the Major's protection, you telegraph Newbury, I think you know the Inspector down there after one of your country jaunts to Berkshire, Hadley.'

'Yes, sir… he's a reliable chap called Wilkes.'

'Right… well get to it, Hadley then come and brief me on your plans for the day.'

'Very good, sir.'

Big Ben struck eleven o'clock as Hadley finished briefing the Chief Inspector after telegraphing Wilkes at Newbury. Bell was alarmed at the news that the killers may possibly be Chinese.

'My God, Hadley, we don't want any more trouble with them hiding in their blasted secret opium dens, we've got enough with the bloody Russians pouring into London.'

'I appreciate that, sir,' said Hadley.

'We don't want to end up trying to keep public order on London streets because of bloody foreigners causing mayhem!' said Bell as Brackley entered the office carrying a buff folder.

'Sir, the Commissioner has listed the officers who are to support you and has called a meeting at midday,' said Brackley as he placed the folder on Bell's desk.

'Thank you, Mr Brackley, we will be there.'

Hadley realised that his plans for the day were altered irrevocably and he hoped that Cooper and Talbot were making some progress.

'So let's see who the Commissioner has given us,' said Bell as he opened the folder and read out the names.

'Inspectors Hanson and Mercer... Sergeants Wells, Sullivan, Harrison and Gibson... do you know any of them, Hadley?'

'I know Hanson quite well, sir, but I've only met Mercer a few times,' replied Hadley.

'What about the Sergeants?'

'I believe that Wells is a reliable officer, but I don't know any of the others, sir.'

'Mmm, well let's hope we can all work together and find these murderers before they kill again,' said Bell.

Hadley returned to his office and briefed George on the latest developments.

'Does that mean I'll have to type the reports for the other two Inspectors as well as yours, sir?'

'I'm afraid so, George,' replied Hadley.

'Well in that case I'll definitely need an assistant, sir.'

'That's out of the question, George, because the Commissioner has given strict orders that nobody is to be told about the Holy Grail and I could not possibly trust another clerk, you are a very special and privileged person,' said Hadley, hoping that the compliment would smooth George over.

'I may be very special and privileged, sir... but I'll still have to do twice as much work as usual!'

'Yes, I'm afraid you will, George, now would you please make a nice pot of tea whilst I write up some notes?'

It was just before midday when Hadley went up to the Chief's office.

'Ah, Hadley, I've decided that Hanson and Mercer should work in your office and Cooper and Talbot will have to move out and join the other Sergeants somewhere else,' said Bell.

'I'm afraid I can't agree to that, sir.'

'Nonsense, Hadley, I'm giving you an order!'

'Sir, with respect, I need my men with me…'

'We haven't got time to argue now, Hadley, the Commissioner is expecting us,' interrupted Bell as Big Ben began to chime twelve o'clock.

When they arrived in the Commissioner's office Hanson and Mercer were already there. The great one introduced them and said 'Chief Inspector Bell is in charge of this important investigation and you will all report to him before he reports to me.' They all nodded and chorused 'yes, sir.'

'Inspectors Hanson and Mercer, I have decided to relieve you of your other duties to assist in this important murder inquiry.'

'Yes, sir.'

'I regard you both as competent officers and this case has far reaching implications for the Force if not brought to a speedy conclusion, namely the immediate arrest of the killers.'

'Rest assured that we'll do our very best, sir,' said Hanson.

'I expect nothing less, Inspector,' said the Commissioner firmly.

'Quite so, sir,' said Mercer.

The Commissioner then briefed them with all the details of the investigation so far and when he told them about the Holy Grail the officers were dumbstruck.

'So it really exists, sir?' asked Hanson in a whisper.

'It would appear so, Inspector.'

'Dear God, no wonder these killers used torture to try and find out where it is hidden, sir,' said Mercer.

'Indeed and if the Grail proves to be genuine, then it is priceless beyond any earthly measure,' said the Commissioner gravely.

'Do you have any doubts that it is genuine, sir?' asked Hanson.

'I can only answer that after it has been recovered by you and authenticated by experts,' replied the Commissioner.

'Recovered by us, sir?' asked Mercer in a shocked tone.

'I'm afraid so, Inspector, not only do you have to arrest the killers of the Porter brothers and find their parents, but you must also recover this priceless relic.'

'But that may be impossible, sir, if William Porter was the only person who knew where it is hidden and he was murdered before telling anyone else... then we have no hope of ever finding it,' said Hanson.

'Inspector Hanson, failure is not an option in this investigation so you all better prepare yourselves for a difficult and dangerous inquiry that lies before you... and ensure that you are armed at all times,' said the Commissioner. They glanced un-easily at each other as they realised the monumental task before them.

CHAPTER 6

After being dismissed by the Commissioner the Inspectors made their way down to Bell's office where he laid out his proposals for the investigation. Hadley was anxious to contact Palmer and find out if any progress had been made in the search for Mr and Mrs Porter but listened patiently as Bell waffled on, often repeating himself. When the Chief Inspector had finally finished giving them his opinions and directions, the three detectives made their way down to Hadley's office where he asked George to make tea and then go to the canteen for sandwiches. The clerk sighed, nodded and disappeared.

Over lunch, Hadley discussed the case and suggested that the Inspectors should read the background notes that Bell had prepared on Porter before deciding how they should carry forward their inquiries. He was determined to be free to work alone with Cooper and Talbot and not be hampered by Hanson, Mercer and the four Sergeants. Hadley thought the Chief Inspector was right when he said that too many officers may complicate matters and this was the result of those in power dictating policy without understanding. However, it would look good when reported in the Press.

Hadley left the Inspectors in his office planning their lines of inquiry and took a Police Coach to Whitechapel.

When he arrived in Palmer's office, the Inspector looked tired and harassed.

'Any developments, Jack?' asked Hadley as he sat opposite.

'I'm afraid not, Jim. I've got my men making house to house inquiries around Limehouse but there's nothing to report so far.'

'Well, I suppose the Porters could be anywhere in London but I've a feeling that they may still be hereabouts,' said Hadley.

'If they are, we'll find them, Jim.'

'I'm sure.'

'Now about the Chinese, I think that we should muster as many officers as we can before attempting to search their premises because there may be violence, Jim.'

'I agree, so let's leave that until my Sergeants have returned from their inquiries and I'll also bring the officers that have just been assigned to the case,' said Hadley.

'You've had more men given to you?' asked Palmer in surprise.

'Yes, on the orders of the Home Secretary, there are another two Inspectors and four Sergeants,' replied Hadley with a grin.

'Blimey, Jim, there's a 'blimmin' army of you now!'

'Indeed there will be, Jack. In the meantime, I'm going up to Islington to speak to Porter's landlady, Mrs Dawkins, to see if she can give any information that might be useful,' said Hadley.

'Right, I'll see you back here later with your army, Jim,' said Palmer with a smile.

When Hadley knocked at the door of 12 Gaskin Street it was opened by a middle aged woman who asked abruptly 'what do you want?'

'Mrs Dawkins?' asked Hadley with a smile.

'No, I'm her sister.'

'Is Mrs Dawkins at home?'

'Who are you and what do you want?' she asked again but before Hadley could answer she said angrily 'you're not another one of them reporters from the newspapers are you?'

'No madam, I'm Inspector Hadley from Scotland Yard and I would like to have a few words with Mrs Dawkins if she's in.'

'Wait here then and I'll see if she'll talk to you,' said the woman as she closed the door. Hadley waited for a few minutes before the door opened and she said 'you'd better come in.' Hadley nodded and followed her into the small parlour where Mrs Dawkins stood up to greet him. After introducing himself, he said to the pale faced, anxious woman 'I know that this must be very upsetting for you, Mrs Dawkins, but if you can tell me anything that will assist me in my inquiries I would be very grateful.'

'Oh dear,' she said quietly before sitting down.

'Please take your time, madam,' said Hadley with smile as he sat opposite.

'Well there's not much to tell, Inspector,' she said.

'Perhaps I may ask you some questions that might help you remember.'

'Don't you go upsetting her like them newspaper men did,' said the sister firmly.

55

'I have no intention of doing any such thing, madam,' replied Hadley glancing at the truculent woman standing with her arms folded.

'I'm pleased to hear it I'm sure.'

'Now tell me Mrs Dawkins, when did Mr Porter move in?'

'It was about two weeks ago, he said he had just left the army and was looking for lodgings for a short time then he said he'd be going away,' she replied.

'Did he say where?'

'No, he didn't.'

'Did he have any visitors?'

'Only one.'

'Do you know who he was?'

'I don't know his name but he was a priest,' she replied and Hadley's blue eyes lit up.

'Tell me more about this priest.'

'Well as I remember he came twice or was it three times? I'm not too sure, Inspector.'

'No matter, did Mr Porter mention his name at all or tell you anything about this priest?'

'No, I just thought that he must have been doing something for the church and of course I approved of that... it was a terrible shock to find him... just terrible,' she broke off and tears began to course down her cheeks.

'I told you not to upset her!' said the sister before sitting beside Mrs Dawkins and putting a comforting arm around the distressed woman.

'I'm sorry, but I do have my duty....'

'You should be sorry! Your duty... fiddlesticks!' she interrupted firmly.

'One final question, Mrs Dawkins, did this priest have an accent?'

'No, not as I remember,' she replied as she wiped her eyes with a handkerchief.

'Thank you for your help, madam, that will be all for the moment,' said Hadley with a smile.

'I hope you're not going to bother her again,' said the sister.

'I may have a few more questions for Mrs Dawkins later,' replied Hadley before he stood up. The sister said nothing but glared at him before she showed him to the front door and slammed it shut after he had stepped out into the street.

On the journey back to the Yard Hadley's mind raced with many unanswered questions as well as the implications of the unknown priest's involvement with Porter. Why hadn't this priest come forward after reading about the Porter brothers' murders? Was he involved in some way? Did the Catholic Church now know of the Holy Grail's existence and recent discovery? Was it all a dark conspiracy by the Church to hide the Grail forever at the Vatican in Rome? He was still trying to answer the questions logically when the coach pulled into the Yard.

Cooper had arrived back and was in conversation with Hanson when Hadley entered the office.

'Any luck, Sergeant?' he asked.

'I'm afraid not, sir, the people I spoke to said they hadn't seen Porter for some time,' replied Cooper.

'Somehow I'm not surprised,' said Hadley as he sat behind his desk.

'Why not, Jim?' asked Hanson.

'Because they are living in desperate fear, Bob and this investigation appears to be getting more complicated and darker by the minute,' replied Hadley.

'You can say that again,' said Hanson.

'I've just come from Islington where I spoke to Porter's landlady, Mrs Dawkins, she says that a priest called two or three times to see Porter,' said Hadley.

'A priest?'

'Yes, I wonder who he is, what did he want, what does he know and why hasn't he come forward?' said Hadley as Talbot arrived back.

'Anything interesting to report, Sergeant?' asked Hadley.

'No, sir, everyone I spoke to is either too frightened to say anything or they really just don't know,' replied Talbot.

'Again I'm not surprised… if they've read the lurid details of the murders reported in the papers then they will all have been struck dumb with fear,' said Hadley as Mercer entered the office.

'I've finished briefing the Sergeants on what we plan to do, Bob,' said Mercer.

'Good,' said Hanson then looking at Cooper and Talbot he said 'now Sergeants, if you would like to join the others in the office down the corridor...'

'My Sergeants are staying here,' interrupted Hadley.

'But Jim, the Chief said that the Sergeants would have to...'

'I don't care what he said, Bob, my men are staying with me!'

'How can we discuss anything private...' began Hanson.

'There is nothing private in this investigation, Bob and we haven't the time to discuss niceties at the moment, there's work to be done!'

'If you say so, Jim,' said Hanson with a resigned sigh.

'Right... Sergeant Talbot would you please ask the other Sergeants to join us?' asked Hadley with a smile.

'Yes certainly, sir,' replied Talbot with a grin.

The Sergeants crowded into Hadley's office and when they were quiet he said 'we have work to do in Whitechapel, gentlemen, we will be searching for Mr and Mrs Porter at various premises owned by the Chinese.' There was a collective sound of drawing breath before Hadley continued 'we will be assisted by Inspector Palmer and some of his men, but be aware that this operation could be both difficult and dangerous as I believe the Chinese may be the killers we're looking for.'

Hanson and Mercer looked anxious, along with two of the younger Sergeants.

'Are we going to be armed, sir?' asked Sergeant Wells, who was a well built, mature officer.

'Yes you are... and whilst Sergeant Talbot arranges the transport for us, I want you all to go to the armoury and draw revolvers and ammunition,' replied Hadley as they looked relieved.

Big Ben was striking five o'clock when the officers set off in three Police Coaches for Whitechapel. During the journey, Hadley remained deep in thought whilst Hanson and Mercer talked incessantly about their plans for the investigation. They often contradicted each other and Hadley was pleased that he had made the conscious decision to remain separate from their intended lines of inquiry. The Inspectors seemed more concerned with what actions they should take to impress the Chief Inspector, so ensuring his favourable report to the Commissioner. Hadley had no time for this political game playing nonsense when lives were at stake and when the coach pulled into Whitechapel Police station he was glad he did not have to listen any more.

When the Inspectors entered Palmer's office, Hadley was pleased to find Agnes and Florrie there as he knew they must have brought some useful information to Palmer.

'Hello, ladies, this is a nice surprise,' said Hadley.

'We're always a nice surprise, Jim,' said Agnes with a smile.

'They've just brought in some interesting information, Jim,' said Palmer.

'Too blimmin' right we 'ave!' exclaimed Florrie.

'Go on,' said Hadley.

'We know who them blimmin' Chinese are who done away with that poor bugger in Turner Street,' said Florrie triumphantly.

'That's excellent news, Florrie, but tell me how you know that for certain?' asked Hadley.

'Well, one of my regulars, who likes to chase the dragon occasionally in one of them smoking dens, told me... after we'd finished our business... that last night when he was 'aving a smoke, he heard some Chinese bloke talking about the 'orrible murder and he said it was the Wang brothers what done it,' she replied.

Agnes added quickly 'and the word down the Lane is that they've got another secret opium den at their warehouse in Mellish Street where all the toffs go.'

'And I bet that's where them poor people who are missing are being kept,' said Florrie with her eyes bright with excitement.

'Well that's only hearsay but we'll start the search there... have you given the addresses of these places to Inspector Palmer?' asked Hadley.

'Too right we have, Jim,' replied Agnes and Palmer nodded. Hadley thanked the women for their help and they both smiled at their favourite Policeman. As they left the office, Agnes told Hadley that she hoped to see him and his Sergeants later in the Kings Head where, over a few glasses of gin, he could tell her and Florrie the outcome of the police search. He just smiled and replied 'I'll see.'

Hadley looked at the Inspectors and said 'gentlemen, let's brief the Sergeants and make a move!'

Palmer, Sergeant Morris and two constables joined Hadley's entourage before they set off for Mellish Street.

Hadley decided that he and Palmer with their Sergeants should lead the raid into the warehouse where the secret opium den was located, whilst Hanson and Mercer led the search at the other address in Tooke Street.

'I just hope we don't find anybody of importance in this den for toffs, Jack, it would be embarrassing,' said Hadley with a smile.

'I shouldn't think we will, Jim, anyone special would have gone back to his club by now for an early dinner,' replied Palmer with a grin and Hadley chuckled.

In the early evening, Limehouse Reach was still busy with costermongers, warehousemen and delivery wagons. The Police coaches arrived in Mellish Street and on Hadley's instruction, the Police drivers pulled the horses up about fifty yards from the alleyway that led to the back of the warehouse owned by the Wang brothers, whilst the third coach with Hanson, Mercer and their Sergeants made its way further along to Tooke Street. The element of surprise was essential if violence was to be avoided. After they stepped down from the coach, Hadley and Palmer led the officers quickly along Mellish Street to Croft Alley. Within minutes they arrived at the entrance to the warehouse were the faded green sign saying 'Ho and Chi Wang. Rice Importers' hung lopsidedly above the door. Without any hesitation Hadley opened the rickety door and stepped into the gloomy interior where he was immediately struck by the strong smell of opium. An old Chinaman was standing at a small counter and behind it was draped a large heavy curtain that blocked off the access to the rest of the warehouse. The man looked up in alarm and asked 'what you want, mister?'

'We're Police Officers and we're here to search these premises,' replied Hadley.

'You can't come in!' said the man in a high pitched tone.

'You will stand aside!' shouted Hadley as another Chinaman

suddenly appeared from behind the curtain and said 'I am owner here, what do you want, Mister?'

'Who are you?' asked Hadley.

'I am Chi Wang, I am owner with my brother,' he replied giving a little bow.

'I'm Inspector Hadley from Scotland Yard and with these officers I intend to search these premises for missing persons,' said Hadley firmly.

'No one here except us,' said Chi Wang.

'We'll see for ourselves and if you're right Mr Wang, you have nothing to be concerned about,' said Hadley. Wang spoke hurriedly in Cantonese to the old man who nodded and immediately disappeared behind the curtain.

'So, who you looking for, Inspector?' asked Chi Wang.

'A couple named Mr and Mrs Porter, do you know them?' replied Hadley knowing that Wang was playing for time.

'No and they not here, no one here, only rice in here,' said Wang with a shrug of his shoulders. Hadley turned to his officers and said 'search every inch of this place right now!'

They all moved forward towards the curtain but Chi Wang attempted to bar them from passing into the area beyond.

'Nothing here… nothing here,' he said forcefully.

'Then you've nothing to fear!' said Hadley as Talbot pushed the Chinaman aside.

'You find trouble!' said Chi Wang but Hadley ignored the remark, drew his revolver and said to a Constable 'stay with this man until we've finished the search.'

'Right, sir.'

Palmer led the way through the curtain into the gloomy interior followed by the Sergeants with the other Constables bringing up the rear. Hadley joined them as they fanned out and began searching amongst the piled high sacks of rice. They moved slowly and methodically along narrow alleyways through the warehouse to the rear of the building but found nothing of significance.

'Where's that old man disappeared to, Jack?' asked Hadley when he caught up with Palmer.

'I've no idea, Jim.'

'I can't see any way out back here and he hasn't passed us, so he must be hiding somewhere,' said Hadley glancing around the dingy building.

'I think I heard a noise coming from under the floor over there, sir... where that cart is,' said Talbot pointing towards a large hand cart full of sacks of rice standing nearby. Hadley said 'let's see if there's anything underneath shall we?' Cooper, Talbot and Morris dragged the hand cart away and Hadley saw a trap door in the floorboards. He pointed at it and said 'this might lead to somewhere interesting, Sergeant.' Talbot bent down and pulled the trap door open by its brass ring to reveal stone steps descending to a cellar below. The smell of opium wafted up and Hadley was sure he heard a muffled sound and said 'someone's down there... find a light quickly!' Sergeant Morris had his acetylene lamp with him and cautiously led the way down the steps, followed by Talbot and Cooper with their revolvers at the ready. When Hadley joined his Sergeants at the bottom of the stairs he was taken aback for a moment when he surveyed the dimly lit, hellish scene before him. The smell and drifting smoke from the opium was overpowering and drugged individuals lay like untidy bundles of clothes on small beds sucking at their long pipes. Women flitted silently about carrying tiny bowls amongst those still smoking and paid little attention to the officers.

'Good God Almighty,' whispered Palmer as he joined Hadley.

'It's a scene of Hell on Earth, Jack!'

'Never a truer word spoken,' said Palmer. Suddenly three men appeared through a door at the back of the curtain draped cellar and rushed towards the officers.

'Hey up lads... I think we've got trouble!' said Hadley as he caught the glint of their knives. Cooper and Talbot moved forward, pointed their revolvers at arm's length whilst Morris shone his torch at them. Cooper shouted 'hold! We are armed Police!' They were stocky, well built men and Hadley guessed that they were Malays. The tallest man was carrying what looked like a Navy cutlass and he began to raise it to strike a blow at Cooper. Hadley thought in a split second that either the men did not understand English or were oblivious to their own mortality. He re-acted instantly by raising his revolver and firing a shot into the ceiling. The muzzle flash and loud report stopped the Malay's in their tracks and momentarily lit the cellar in a flash of light that

62

made the ghastly scene seem unreal. Some of the women screamed whilst the smokers who were still conscious jumped at the sound. Suddenly the old Chinaman appeared from behind a curtain at the back of the cellar where he had been watching the events unfold and shouted in Cantonese at the Malay's. They drew back whilst he came forward and confronted the officers, shouting 'you get out! Get out now!' as he waved his arms at them.

'Arrest that man and handcuff him along with the rest of them!' said Hadley firmly. Talbot grabbed the Chinaman whilst Palmer, Morris, Cooper and the Constables rushed at the Malay's who resisted by slashing out at them with their knives. Hadley fired again into the ceiling but it had no effect so he raced forward to assist his men being attacked by the Malay's. Morris caught one of them around the neck and as the man attempted to stab him, Cooper struck the Malay a heavy blow to his head with the butt of his revolver and he collapsed to the floor with Morris still hanging onto him. At that moment the other two stopped struggling, dropped their weapons and surrendered. They were quickly hand cuffed and led away up the stairs out of the dingy cellar.

Hadley surveyed the scene and said to Palmer with a grin 'well, I'm glad that all ended happily, Jack!'

'Yes indeed,' chuckled Palmer.

'So I think we'll leave this lot stewing in their own juice whilst we get our violent friends away then we'll search the place thoroughly.'

'Right you are, Jim.'

Making their way out of the cellar to the entrance of the warehouse they found Morris and Cooper helping the Constable, who had been left guarding Chi Wang, to his feet.

Hadley looked quizzically at Cooper before asking 'where is he, Sergeant?'

'I'm afraid he's attacked the Constable and scarpered, sir,' replied Cooper apologetically.

CHAPTER 7

The coach with Hanson, Mercer and their Sergeants pulled up right outside the Wang Emporium in Tooke Street. The narrow shop front was painted a dull red and the window was full of decorated tea boxes, bone china tea sets, gold painted dragons and other Chinese bric-a-brac. Hanson led his men into the shop where an Oriental woman looked up in surprise from behind the high counter, which ran down the length of the shop.

'Yes, mister?' she said nervously.

'We're police officers from Scotland Yard and we intend to search these premises,' replied Hanson.

'What you do that for?' she asked.

'We have reason to believe that missing persons may be held here against their will,' he replied.

'Nobody here except me and girl,' she said hurriedly before ringing a small hand bell.

'Well we shall see about that,' said Hanson as a door at the rear of the shop opened and a small Chinese girl appeared. She looked anxiously at the officers, gave a little bow to them then went behind the counter and stood next to the woman.

'See, nobody here, mister, only Tai Lu and me.'

'Do you know if the Wang brothers are here?' asked Mercer.

'They not here,' she replied shaking her head.

'But do you know where they are?' Mercer persisted.

'They not here,' she repeated nervously, looking from one Inspector to the other with wide-eyed apprehension. Hanson glanced up at a large gold framed sepia photograph on the wall of the Wang brothers standing outside the Emporium.

Hanson pointed at the photograph and asked 'is that them?' The woman looked and nodded replying 'yes, mister.'

'Then we'll take that for identification purposes... Sergeant Wells, seize that photo and take it out to the coach,' said Hanson.

'Right sir.'

'Now men, let's begin the search,' said Hanson.

Mercer led Sergeants Harrison and Gibson to the door at the back of the shop whilst Hanson and Sullivan went behind the counter.

The woman pushed passed them and hurried to the back door attempting to stop the officers by shouting 'you no go in there, private!'

'Please stand aside!' said Mercer firmly.

'You no go in!' she screamed as she stood in front of the door. Sergeant Harrison grabbed the woman and moved her forcefully out of the way. Mercer opened the door and went through into a dingy corridor, followed by the Sergeants. Wells returned to the shop as Hanson said 'let's see what she's trying to hide from us.' They hurried on and followed the others into the corridor as Tai Lu ran out of the shop and disappeared into the busy street.

At the end of the corridor was a flight of rickety stairs that led up to the floor above and a door that led down to a cellar.

'I'll take the upstairs whilst you search the cellar,' said Hanson to Mercer.

'Right, Bob,' replied Mercer before he led his men down the stone steps to the dimly lit cellar. The smell of opium grew stronger as they neared the final step and when they stood at the cellar entrance they were transfixed by the hellish sight before them. The walls were draped in dark red, heavy curtains and a number of beds were in rows, lying on them were smokers, drifting in and out of consciousness. Two Chinese women, carrying small bowls, stopped what they were doing and stared at the officers.

'I doubt if the Porters are amongst this lot but they could be in another room behind these curtains,' said Mercer.

'Right, sir, we'll look behind them all,' said Gibson.

Hanson climbed the stairs to the landing which had several packing cases of various sizes piled up against the wall. There were two small rooms either side of the landing with more cases and the rooms were searched thoroughly before Hanson led his men up another flight of stairs to the top of the building. There was a single flickering candle in a wall holder to light the windowless landing and only one door leading from it. Hanson opened it and stepped into a dimly lit attic where several opium smokers lay about like rags on small beds. He noticed two Oriental women attending to the clients nearest the door but suddenly he was aware of a well built man stepping forward out of the smoke filled gloom.

'Hello, mister, you want smoke okay?'

'No, we're Police officers and we intend…' Hanson began but was interrupted by the man shouting in Cantonese.

'And you're under arrest… cuff him Sergeant!' shouted Hanson and as the man began to struggle with Sullivan, two men carrying batons appeared from behind a curtain at the far end of the attic. They raced forward as Sullivan attempted to handcuff the first man and Wells drew his revolver and pointed it at the men.

'No trouble now, so come quietly,' said Wells firmly but they took no notice and struck out at Sullivan with their batons. One missed but the other caught the Sergeant on his shoulder which caused him to cry out in pain. Wells hesitated for a moment but fired into the ceiling as Hanson rushed forward to assist Sullivan. When Mercer and his men heard the shot they stopped their search and raced upstairs to the attic where they found the officers struggling with the three men. The women had dropped their bowls and joined in the fight, biting and scratching the officers. The speed and fury of the attack had left the Police floundering until Mercer's men arrived and lashed out with their truncheons, striking the assailants repeatedly about the head. The women were not spared and one of them fell unconscious to the floor before being trampled in the melee. The attackers were eventually overpowered and two lay on the floor with heavily bleeding head wounds, whilst the third sat dazed and disorientated.

'We'd better send for an ambulance, Bob, and get them away to hospital,' said Mercer.

'It would be quicker if we took them in our coach,' said Hanson.

'Right, let's do that,' said Mercer.

After the injured men were all handcuffed, the officers assisted them downstairs along with the two women. On reaching the shop they were confronted by a number of Malay and Chinese men carrying batons and clubs of various sizes.

'Where you take them, mister?' asked the foremost Chinaman in a threatening tone.

'To hospital and then to Whitechapel Police station,' replied

Hanson.

'No, we take care of them,' said the Chinaman.

'They're all under arrest, so stand aside if you don't want to join them!' said Hanson firmly.

'They stay here, mister.'

'Listen to me, whoever you are, we're armed Police officers and will not hesitate to shoot anyone attempting to stop us carrying out our duties!' said Hanson forcefully.

'You not take them!' shouted the Chinaman.

'Oh yes we will!' shouted Hanson before he attempted to push the Chinaman aside. Then all hell broke loose as the men attacked the officers whilst Tai Lu looked in through the shop front door and smiled at the escalating fracas.

Palmer had sent Morris with two Constables back to Whitechapel with their prisoners whilst he, Hadley, Cooper and Talbot hurried round to Wang's Emporium to see if Hanson and Mercer had managed to find the Porter's or the Wang brothers. A sizeable crowd had gathered outside the shop watching the unfolding violence within and some bystanders had joined the Chinese in fighting the officers.

As their coach pulled up at the edge of the fast growing crowd, which had now spilled into the road, Hadley shouted 'we've got to control this situation before it really gets out of hand so when we're outside the shop fire your weapons in the air!'

'Right, sir,' the Sergeants shouted in chorus before they followed the Inspectors out of the coach. Hadley and his men pushed their way through the crowd shouting 'Police! Make way! Make way!' They struggled to reach the shop doorway and did so after exchanging a few blows with spectators who were intent on stopping them. They fired their revolvers into the air which brought a momentary halt to the fighting inside. Hadley and Palmer led the way into the shop with Cooper and Talbot. The Inspectors pulled one man after another away from the struggling melee, which had renewed, whilst the Sergeant's struck them down with the butts of their revolvers. Soon it was all over and Hanson, Mercer and their Sergeants looked relieved.

'You've arrived just in time Jim, thanks,' said Hanson with a smile as he surveyed the injured and groaning men on the floor.

'You're welcome, Bob,' said Hadley.

'This little lot will take some sorting out, Jim, so I'd better get more help,' said Palmer with a sigh.

'If you would, Jack.'

Palmer raced back to Whitechapel Police station to summon more men, two prison wagons and ambulances from The London Hospital. Meanwhile, Hadley and the officers identified the main suspects for the unprovoked attack and let the bystanders leave after a strict Police warning for foolishly joining in the affray. Hadley questioned the Orientals who understood English, regarding Chi Wang, his brother and the Porter's, but they denied all knowledge of their whereabouts, which did not unduly surprise him.

When Palmer arrived back with Morris and all the men he could muster, the prisoners were escorted out through the hostile, jeering crowd to the wagons. Two ambulances arrived moments later and took away the men and women who had been injured. Before they left for The London, Hadley gave strict instructions to the Constables escorting them that they should be kept under close guard until he arrived at the hospital.

After the prisoner wagons and ambulances had departed, it was decided to leave Sergeant Morris with two Constables at the warehouse and Talbot with two more men at the Emporium in case Chi Wang or his brother returned. The Inspectors, along with the remaining officers, then made their way to Whitechapel Police station to debrief and plan the next move in the search for the Wang brothers and the Porters.

On arrival at the station Hadley telegraphed Inspector Bromwich at Mile End, requesting his assistance and also asked the Duty Inspector in the Watch Office at the Yard for six more armed men to relieve Morris and Talbot.

They were enjoying a much needed pot of tea and some sandwiches from the canteen, when Bromwich arrived. Hadley introduced him to the other Inspectors then quickly briefed him on the day's events, he looked quite shocked when Hadley finished.

'So, how can I help you, Jim?' asked Bromwich.

'Arrange for an immediate house to house search from

Limehouse Reach up to the end of your patch for these Chinese brothers and the Porter's, Phil,' replied Hadley.

'Blimey, that's a tall order, Jim, I'm not sure I can do that without getting permission from the Chief and he's gone home now,' said Bromwich.

'The Commissioner told me that I was to use all possible means to crack this case and that's why he ordered Hanson and Mercer here, along with four Sergeants to join me in this investigation, Phil,' said Hadley firmly.

'Then it must be done,' whispered Bromwich.

'Time is of the essence, Phil,' said Hadley.

After Bromwich left to arrange for his men to begin the search from Mile End, Hadley decided to go with Cooper to The London, then to the warehouse and Emporium, whilst Palmer, Hanson and Mercer started interviewing the prisoners.

As the coach rattled over the cobblestones Hadley said 'today we've seen that violence awaits us at every turn, Sergeant and I'm very fearful for our future.'

'But we are armed, sir, so if push comes to shove we can shoot the buggers down... the Commissioner said so,' replied Cooper.

'He did indeed, Sergeant, but in my experience, blame for the unlawful killing of criminals, however justified, can ruin promising careers.'

At The London, Hadley spoke to the duty Doctor and was told that all the prisoners had sustained injuries serious enough for them to remain in hospital for several days. Hadley then asked about the condition of Mrs Jane Porter and the Doctor said that she was still under sedation and could not be disturbed. Hadley made the Doctor aware that Mrs Porter was now more likely to be the target of attack by her husband's killers, which alarmed the Doctor.

'Good God, Inspector, this is a hospital and not a place for such outrageous behaviour!'

'Quite so, Doctor, that's why you have the armed Policemen here to guard against such eventualities,' said Hadley with a smile whilst making a mental note to increase the number of officers.

The detectives left the hospital and made their way to the

warehouse in Mellish Street and were pleased to see that the armed officers from the Yard had just arrived. Sergeant Morris and his men were relieved from duty and returned to Whitechapel station whilst Hadley briefed the Yard officers before going down to the opium den. He and Cooper carefully studied each comatose smoker and Hadley decided to let them remain undisturbed. If there was anybody of importance laying there it would be best to leave them and hope that the Press did not get wind of their addiction.

Talbot was telling the Yard officers, in graphic detail, about the fight when Hadley and Cooper arrived at the Emporium. The crowd outside had dwindled to a few curious onlookers which was a relief to the detectives. Talbot confirmed that neither Chi Wang or his brother had been seen at the shop and the Oriental woman and Tai Lu had disappeared. Hadley briefed the officers and then returned to Whitechapel with his Sergeants and Constables.

Hanson and Mercer were still questioning the last of the prisoners when Hadley arrived with his men. Entering Palmer's office, he thought that his friend looked tired and frustrated.

'Well, what a day, Jack,' said Hadley as he slumped down in a chair.

'Yes, Jim and it's not over yet!'

'True... have you discovered anything significant from the prisoners?'

'Not really, they deny everything and none of them know where the Wang brothers are... and say they have never heard of the Porter's,' replied Palmer.

'It's to be expected.'

'The problem is that these bloody Orientals are violent and have no respect for the law.'

'That's obvious, Jack.'

'I'm afraid that we'll have plenty of trouble from them before this investigation is over,' said Palmer as Hanson and Mercer entered the office. Hadley looked up at them and asked 'well?'

'Nothing of any relevance, Jim,' replied Hanson.

'They all pretend they don't really understand English, shake their heads and say 'no' to everything,' added Mercer.

'Well we can hold them all and charge some of them with running the opium dens... that'll keep them behind bars for awhile,' said Hadley.

'True, but it won't help us to find the Porter's or the Wang brothers,' said Hanson.

'I think the Porter's are probably dead by now,' said Mercer.

'And the Wang boys are responsible,' added Hanson.

'If they are then we'll catch them and hang them for certain,' said Palmer.

The detectives discussed the investigation and their plans for the next day until Hanson glanced at his fob watch and announced it was almost ten o'clock and he was going home. Mercer also said that he'd enough for one day and left with him.

'Fancy a pint, Jack?' asked Hadley when they were alone.

'No thanks, Jim, I think I'll go home and get some rest as I'm sure tomorrow will be another busy day,' replied Palmer.

'That you can be sure of,' said Hadley with a smile before saying 'goodnight'.

Talbot and Cooper did not need much persuading to join Hadley for something to eat and a pint at the Kings Head before they went home. Hadley hoped that Agnes and Florrie were still there so he could talk to them about the day's events.

The pub was busy as usual and they had to push their way through to the bar where Vera was doing her best with the girls to serve everyone at once.

'Evening, Vera,' said Hadley loudly above the noise.

'Be with you in a minute, guvnor,' replied Vera as she pulled a foaming pint for a soldier and Hadley nodded before asking his Sergeants 'what do you want to eat?'

'I'm starving, so anything hot, sir,' replied Cooper.

'Same here, sir,' said Talbot.

Vera smiled as she asked 'your usual is it, gents?'

'Please, Vera, and what have you got to eat?'

'Not much now... it's late,' she replied as she began pulling their pints of stout.

'We're all starving Vera,' said Hadley.

'Right guvnor, I'll go in a minute and see what's left,' she replied as placed the first pint on the wet counter.

'Anything hot will do,' said Hadley and Vera nodded as Agnes appeared behind him, tapped his shoulder and asked 'will we do, Jim?' Hadley turned and laughed before replying 'you and Florrie will always do!' The women laughed and Florrie asked 'so are you ready for one of my hot 'specials'?'

'Not tonight, Florrie,' replied Hadley.

'Oh why not?' she asked.

'Because I'm still on duty!' replied Hadley with a grin as Vera placed the other pints on the counter and asked 'is it gins for the ladies, guvnor?'

'If you please, Vera.'

When they all had their drinks they said 'cheers' whilst Vera disappeared to the kitchen. She came back moments later and said 'we've got two steak and kidney pies left with some gravy but no mash, no peas but plenty of ham and cheese, so what's it to be?'

'The pies for my lads and I'll have a cheese sandwich with pickles, what do you want ladies?' said Hadley.

'Oh nothing thanks Jim, we've already had some jellied eels from Isaacs,' replied Agnes.

'Then it's two hot pies and a cheese and pickle sandwich, please Vera,' said Hadley.

'Right you are, guvnor.'

The door to the back room was open and Hadley could see several people at the table but said 'let's go and talk in there, it's a bit quieter.' The ladies nodded and led the way through to the back of the room where there was a small round table in the corner. The other drinkers looked suspiciously at them as they walked by and sat down round the table.

'So, I hear that our Bobbie blue eyes had plenty of trouble down at Limehouse tonight,' said Agnes.

'Just a little,' said Hadley with a smile.

'And did you find them missing people?' asked Florrie.

'No not yet.'

'Well I bet them blimmin' Chinese Wang brothers have got them somewhere,' she said firmly.

'I think you may be right, Florrie, and we need all the help we can get, so if you or any of the girls hear anything, let Jack Palmer know right away,' said Hadley.

'We will, Jim,' said Agnes as a barmaid arrived with a tray. The steaming pies, covered in gravy, were put in front of the Sergeants and Florrie said to Cooper 'that looks tasty, can I have a little bit?' He smiled and replied 'of course you can.'

'Careful, Sergeant, you never know what she'll be after next,' said Hadley with a grin.

'It's alright, sir, I'm quite safe because I'm married and on duty!' said Cooper and they all laughed.

Sitting in a Hansom cab on his way home, Hadley felt that little had been accomplished in the investigation and was very concerned at what lay ahead. The Wang brothers had to be found and arrested as they were suspects for the Porter's kidnapping. He knew that would be a very difficult task as the Chinese community were so hostile towards the Police and he was sure that they would not give the Police any assistance in finding the Wang brothers. However, he thought it more likely that the murders were committed by the men who had attacked Major Fielding outside his home. There were many unanswered questions spinning around in his head when he eventually arrived home to be greeted by Alice.

'I've saved some broth for you, Jim,' she said as she helped him off with his coat.

'Thank you, dear,' he replied.

'Your coat's heavy, what have you got in it?' she asked and he smiled then took out his revolver.

'Oh Jim, you know how I worry when you've got a gun,' she said.

'I know dear, but it's on the Commissioner's orders.'

'In that case whatever you are investigating must be dangerous,' she said and he just smiled and went through to the warm parlour.

CHAPTER 8

Hadley slept well and arrived in his office just before eight o'clock ready for another hectic day. George was already there with the kettle on and Cooper and Talbot arrived together as Big Ben struck the hour. The first thing Hadley asked them to do was write reports on the previous day's events for George to type whilst he went up to give a verbal account to the Chief Inspector.

When he had finished his tea, Hadley was just leaving to go up to Bell's office when Hanson and Mercer arrived. He told them where he was going and Hanson asked 'shall we come with you, Jim?'

'If you wish, but knowing the Chief, I'd advise you to stay here and write your reports because he's not best pleased with officers disturbing him first thing in the morning with bad news,' replied Hadley with a smile.

'Right you are, Jim.'

'Then we'll let you be the bearer of the news,' said Mercer.

'Yes, quite so… George will make a pot of tea for you and type your reports,' said Hadley and George sighed.

Chief Inspector Bell looked up from the newspaper on his desk and glared at Hadley when he entered the office.

'Good morning, sir,' said Hadley with a smile.

'What have you got to smile about, Inspector?' asked Bell angrily but before Hadley could reply, Bell continued 'something good I hope regarding the riots you caused in Limehouse last night, which are so extensively and comprehensively reported in this morning's Press!'

'Sir, with all due respect…'

'Respect Hadley… I think you must be deranged these days!'

'Sir, I haven't seen the papers but I expect the Press have exaggerated the events as usual…'

'But the public read and believe what they report Hadley!' interrupted Bell.

'I'm sure they do, sir, but it is not the truth!'

'And what is the truth may I ask?'

'Sir, if I…'

'The truth is, Hadley, that there was a fight last night between Police officers and Chinese immigrants where guns were fired in the street, endangering the general public and frightening the horses!'

'Sir...'

'That was before the casualty department at The London Hospital was overwhelmed by people injured by your men!' interrupted Bell angrily.

'On information received...'

'From one of your dubious and unreliable, drunk, street walkers no doubt,' interrupted Bell but Hadley ignored the remark and continued 'we were carrying out a search of premises owned by two Chinese brothers named Wang...'

'And did you find anything worth reporting to the Commissioner after causing this riot? The answer is 'no', Hadley!'

'But, sir...'

'According to the Press, all you found was a couple of opium dens!'

'We were searching for the Porter's sir and anything that could lead us further in our murder investigation.'

'Well it's simply not good enough, so be prepared for a very difficult meeting with the Commissioner,' said Bell.

'Oh very good, sir,' sighed Hadley.

'I'm expecting him to summon me at any moment so you'd better stay here and report everything in detail before we go up and try to give him some sort of coherent explanation of this latest mess,' said Bell.

Hadley had just finished speaking and Bell was about to question him further when Mr Brackley entered.

'Good morning Chief Inspector... Inspector, the Commissioner would like to see you both as soon as possible,' said Brackley. Bell sighed and replied 'thank you, Mr Brackley, we'll come immediately.'

The Commissioner was standing at the window looking out at the Thames when they entered his office. He did not turn to face them even when Bell cleared his throat and wished him 'good morning, sir.'

'I'm not sure it is, Chief Inspector,' said the great one calmly, still gazing out at the river. Hadley and Bell looked anxiously at each other knowing that the omens were not good.

'Sir, Hadley has explained everything...'

'Well it's a shame that he didn't explain it to the damned Press, Chief Inspector!' interrupted the Commissioner angrily as he whirled round to face them. There followed a few moments of shocked silence before the Commissioner sat at his desk and waved them to sit. They waited anxiously for him to speak.

'It is now two days since William Porter was murdered in Islington, his brother in Whitechapel and their parents kidnapped and both of you are fully aware of the seriousness of this investigation.'

'Oh yes indeed we are, sir,' whispered Bell hesitantly.

'So far there have been no arrests, no suspects and nothing positive to show, despite the enormous manpower resources put at your disposal to find these killers...'

'We are making some progress, sir,' interrupted Bell hesitantly.

'Chief Inspector, all I have to report to the Home Secretary at the moment is that we have the Bishop of London and the Archbishop of Canterbury under armed guard for their protection at Lambeth Palace and a riot in Limehouse!'

'We realise it looks bad...'

'Bad is not a word I would use to capture even the merest essence of your failure, Chief Inspector!' interrupted the Commissioner.

'But, sir...'

'Disastrous might be more suitable!' thundered the great one with his side whiskers bristling as never before.

Hadley took a deep breath and said 'I'm preparing a full and detailed report for you, sir and you'll have it on your desk by midday,' hoping that would placate the Commissioner.

'By God it had better be good, Hadley!'

'It will be, sir.'

'Now tell me what's in this report of yours that will calm my shattered nerves,' said the Commissioner in a soft voice as he narrowed his eyes, which quite unnerved Hadley.

Big Ben was striking nine o'clock when Hadley and the Chief

Inspector left the Commissioner and made their way down to Bell's office.

'I think we did our best to placate him,' said Bell as he slumped behind his desk.

'Yes, sir, and I believe we succeeded a little.'

'Only time will tell.'

'I'm sure that deep down he has some sympathy for us,' said Hadley.

'I do hope so, otherwise we'll both be on horse traffic duties by the end of the month,' said Bell wearily.

'That's not something I'd look forward to, sir.'

'Quite so, Hadley, now I suggest you get on with writing your report and leave me to worry about what the hell we do next,' said Bell.

When Hadley arrived back in his office Hanson and Mercer had left with their Sergeants to follow up further lines of inquiry in Whitechapel. He was relieved to be alone with Cooper and Talbot, telling them of the Commissioner's anger at their slow progress before beginning to write his report. Hadley had just put the final touches to it and given it to George to type when a messenger arrived from the telegraph office.

'This just came in for you, sir,' said the boy as he handed the buff envelope to Hadley.

'Thank you.'

Opening the message he read it and said 'good God Almighty!'

'What is it, sir?' asked Cooper in alarm.

'It's from Inspector Graves in Oxford and it says '*Inspector Hadley, I was called to Christ Church University in St. Aldates this morning where the body of Professor Horace Pennington was discovered. First indications at the crime scene showed that he had been cruelly tortured in a similar fashion to the Porter brothers, which was widely reported in the national Press. I believe that the killings may be linked and your presence here would be appreciated, yours, Inspector George Graves, Oxford Police.'*

'Blimey, sir!' exclaimed Talbot.

'If it is the same people who killed the Porter's then it probably rules out the Wang brothers, sir,' said Cooper.

'Maybe, Sergeant but they could have gone to Oxford last night after the disturbances.'

'So, it's off to Oxford post haste for us, sir,' said Talbot with a grin.

'Yes, Sergeant, I'll just let the Commissioner and the Chief know,' said Hadley.

'I'll look up the train times, sir,' said Cooper.

'Right.'

'Can I do anything, sir?' asked Talbot.

'Yes, Sergeant, draft a telegraph message to Inspector Palmer letting him know what has happened and ask him to tell Inspectors Hanson and Mercer,' replied Hadley before he hurried out and up the stairs to Bell's office.

The Chief read the message and his face drained of colour before he whispered 'my God, Hadley, the madness begins again.'

'Yes, sir.'

'The Commissioner must see this at once.'

'I agree, sir, and we all are ready to go up to Oxford to...'

'Go to Oxford? No, certainly not Hadley, you must stay here and let Inspector Graves investigate this murder,' interrupted Bell.

'But, sir, I believe it's vital that I...'

'Not another word, Hadley.'

The Commissioner read the message then looked at Hadley and said 'get up to Oxford as quick as you can, Inspector!'

'Very good, sir,' replied Hadley with a contented smile.

'We can't leave these provincial police people to investigate this murder - they'll probably miss something which could lead to the immediate arrest of these maniacs,' said the Commissioner firmly.

'Quite so, sir, and I fear none of them are as highly trained as us in such important murder inquiries,' said Bell before he glanced at Hadley who raised his eyebrows.

'I'm afraid you're right, Chief Inspector.'

'Thank you, sir,' beamed Bell.

'Return tonight if you can, Hadley and give me a report before my meeting with the Home Secretary... I'm due to see him at seven o'clock this evening.'

'Yes I will, sir and if necessary, one of my Sergeants can stay at Oxford to follow up any leads.'

'Good, now go to it gentlemen and let's hope that by tonight I have something positive to report to the powers that be.'

Hadley returned to his office and drafted a quick reply to Inspector Graves advising him that he and his Sergeants would be arriving at Oxford station on the train at eleven thirty. The detectives took a Police coach to Paddington and arrived just in time to catch the ten fifteen express. They had a compartment to themselves and so were able to discuss the case at length during the journey.

Inspector Graves and Sergeant Williams were at the station to meet them and after a brief summary of the investigation so far, Hadley asked to see the body. Graves ordered the Police coach to take them to the Radcliffe Infirmary where Professor Pennington's tortured remains lay in the mortuary.

'I've never seen anything like it, Inspector Hadley, he'd been tied to a chair, there was blood everywhere and his room had been ransacked,' said Graves as the coach hurried up St. Aldates and passed Christ Church University.

'Are there any witnesses who saw or heard anything unusual last night?' asked Hadley.

'No one has come forward yet, but my men are making inquiries throughout the university,' replied Graves.

'Good, let's hope they discover some useful information.'

'It has come as a great shock, the Professor was a very well liked and respected academic, and I'm sure he had no enemies,' said Graves as the coach turned in through the gates of the Radcliffe Infirmary.

'What did he study?' asked Hadley.

'I believe it was French medieval religious history,' replied Graves. Hadley's mind raced and made connections to the priest who visited Porter and the Catholic Church.

Doctor Morton led the detectives from his office in the morgue to the white tiled dissecting room and uncovered the body of Professor Pennington. Hadley looked at the flesh that had been cut in strips from his chest down to below his navel then at the large red weal around the neck signifying that the Professor had been garrotted. The injuries were identical to those inflicted on the Porter brothers.

'I've never seen such a mess, Inspector,' said Morton.

'I'm afraid that we have, Doctor,' said Hadley as he glanced at his Sergeants who nodded.

'Good heavens,' said Morton.

'We're investigating two murders in London where the victims died after similar torture and strangulation as the Professor,' said Hadley.

'This is barbaric and they must have endured an agonising death,' said Morton.

'I'm sure they did.'

'Well who ever committed these appalling crimes must be brought to justice then hanged without mercy,' said Morton.

'They will be caught, Doctor.'

'I do hope so.'

'Inspector Graves alerted me after linking the torture and murder of the Professor with my investigations into the killing of the Porter brothers, hopefully this will help close the net quickly on these maniacs' said Hadley and Graves smiled appreciatively when Morton looked at him.

'I'm pleased to hear it, Inspector,' said Morton.

'Indeed, Doctor, now would you please send a copy of your autopsy report to me at Scotland Yard?'

'Yes of course, Inspector.'

The detectives left the Radcliffe Infirmary and made their way to Christ Church University where, upon arrival, Graves led them to the crime scene. Hadley was pleased to see Constables stationed at various entrances talking to students and making notes, whilst two were guarding the door to the room where the murder had been committed. Graves opened the door and stood aside for the detectives to enter the ransacked, bloodstained room. The ropes, which had been cut to allow for the removal of the body, were still attached to the chair.

Hadley turned and asked Graves 'have you carried out a thorough search yet?'

'No, only a cursory one looking for a weapon, Inspector,'

replied Graves.

'Did you find anything?'

'No, I'm afraid not.'

'Right.'

'After I received the telegraph saying that you were on your way I thought it best to leave it to you, Inspector,' said Graves.

'Thank you.'

'I presume you would like to question the other members of staff and the Professor's students?' asked Graves.

'Yes please, Inspector.'

'I'll organise it immediately.'

'Thank you,' replied Hadley and Graves nodded then disappeared.

'So let's begin Sergeants and see what we can find that may shed some light on our darkness,' said Hadley.

The Professor had been untidy with books, papers and folders strewn about his desk even before the room was ransacked. The bookshelves along two walls of the large study were crammed full with leather bound books on French medieval history which had not been disturbed by the killers. The detectives searched methodically round the room before paying particular attention to the contents of a bureau and desk drawers. Cooper found several letters on the top of the desk and drew Hadley's attention to them.

'They're from a priest in Scotland, sir,' said Cooper as he handed them to Hadley. The first was dated three weeks ago and read:

Dear Professor, I am very pleased to learn the interesting information that you have managed to glean from the Abbey at Montauban and I believe that our quest will soon be fulfilled in glorious triumph. Please let me know immediately you have more news. Yours truly, Andrew Sinclair.

Hadley then read the next letter dated a week after the first.

Dear Professor, I am troubled by the news that you believe some information has been passed to the French authorities by the Abbey at Montauban. It is of the utmost importance that we move swiftly to protect our quest so please do not delay for a moment, yours truly, Andrew Sinclair.

The final letter dated just four days ago and said:

Dear Professor, after reading your last letter I am very concerned so I suggest you come to Stirling as soon as possible for your own safety. I will make all the necessary arrangements for you, yours truly, Andrew Sinclair.

The letters were written on headed paper giving the address of Saint Mary's Church in Stirling and were signed in a scrawl by the priest, Andrew Sinclair. Hadley's mind raced as he made the connections to the man with a Scottish accent who had attempted to kidnap Major Fielding. He was concerned by the obvious involvement of the French and he wondered if the Grail had been taken back to France in medieval times. His thoughts were interrupted by Cooper who said 'there's some letters here in French, sir, they're all from an Abbey at a place called Montauban near Toulouse.'

'We'll take them back to the Yard, get them translated and find out precisely what's been going on, Sergeant.'

'Very good, sir,' replied Cooper as Talbot suddenly exclaimed 'blimey, sir, there's a note here from William Porter!'

Talbot handed the note to Hadley and at that moment Graves re-appeared and said 'I've assembled all the Professor's colleagues in the Master's study for you, Inspector.'

'Thank you, I'll be with you in minute,' replied Hadley before he read Porter's note:

Dear Professor, thanks for all your help but I think you may in danger now so be on your guard, yours truly, William Porter.

CHAPTER 9

Hadley left Talbot to continue searching the room whilst he and Cooper followed Graves to the Master's study where the staff and a few students had been assembled. The anxious and shocked gathering of academics sat quietly as Graves introduced the detectives.

The Master said 'this is a truly horrific crime, Inspector, so please be assured that we will do everything in our power to assist you in bringing this mindless killer to justice.'

'Thank you, sir, any help that you can give us will be greatly appreciated,' said Hadley with a smile.

'Who could have done this to Horace? He was such an unassuming person,' said one elderly academic and others murmured 'hear, hear.'

'That's what we have to discover, sir, now did any of you see any strangers last night?' asked Hadley and they all shook their heads before glancing at one another.

'Who was the last person here to see the Professor?'

'I think it must have been me, Inspector,' said a young man nervously.

'And you are, sir?'

'James Prentice, reader in medieval history,' he replied and Cooper started making notes.

'What time was that?'

'About ten o'clock, Inspector, the Professor and I were discussing the persecution of the Knights Templar's by Philip IV,' replied Prentice.

'Where did this discussion take place, sir?'

'In his study... where he was murdered,' replied Prentice in a faltering whisper.

'Did the Professor appear to be his normal self?'

'Yes, he seemed quite relaxed.'

'Exactly what time did you leave him in his study?'

'Just before ten because I heard the College clock strike the hour as I made my way back to my lodgings, Inspector.'

'Did you see any strangers or notice anything untoward on your way home, sir?'

'I didn't see any strangers, Inspector but I did notice a large coach drawn by four horses standing near the College entrance in St. Aldates,' replied Prentice.

'And what drew your attention to this particular coach?'

'Well, as I said, it was a large stage coach, the old type with the four horses, and we don't often see them anymore.'

'Did you notice the occupants?'

'No, Inspector, I just hurried on by, I'm afraid,' replied Prentice, Hadley nodded and said 'thank you, sir.' He paused for a few moments then asked 'is the Lodge Porter, Mr Baker here?'

'Yes, sir,' came the reply from a stout, ruddy faced man standing behind the Master.

'I understand from Inspector Graves that you found the Professor this morning.'

'I did indeed, sir and it gave me a terrible shock to see him there like that... all covered in blood,' replied Baker.

'I'm sure it did, Mr Baker... so tell me, what time was that?'

'Eight o'clock, sir.'

'Why did you call on him at eight?'

'Well, sir, yesterday the Professor asked me to purchase a train ticket to London, then collect him this morning and take him to the station in the trap to catch the nine o'clock train to Paddington, sir.'

'Did the Professor tell you why he was going to London, Mr Baker?' asked Hadley.

'He didn't, sir, but if it is of any help, he instructed me to only purchase a single ticket so I presumed he did not intend returning today,' replied Baker.

'When you were carrying out your various duties about the town did you see this stage coach that Mr Prentice noticed in St. Aldates last night?' asked Hadley.

'I saw a stage coach in the London Road when I went to purchase the Professor's ticket in the afternoon, sir, but I couldn't say whether it was the same one that Mr Prentice noticed,' replied Baker.

'Would you say it was unusual to see such a coach in Oxford these days?'

'Yes, sir, I mean the trains are so quick and easy to London now, so the big old stage coaches have had their day,' replied

Baker.

'Quite so, Mr Baker... now, can you remember if the Professor had any visitors in the last week?'

'Yes, sir, last Thursday a priest called at my Lodge and said that the Professor was expecting him, so I showed him to his study,' replied Baker as Hadley's eyes lit up and he glanced at Cooper who raised his eyebrows.

'Did this priest give you his name?'

'Yes, sir, his name was Father Murphy, he said he was up from London.'

'Can you tell me anything else about Father Murphy?' asked Hadley.

'No not really, sir, he was very quiet person and just thanked me when I took him to see the Professor,' replied Baker.

'How did the Professor react when he met Father Murphy?'

'Well he obviously hadn't seen him before because he said 'so you're Father Murphy... we meet at last'.'

'Do you know what time the priest left?'

'No, sir, I had some other duties to attend to, so I was away from my Lodge until early evening and he must have left before I returned.'

'Did the Professor have any other visitors from London?'

'The only other one I can think of came to see him about two weeks ago, sir.'

'And do you remember his name?'

'I'm not sure, sir, but I think it was something like Proctor, he said he'd just left the army, but it'll all be in the visitors book,' replied Baker and Hadley smiled realising that some of the pieces in the puzzle were beginning to fit.

Hadley thanked them all for their assistance, sent Cooper to check the visitor's book with Baker for the dates of Porter's and Murphy's visits, whilst he and Graves returned to the Professor's study where Talbot had finished his search.

'I've found nothing of any significance, sir, just lots of student's papers on history and I can't understand most of it,' said Talbot.

'No matter, Sergeant... have you seen a travelling case or portmanteau of some sort hereabouts?'

'No, sir… is one missing?'

'I think it may be.'

'Well it's not here, sir,' replied Talbot, Hadley nodded and said 'that's strange… but never mind, we have some new and interesting lines of inquiry to follow up.'

'Oh good, sir.'

'It seems that Porter has been here as well as our mysterious priest.'

'Well that's a turn up for the book I must say, sir.'

'Indeed it is, Sergeant.'

'So what's next, sir?'

'I plan to return to the Yard with Cooper but I'd like you stay here and assist Inspector Graves searching for an old stage coach that may still be lurking about Oxford.'

'Very good, sir.'

'Check all the blacksmiths, farriers and wheelwrights in the town to see if they can remember seeing this coach, try and find out who the passengers were and where they came from.'

'Right, sir, and when do you want me back at the Yard?'

'As soon as possible, Sergeant, because I've a feeling that things will move swiftly from now on,' replied Hadley.

After discussing the investigation and further lines of inquiry at the Police station over a lunch of tea and sandwiches, Hadley thanked Graves for his assistance and caught the train back to London with Cooper, arriving at Paddington in the late afternoon.

Once back in the office, Hadley asked George to prepare a list of all the Catholic priests in London named Murphy.

'That'll be a long job, sir,' said the clerk.

'Then the sooner you get started the better,' said Hadley.

'Very good, sir,' sighed George.

'Sergeant, whilst I prepare a quick report for the Chief and the Commissioner, please get the letters from the Abbey in France translated.'

'Right, sir.'

'I think they'll make interesting reading.'

Big Ben was striking five o'clock when Hadley made his way up to the Chief's office with his report. Bell looked up and said 'I see you're back already, well that's a relief.'

'Yes, sir,' said Hadley as he placed the report on the desk and sat in the creaking chair.

'Well, what news from the dreaming spires of Oxford?'

'Pennington was tortured and murdered in the same way as the Porter brothers, sir.'

'I feared as much. So what else?'

'A priest named Murphy called to see the Professor before he was murdered and about two weeks ago William Porter also saw Pennington and later wrote a short note telling him he was in danger, sir,' replied Hadley.

'Ah, now at last we're getting somewhere,' said Bell with a smile.

'And that's not all, sir, the Professor had recent correspondence from a priest in Stirling named Sinclair, as well as an from an Abbey in France,' said Hadley.

'An Abbey in France?... Oh, good blasted French aren't involved!'

'Cooper is having the letters from sir.'

'As if we haven't got enough on without the frogs sticking their no complicating matters,' said Bell shaking

'Quite so... but I believe that it's all

'You may be right Hadley, but I needn't remind you that these mad killers are still at large and roaming around the country.'

'Yes, sir.'

'And it's our duty to find and arrest them pretty damned quick!'

'Of course, sir.'

'The sooner these blackguards are in custody and have a fair trial before they're hanged, the better, Hadley.'

'Yes, sir.'

'The Commissioner is a very worried man and there is no doubt he will come under great pressure from the Home Secretary tonight for news of some positive progress towards the killer's arrest,' said Bell firmly.

'I quite understand, sir.'

'So before we go up to see him, tell me quickly what's in your report,' said Bell and Hadley gave a succinct version of the events at Oxford.

Lord Stillwell was with the Commissioner when Bell and Hadley entered his office.

'I beg your pardon, sir, I didn't know that you had his Lordship with you,' said Bell as he bowed and began to withdraw.

'It's alright, Chief Inspector, please come in... and you too, Hadley,' said the great one.

'Thank you, sir... good afternoon my Lord,' said Bell.

'Good afternoon, Chief Inspector... Inspector,' replied Stillwell.

'Good afternoon, sir,' said Hadley.

'I'm sure that his Lordship will be as interested as I am in your report, Chief Inspector,' said the Commissioner as he waved them to sit.

'Indeed, sir,' said Bell and Hadley realised that the great one would make as much advantageous political capital out of the situation as he could. If he impressed Stillwell with their efforts to catch the killers, which would undoubtedly be reported to his Grace the Archbishop, then the Commissioner could count on these powerful clergy for support should things become even more difficult.

'I have already informed his Lordship of your efforts with your team of extra officers, Chief Inspector,' said the Commissioner with a smile.

'Yes, sir, and we are making substantial progress,' said Bell and the great one beamed but Stillwell did not look duly impressed.

'That's good to hear, now tell us of the developments in Oxford, Chief Inspector.'

'Well, sir, as Hadley has only just arrived back, he has not yet had time to give me a full report,' replied Bell.

'In that case let's hear it directly from him,' said the Commissioner as he beamed at Hadley.

'Yes, sir,' said Hadley and he proceeded to give an account of the investigation into Pennington's murder when Stillwell interrupted him in horror.

'You mean to tell me that there's been another horrific

murder?' gasped Stillwell.

'Yes, my Lord,' replied Hadley and then Stillwell glared at the Commissioner and said 'this is not what I would call progress towards arresting these killers who have now murdered again and threaten to harm his Grace and myself, Commissioner!'

'My Lord, I assure you that the net is tightening and it will not be long before we have these maniacs in custody,' said the Commissioner in a soothing tone.

'Well I look forward to that blessed moment,' said Stillwell.

'Please continue, Hadley.'

'Yes, sir... now we know that William Porter visited the Professor and also a Catholic priest called Murphy...'

'A Catholic priest?' interrupted Stillwell in alarm.

'Yes, my Lord, we know that he came from London and my clerk is preparing a list of all the priests with that name for questioning,' replied Hadley.

'Oh, dear God,' whispered Stillwell.

'We also have proof that the Professor had been corresponding with a Catholic priest in Scotland along with an Abbey in France...'

'This is all very worrying, Commissioner and too much for me to comprehend at the moment,' interrupted Stillwell.

'I'm sure it is, sir, especially this unwelcome French connection'

'If the Grail should fall into the hands of Rome... well, I just dread to think of the consequences for us all,' said Stillwell shaking his head as the Commissioner's face drained of colour.

'I'm sure that we can prevent that, sir,' said Hadley in a confident tone.

'I pray to God that you can, Inspector,' said Stillwell.

'Well I'm confident that it's only a matter of time before we arrest the killers and recover the Grail, your Lordship,' said Bell and the Commissioner's face began to look a little rosier after hearing that.

'I assure you, my Lord that the Chief Inspector and his officers will have this investigation brought to a successful conclusion within the next few days,' said the Commissioner firmly.

'Then with that encouraging news I will leave you Commissioner and return to Lambeth Palace to inform his Grace of the developments so far, although I must confess that I'm not as optimistic as you appear to be regarding the successful outcome of your investigation 'within days',' said Stillwell.

'I assure you, sir...' began the great one but the Bishop stood up, gave a little bow as they all scrambled to their feet and he left the office without bothering to listen to any more.

The Commissioner looked hard at the detectives and waved them to sit.

'This investigation is not going at all well, gentlemen, the Bishop is obviously not convinced and will inform his Grace of his concerns and there is now a further complication, which I'm sure is connected with this case,' he said.

'May we know what it is, sir?' asked Bell.

'Yes, Chief Inspector,' and the Commissioner paused, glanced down at the paperwork on his desk and picked up a telegraph message.

'I have just received this message from the Commissioner of Gendarmerie at the Palace du Justice in Paris and it says *'Monsieur Commissioner, I have to advise you that two of my most trusted officers, Captain Marcel Devaux and Sergeant Michel Rousseau, will travel to London and arrive at Scotland Yard on the 21st of May with a sealed envelope containing secret information to be read by you only. Please give the matter contained in this letter your most urgent attention and advise me accordingly of what action you propose to take, yours, Rafael de Montefiore, Commissioner du Gendarmes, Paris.''*

'Oh Good heavens, sir, another unwelcome French complication,' said Bell.

'I fear so, Chief Inspector,' the Commissioner sighed.

'Well Captain Devaux and Sergeant Rousseau were a great help in the Russian murders investigation and they also gave assistance when Cooper and I were in France tracking down Doctor Schimmler,' said Hadley brightly. He was genuinely pleased that the popular French officers were about to arrive the next day and he guessed their mission would be connected to the Holy Grail.

'They may have previously helped in routine investigations, Hadley, but what we're engaged in at the moment is somewhat far removed from our usual activities,' said the Commissioner firmly.

'I agree, sir, these French officers are generally so unruly, undisciplined and have no sense of decorum, so it is very difficult to work with them,' said Bell glancing disapprovingly at Hadley.

'Quite so, Chief Inspector, but we must set them an example of how to behave in all circumstances... after all, we do have the advantage of being British,' said the great one pompously.

'And I thank God we are, sir, but getting these Frenchmen to behave properly... well, in my experience that's much easier said than done,' Bell persisted whilst Hadley glanced out of the window and smirked.

'We must persevere, Chief Inspector,' the Commissioner sighed.

'Of course, sir.'

'Now Hadley, what are your immediate plans to find and arrest these killers?' asked the Commissioner.

Hadley said that his next move was to find Father Murphy and question him, read the letters from the Abbey in France and telegraph the Police in Stirling to question Father Sinclair, all of which he believed would ensure closer links to the killers and lead to their arrest. When he had finished speaking the Commissioner said with relief 'well that's all positive news I can give the Home Secretary at our meeting this evening.'

'I'm sure that Hadley will have these maniacs in custody by the end of the week, sir,' said Bell and Hadley groaned silently.

'I do hope so Chief Inspector, now I will not detain you any longer, gentlemen, so go to it and keep me well briefed,' said the Commissioner with a smile.

CHAPTER 10

When Hadley arrived back in his office Cooper was helping George list the names of priests in the London area.

'We've found four Murphy's so far, sir and we've nearly finished going through the register,' said Cooper.

'Well done, gentlemen and when you've completed the list we'll decide who to call on first,' said Hadley.

'Right, sir. I took the Abbey letters for translation and they'll be ready in the morning,' said Cooper.

'Well, what progress we're making today and it's not over yet,' said Hadley with a smile.

'No, sir it's not... so tell me, how was the Commissioner?'

'He was in a much better frame of mind when I left him than when I arrived, Sergeant.'

'That's good to hear, sir.'

'It is... and the other news is that Captain Devaux and Sergeant Rousseau are arriving tomorrow from Paris with a sealed letter for the Commissioner.'

'Well that's a surprise, sir, they must be onto the Grail as well,' said Cooper.

'Indeed they must, Sergeant.'

'But it'll be good to see them again, sir.'

'Yes, I'm looking forward to it,' said Hadley as Hanson and Mercer arrived.

'So... any luck gentlemen?' asked Hadley and Hanson sighed and shook his head.

'We've traipsed around everywhere in Whitechapel and gone to Mile End then Bishopsgate, but there's no sign of the Porters or the Wang brothers,' said Mercer.

'Any news from Bromwich and his men?' asked Hadley.

'No, I'm afraid not, Jim,' replied Hanson.

'So how did you get on in Oxford?' asked Mercer.

'Professor Pennington was murdered in the same cruel manner as the Porter brothers...'

'Good God,' interrupted Hanson.

'And our mysterious priest, who's called Murphy, went to see him last Thursday and Porter visited two weeks ago,' said Hadley.

'Now we're getting somewhere,' said Mercer.

'I think so... and two other interesting pieces of information that have come to light in this puzzle are that Pennington was in correspondence with a priest in Scotland and an Abbey in France.'

'Good heavens! That means that the Grail is probably still in Scotland!' said Hanson.

'I think you're right but there is yet another twist in this tale...'

'Go on.'

'I've just been told that two French police officers are arriving here tomorrow with a sealed letter for the Commissioner's eyes only.' The Inspectors' jaws dropped in unison.

'Do you think it's in connection with the Grail?' asked Mercer.

'I'm sure it is.'

'Blimey, Jim, this is getting very complicated,' said Hanson.

'It will be if the bloody French are involved!' said Mercer.

'Normally I'd agree with you, but these two officers are known to us and have always been very helpful with our investigations in the past,' said Hadley with a smile.

'Well, we'll wait and see just how helpful they are this time round, Jim,' said Hanson.

'They're good men and I've every confidence in them,' said Hadley.

Mercer shook his head slightly and said 'well, remember they're coming from a Catholic country so I'm sure that they'll want to recover the Grail themselves and claim it as theirs before taking it back to Paris.'

'You may be right.'

'I'm sure of it,' said Mercer and Hadley gave a little smile.

'Now we have a list of priests in London called Murphy, so I suggest we split up, take the Sergeants and question these priests about their movements last Thursday, as well as any links they may have had with William Porter,' said Hadley.

'Right Jim,' nodded Mercer.

'And bring in any of them who raise your suspicions.'

'Very good,' said Hanson with a nod.

Hadley gave each Inspector two addresses of the priests, leaving himself and Cooper to call on the others they found listed in the Catholic register. Half an hour later, Hadley and Cooper set off in

Police coach to the first of three addresses and discovered that the priests at the first two addresses had alibi's for last Thursday and denied all knowledge of knowing William Porter. However, at the third address in Hoxton, Father Patrick Murphy was not at home and the detectives were informed by his housekeeper that he had been called away unexpectedly on important church business. When Hadley asked where Father Murphy had gone, the housekeeper claimed that she did not know but said that he was expected to return within a few days. The detectives left and on their way back to the Yard Hadley said 'I think that he's our man, Sergeant.'

'I'm sure of it, sir and of course Hoxton is not far from Islington, so it would be reasonable to assume that any orders from the Catholic hierarchy to visit Porter would be given to the nearest priest.'

'Indeed, Sergeant.'

Big Ben was striking nine o'clock when they arrived back in the office. On Hadley's desk was a hastily scribbled note from Hanson saying that he and Mercer had called on all the priests and their inquiries had been fruitless.

'Well that confirms to me that our renegade priest is likely to be Father Patrick Murphy, Sergeant.'

'It would seem so, sir.'

'And the next difficult question is… where the devil is he?'

'In Scotland, sir?'

'Possibly… so now I think it's time we telegraphed our colleagues in Stirling and ask them to pay a visit to Father Andrew Sinclair, find out if Murphy is with him and question them closely about their involvement with Pennington and Porter.'

Hadley sent Cooper home before sitting and composing a detailed message to the Duty Inspector at Stirling Police station. When it was finished he took it up to the telegraph office where it was immediately dispatched.

It was ten o'clock when Hadley arrived home and a worried Alice was waiting anxiously for him.

'What a day,' said Hadley with a sigh as he took off his coat and followed Alice into the parlour.

'I don't expect you've eaten much today have you, Jim?'

'No, just a few sandwiches, dear.'

'Well, I've saved you some soup to warm you up and a slice of meat pie.'

'You're an angel,' said Hadley as he slumped down in a chair by the fire.

'And you'll be one if you don't stop soon, Jim, this job is killing you slowly and you can't see it,' she said firmly.

'Now, now Alice…'

'Don't you 'now now' me, Jim Hadley! I want a husband who stays alive until he's old and full of wrinkles!'

'Alice dear…'

'I'm not ready to be a widow just yet and the way you're carrying on at the moment it won't be long before I am one… and I don't look good in black!' she interrupted.

He shook his head slowly knowing that his wife's fear was true, but he was too tired to argue 'Alice dear… just get the soup.'

After a restless night Hadley struggled to get out of bed the next morning. Over the breakfast table he decided that when the investigation was over he would request a week's leave and take Alice and the children to Bognor Regis for a holiday. He glanced at Alice, then his son, Arthur and Anne, his pretty young daughter, before announcing his intentions.

'I've been thinking that we could all do with a week away, so I will put in for a spot of leave as soon as this investigation is over,' he said with a smile and he watched Alice's face light up with relief.

'Oh that will be wonderful, Jim,' she said and Arthur asked 'can we go to Bognor again, Pa?'

'Yes, why not, we all like it there,' replied Hadley.

'And can we ride on the donkeys?' asked Anne.

'Of course,' Hadley smiled and gave a nod to Alice who wiped a little tear away from her moist eyes.

'So when are we going to go, Pa?' asked Anne.

'In a week or so if all goes well,' he replied hopefully.

Feeling much better after seeing Alice happy and relieved, Hadley left his home in Camden and hailed a Hansom to take him to Scotland Yard. He knew that the day ahead would be full of incidents and he wondered what time the French officers would arrive. He knew that their sudden appearance with a secret document would cause upheaval in all quarters but he looked forward to seeing them again. He hoped that the translations of the Abbey letters would give some leads in the hunt for the killers as well as Talbot's inquiries in Oxford. As he had no previous experience with the Scottish Police he was concerned that if they did not act quickly enough and question Sinclair today, then valuable time would be lost.

When he arrived in the office, just before eight o'clock, Cooper was already there and George had the kettle on for tea.

'It's going to be a busy day with the arrival of our French colleagues, sir,' said Cooper brightly.

'Indeed it is, Sergeant.'

'Do you know what time they're coming, sir?'

'No, Sergeant, but I would guess about lunchtime,' replied Hadley as George brought in their tea.

'Of course they'll be with the Commissioner for awhile before we see them,' said Cooper.

'Possibly... but knowing them they might surprise us first,' said Hadley with a grin.

'It'll be good to see them again, sir,' said George as he placed Hadley's cup on his desk.

'Indeed it will, George.'

'They always liven the old place up a bit.'

'They certainly do... now Sergeant, when you've had your tea please see if the translations are finished.'

'Yes, sir,' replied Cooper as Hanson arrived. Hadley waited until Mercer arrived a few minutes later before telling the Inspectors what had transpired after they left the office last night.

'Well it seems that Father Patrick Murphy is our man, Jim,' said Hanson.

'I believe that is certain, Bob.'

'Do you have any idea where he is?' asked Mercer.

'No I haven't... but his housekeeper expects him back within the next few days,' replied Hadley.

96

'Well Scotland is my best bet,' said Hanson.

'I agree… that's why I've telegraphed the Stirling Police to find out if Murphy is with Sinclair,' said Hadley.

'Those two have got a lot of questions to answer,' said Hanson and Hadley nodded.

After further discussions about the case over another pot of tea, Hanson and Mercer left with their Sergeants to continue their lines of inquiry and assist in the search for the Wang brothers and the Porters. Hadley wrote a quick report for Bell and the Commissioner regarding the events of last night and George began typing it.

Cooper arrived back with the translations and handed them to Hadley, who was eager to read them. He arranged them in date order as Cooper drew up a chair and sat beside him to make notes.

'Right, Sergeant, here we go… the first letter is dated the 2nd of April and it says: *'Dear Professor Pennington, your letter of the 15th of March concerns us greatly and we have made inquiries on your behalf to discover if what you claim is true and can be substantiated. We sent an envoy from this Abbey to question Father Latour at Sainte Girons regarding the alleged recorded actions of a certain Knight Templar named Guillame de Rieux in the year 1320. Our envoy reports that there is only rumour surrounding your assertion that a holy relic was brought to Sainte Girons by Guillame de Rieux from Scotland. There are no records of this in our Catholic church at Sainte Girons and we can state without fear of contradiction that if such a holy relic existed and was discovered, it would be the property of the Holy Roman Catholic Church, yours, Cardinal Pierre Lefevre, Abbey de Montauban.'*

'Well it seems that the Professor believed he was onto something, sir.'

'It certainly looks like it… now the next letter is dated the 12th of April and says: *'Dear Professor Pennington, your insistence that a holy relic is somewhere in the area south of Toulouse is very troubling to us. After careful consideration of your latest request we reluctantly sent our envoy to question Father Dalmas at Foix and search the church records for any information regarding Guillame de Rieux after his return from Scotland. We can now report that there is no evidence to support your assertions and we now consider the matter finally closed, yours, Cardinal Pierre Lefevre, Abbey de Montauban.'*

'Well what do you make of that, sir?'

'I'm not sure, Sergeant, but it begs many questions.'

'Do you think that the French realise that it's the Holy Grail that the Professor is talking about, sir?'

'Well there's no mention of it in the letters but I'm sure that they must have an idea and that links in with the visit of our friends from Paris,' replied Hadley.

'Perhaps that's why they say the matter is closed, sir.'

'Yes, it seems as if they want to stop the Professor digging any deeper.'

'What does the next one say, sir?' asked Cooper.

Hadley picked it up and read *'Dear Professor Pennington, in our last letter we stated clearly that we regarded the matter as now finally closed and it is only out of courtesy that we make this reply. Your repeated assertions that a holy relic was brought to this region from Scotland by Guillame de Rieux are totally without foundation. We have sent our envoy to investigate your claims and can confirm that nothing whatsoever has been discovered that might give credence to your theories. Finally, we have advised Cardinal Charnay, our Holy Father in Toulouse, of your assertions, yours, Cardinal Pierre Lefevre.'*

'Well, it seems that the Cardinal has handed the whole thing over to his superior in Toulouse to deal with, sir.'

'Yes, and I'm sure that he contacted the powers that be in Paris, hence our friends hasty visit today, Sergeant.'

'They must have some further information about Scotland because why else would they come here, sir?'

'We shall see, Sergeant.'

Hadley took the letters along with his report up to Bell's office.

'Have you some positive news, Hadley?'

'I think so, sir,' he replied as he placed the buff folder on Bell's desk before he sat in the creaking chair. Bell quickly opened the folder, read the report and the letters. Other than occasionally whispering 'dear God', Bell said nothing until he had finished reading.

'Well, I'm sure the Professor was onto something and the French know more than they're admitting, Hadley.'

'Quite possibly, sir.'

'I don't trust them an inch.'

'I realise that, sir.'

'They're our natural enemies, Hadley and have been for hundreds of years.'

'Yes, sir.'

'I see you've discovered who this mysterious London priest is and telegraphed the Police in Stirling to question the other priest, Sinclair.'

'I have, sir, because it's possible that Murphy is with him.'

'Good... and let the Police in Stirling handle this because I don't want you to go on another wild goose chase all the way up there,' said Bell firmly.

'No, sir.'

'You're needed here because I'm sure that the killers are in London and it is imperative that we arrest them soon.'

'I'm sure we will, sir.'

'Where are Hanson and Mercer at present?'

'They've gone to the East End, sir, to carry on the search for the Porters and the Chinese,' replied Hadley.

'Good... so stay in your office for the time being, just in case the Commissioner wishes to speak to you after I've shown him your report and these letters from France.'

'Very well, sir.'

Big Ben was striking eleven o'clock when the messenger came from the telegraph office and gave Hadley a buff envelope.

'It's marked 'urgent', sir,' said the boy.

Hadley thanked the boy then read the message aloud to Cooper and George, as he was bringing in their mid-morning tea.

'It's from Inspector Palmer and he says: *'Pleased to inform you that Mr and Mrs Porter have been found alive but in distress. They have been taken to The London where they are receiving medical treatment under Police armed guard. Suggest you attend, yours, Inspector Palmer.''*

'Ah, some good news at last, sir.'

'Indeed, Sergeant, I'll let the Chief know immediately and then we'll get over to The London,' said Hadley.

'What about your tea, sir?' asked George.

'No time for that now, George,' replied Hadley as he strode out of the office.

The Chief was not in his office and Mr Jenkins told Hadley that he was still with the Commissioner. Hadley raced up the stairs and entered the spacious office.

'What is it now, Hadley?' asked the Commissioner testily.

'Sorry to disturb you, sir, but I've some good news from Inspector Palmer,' replied Hadley as he handed the message to the great one.

'Good heavens! The Porter's have been found alive, Chief Inspector!'

'That's very good news, sir, where were they?' asked Bell.

'It doesn't say, but they've been taken to The London, where I presume Palmer is now,' replied the Commissioner.

'I'll get over there right away, sir,' said Hadley.

'Good... then get back with a full report as quickly as you can, Inspector.'

'Yes, sir,' replied Hadley as Mr Brackley entered and said 'the two French Officers you're expecting have arrived, sir.'

'Then show them in Brackley.'

'Very good, sir.'

'You stay here, Chief Inspector... and you too Hadley,' said the Commissioner.

CHAPTER 11

Brackley stood aside to allow Captain Devaux and Sergeant Rousseau to enter as the Commissioner stood to greet them. Both officers were immaculately groomed and dressed in well fitted grey suits, high winged white collars and blue silk ties studded with diamond pins. They both smiled broadly when they caught sight of Hadley standing next to Bell.

'Bonjour Monsieur Commissioner... Chief Inspector... Inspector,' said a smiling Devaux, giving a little bow.

'Good day to you, Captain, and I trust you've had a pleasant journey from Paris,' replied the Commissioner.

'Oui, Monsieur Commissioner, the ferry crossing was smooth but the train from Dover was a little slow,' replied Devaux and Bell pulled a face.

'Please sit down, gentlemen.'

'Merci,' replied Devaux before he sat down, placing a small black case on his lap.

'Now I understand from your Commissioner in Paris that you have journeyed here with a secret letter for me in a sealed envelope, Captain.'

'Oui, Monsieur, the message was deemed too important and sensitive for it to be sent by telegraph so it was decided that we should bring it to you personally,' said Devaux. He opened the case and took out a large white envelope that had been sealed with red wax.

'Do you happen to know what the message is, Captain?' asked the Commissioner as Devaux handed it to him.

'Oui, Monsieur... but I have been sworn to the utmost secrecy,' replied Devaux.

The Commissioner broke the seal, opened the envelope, took the letter out and read it very carefully. He placed it back in the envelope and his expression gave no hint of what was contained in the secret message.

'I will discuss this with Sir George West, our Home Secretary, and give a written answer for you to take back to Paris, Captain,' said the Commissioner in a solemn tone.

'Très bien, Monsieur Commissioner.'

'So I suggest that as you know Inspector Hadley, you remain in his office until I send for you,' said the Commissioner and Bell 'tut-tutted' quietly whilst Hadley smiled.

'Oui, Monsieur.'

'But please do not interfere with his duties, Captain.'

'Non, Monsieur.'

'I will make arrangements for you to stay overnight in our rooms here that are reserved for special guests,' said the Commissioner.

'Merci, Monsieur, that is very kind of you.'

'Not at all... we're always pleased to offer hospitality to our colleagues from other countries,' said the great one. Bell rolled his eyes and was barely able to contain his annoyance. Hadley thought that the Commissioner had made the offer to the Frenchmen so he could keep an eye on them.

'Merci beaucoup, Monsieur Commissioner.'

'So I will not detain you any longer, gentlemen,' said the Commissioner brusquely and the French officers stood up and gave a nod before leaving the office, followed by Hadley.

Once outside in the corridor, Devaux flung his arms around Hadley and said 'it's so good to see you again, mon ami!'

'Likewise Marcel... and you too Michel.'

'And how is everybody?'

'All very well,' replied Hadley as they descended the stairs.

'And the ladies?'

'They're well too and will be surprised to see you no doubt,' said Hadley with a grin.

'Très bien, I look forward to meeting them again, Jim.'

Both Cooper and George were all smiles when the Frenchmen entered Hadley's office and hugged them both. After noisy greetings and inquiries about their health and well being, Devaux said to George 'now may we have a cup of your wonderful tea, George?'

'Oh most certainly, sir!'

'Bon, on the train from Dover, Michel and I agreed that when we got to the Yard the first thing we needed was a cup of your special tea to revive us,' said Devaux with a smile.

'It's coming right up, sir,' said a smiling George before he hurriedly disappeared.

'You old charmer you,' said Hadley with a chuckle.

'Let me tell you, Jim, you catch more bees with honey than vinegar,' replied Devaux as he made himself comfortable on a chair.

'So true, now whilst you're confined to my office…'

'Oh non, we're not confined at all, Jim, we look forward to going out tonight for dinner with you and seeing the ladies,' interrupted Devaux.

'I think the Commissioner expects you to stay here, Marcel,' said Hadley.

'Then his expectations will be dashed, Jim!'

'Marcel you must…'

'Jim, we have done our duty and delivered a secret message to your Commissioner so we are now free to go out with you,' interrupted Devaux and Hadley sighed then grinned.

'Right you are, Marcel. Now Cooper and I have to go to The London Hospital…'

'Are you ill, mon ami?'

'No, we have to interview some people who have just been found after being kidnapped and they have been taken to the hospital,' replied Hadley.

'Bon, after we've had our tea we'll come with you!'

'Marcel, I think you should stay…'

'Nonsense, mon ami,' interrupted Devaux and Hadley shrugged his shoulders as George arrived with their tea.

Hadley waited for a few moments after they had sipped their tea before he said 'I think I should tell you Marcel that we are investigating three murders, which I believe may be connected to your secret message and…'

'You want to know what's in the letter?' interrupted Devaux.

'If you can say… then I think it would be helpful.'

'Bon, then I will tell you.'

'Thank you… but before you do, I must tell you that Cooper and George are sworn to secrecy with regard to our investigation so anything you tell us will be kept strictly confidential,' said Hadley.

'Très bien but I would trust them anyway, Jim,' replied Devaux.

'Thank you, Marcel.'

'So, mon ami, it all started when our Commissioner received a letter from Cardinal Charnay of Toulouse saying that a Professor Pennington from Oxford had been making inquiries about a holy relic that he believed was to be found in the region. The Abbey at Montauban sent envoys to churches in the area to make inquiries and check the records held by them concerning a Knight Templar called Guillame de Rieux. It appears that the envoys found out that there was a relic brought back from the holy land during the crusades but it was taken to Scotland when the Knights were disbanded by King Philip. To protect the discovery of this relic the Cardinal at Montauban did not inform the Professor that the record showed it was probably still in Scotland. The message to your Commissioner is to help us find it and stating clearly that the relic belongs to France,' said Devaux.

Hadley waited for a moment before he said 'I'm afraid that Pennington was found murdered...'

'Mon Dieu!'

'Along with two brothers, one of whom informed the Bishop of London, that for a reward, he would tell him where it was hidden.'

'Then it is true that this relic is still in Scotland, Jim?'

'It would appear so, Marcel... and do you know what this relic is?'

'Oui, mon ami, it is supposed to be the Holy Grail and if it exists it belongs to France.'

'That may be the major problem that the Commissioner has to discuss with the Home Secretary,' said Hadley.

'This could be very difficult, Jim.'

'I agree, now let's leave that for the moment and get off to The London.'

Palmer was waiting outside the ward with two armed constables when the detectives arrived. Palmer explained briefly that the Porter's had been discovered bound and gagged on a disused coal barge that was moored up just beyond Limehouse Reach.

'Who found them, Jack?'

'A passing lighter-man noticed that the cabin door had been forced open, went to investigate, heard a noise and found them tied up, Jim,' replied Palmer.

'Well that was lucky for them,' said Hadley.

'It was, because in another day or so they would have probably died.'

'Have they been tortured?'

'Mr Porter has bruises on his face but Mrs Porter seems alright, except for her mental state, the poor woman is half demented with everything that's happened,' replied Palmer.

'I'm not surprised, have they said who did this?'

'I've not been allowed to question them yet, Jim, because they were brought straight here after the lighter-man called a Constable.'

'Right, let's ask the Doctor if we can see them,' said Hadley.

'I'll find him,' said Palmer before hurrying away.

'Marcel, would you and Michel wait here whilst we have a word with these people?'

'Bien sûr, Jim, we have all the pretty nurses to watch and that will keep us occupied,' replied Devaux with a smile.

Mr Porter was sitting at his wife's bedside when the detectives arrived in the side ward with the Duty Doctor and the formidable Matron. The couple looked pale and distressed but before Hadley could say anything to them, the Doctor said 'I can't allow you any more than five minutes with my patients, Inspector.'

'Very well, Doctor.'

'Matron, will you stay here and ensure that Mr and Mrs Porter do not become distressed?'

'Yes, Doctor, you may rely on me,' she replied firmly before glancing at the detectives and they knew instantly that Matron's word was law and could not be challenged.

Hadley looked at the couple and said calmly 'I'm glad to see that you're safe now and I want you to know that we were searching for you ever since our liaison officer told us that you had been collected by another coach.'

'We thought it was the Police coach, but it blimmin' wasn't!' said Porter.

'Quite so. Do you know who the kidnappers' were?'

'Never seen either of them before,' replied Porter.

'Can you describe them for us?' asked Hadley as Cooper took out his notebook.

'They were big fellas, one had a moustache and the other a beard,' replied Porter.

'What else?'

'They were nasty bastards, especially the Scotch one…'

'Tell me about him,' interrupted Hadley.

'Well he seemed to be the guvnor and told the other one what to do all the time.'

'Can you remember anything he said?'

'He kept asking me what our Billy had said to us about some relic or something but I didn't know what he was on about and kept telling him that Billy hadn't said anything. Then he started knocking me about, calling me a liar… as Gawd's my judge I never tell lies… not to anybody,' replied Porter as a tear coursed down his bruised cheek.

'I think that's enough now,' said Matron firmly.

'Just one more question Matron,' said Hadley.

'Just the one then,' she said.

'Mr Porter, did you hear these men say they were going to Oxford?'

'No, but after the big fella stopped blimmin' well knocking me about he said something like 'I don't think they know' and then they left… we could have died on that old barge if the lad hadn't found us,' replied Porter as his tears flowed and his wife began to sob.

'That's enough, Inspector… so out you go… right now!' said Matron loudly.

'Yes Matron… and thank you, Mr Porter, you've been very helpful,' said Hadley as they left the side ward.

The detectives made their way through the main ward, closely followed by Matron, Hadley said 'I think that rules the Chinese out of the murder investigation, Jack.'

'It does, Jim and I must admit I'm relieved,' replied Palmer, Hadley nodded and said 'but when you find them, Jack, you can charge them with running illegal opium dens and affray.'

'Yes I can… when we find them, Jim.'

They returned to Palmer's office where he invited them to join him for a lunch of tea and sandwiches whilst they discussed the case. When they were all seated Palmer looked at the French officers and asked 'so tell me, Captain, what brings you all the way from gay Paris to London?' Hadley and Cooper waited with bated breath for Devaux's answer and were relieved when he replied with a smile 'ah, officially we're here to study the famous Scotland Yard's methods of detection, mon ami.'

'Blimey, if that's the case then I'm sure your stay won't be long!' said Palmer and they all laughed.

'Actually, mon ami, I am on a secret mission,' said Devaux in a loud whisper as he glanced furtively about.

'I guessed as much,' said Palmer.

'Oui, and Jim is helping me.'

'To do what?' asked Palmer and Hadley held his breath.

'Can you keep this a secret, mon ami?'

'That depends on what it is, Captain.'

'Then because I'm sure you'll understand... I will tell you.'

'Go on,' said Palmer.

'It is to persuade Florrie to come with me to Paris to give our Commissioner one of her 'specials',' said Devaux as he winked at Palmer.

'You bloody French!' exclaimed Palmer with a grin and Hadley laughed out loud.

'Mon Dieu... I'm serious, after my last visit I told him all about Florrie, so he gave me orders to come here and bring her back to Paris for a weekend.'

'With all expenses paid no doubt,' said Palmer.

'Bien sûr, and a little extra for her troubles!' said Devaux with a smile as the tea and sandwiches were brought in.

Over lunch Hadley discussed with Palmer the lines of inquiry they should follow to discover who the two kidnappers were and their possible whereabouts. Hadley was convinced that they were the murderers and he hoped that Talbot would return with positive leads from Oxford. Palmer agreed to make inquiries around Limehouse Reach to discover if there were any witnesses to the kidnapping as well as finding any link between the owner of the barge and the two men.

Big Ben was striking two o'clock when they all arrived back at the

Yard. Hadley wrote a short report on the Porter's kidnapping for George to type before he took it up to the Chief. He had just finished reading it through when the messenger came from the telegraph office and placed a buff envelope on his desk.

Hadley thanked the boy then read it out loud *'Inspector Hadley, Scotland Yard, Sir, at your request I went to Saint Mary's Church this morning to interview Father Andrew Sinclair with regard to the matters contained in your telegraph. Father Sinclair was not at the church or at home and his housekeeper, Mrs Murray, informed me that last night another priest had called him away by on urgent Church business for a few days. Mrs Murray did not know when Father Sinclair would return. I regret that I cannot be of more assistance to you this time but I will call at the house again and speak to Father Sinclair when he has returned. Please advise me of any other action that you wish me to take, yours truly, Inspector Ross MacKay, Stirling Police.'*

'I bet the other priest is Murphy, sir,' said Cooper.

'I'm sure you're right, Sergeant, and he knows where this relic is hidden.'

'Mon Dieu, then we must go to Scotland right away, mon ami,' said Devaux.

'Hold your horses for a moment, Marcel, while I let the Chief know what's happened and then we'll decide what's to be done,' said Hadley.

'Très bien… meanwhile we will find out the times of the trains to Stirling,' said Devaux and Hadley sighed.

Chief Inspector Bell read the report first and then the telegraph from MacKay.

'Well it appears that the Grail is somewhere in Scotland and Murphy is the man who knows where it is,' said Bell.

'Indeed it does, sir, but it seems strange that Porter would have told him where it was hidden whilst he was engaged in financial negotiations with Lord Stillwell.'

'That's true Hadley, but you never know how the mind of a lower working class person works these days, they all think they're too clever by half but they really don't know their proper place in the social order of things,' said Bell pompously.

'Nevertheless, sir, I think it's more than a little strange.'

'Well perhaps this French Cardinal in Toulouse knows where it is, has informed Murphy and he's rushed off hot foot to Stirling to retrieve it with the help of Sinclair. Meanwhile our two murderers are busy killing everybody who may know anything about the Grail's hiding place,' said Bell.

'Yes indeed, sir.'

'So what are you planning to do next, Hadley?'

'Now that we know the Wang brothers didn't kidnap the Porter's, sir, concentrate on finding the two men who did, I'm pretty sure that they are our killers.'

'Good, because I don't want you rushing off to Scotland on a wild goose chase that will lead to nothing,' said Bell.

'Right, sir, but I think the French officers will want to go...'

'Don't tell me you've discussed this investigation with them!' interrupted Bell angrily.

'Sir, Captain Devaux is fully aware of this situation...'

'Good God Hadley! The Commissioner gave you strict instructions not to discuss this case with anyone... let alone the blasted French!'

'Sir, if I may...'

'No you may not Hadley! You heard the Commissioner tell them to stay in your office until he sent for them!'

'Yes I did, sir.'

'Then they will take his written reply back to Paris on the next train out of London!'

'I think that they may have other plans, sir.'

'Well I hope not for your sake, Hadley, because they are your responsibility!' exclaimed Bell angrily and Hadley replied with a sigh 'yes, sir.'

There followed a few moments of silence before Bell said 'now that the Porters have been found it will free up Hanson and Mercer to assist you in finding these maniac killers before they strike again, so I suggest you concentrate on that, Hadley and I'll brief the Commissioner on this latest development.'

'Very good, sir.'

When Hadley arrived back in his office he found that Talbot had returned from Oxford and was busily engaged in conversation.

'I've some good news to report, sir,' said Talbot with a smile.

'Then let's hear it, Sergeant.'

'I questioned several farriers in Oxford and found that one of them, named John Timken, had shoed a horse for two men who pulled up in an old stage coach the day of Pennington's murder, sir.'

'Please go on, Sergeant,' said Hadley.

'Timken said that one of the men in the coach had a Scottish accent and was quite rude to the other, who he called 'Doyle', sir.'

'At last we have a name,' whispered Hadley his eyes shining brightly.

'We have two names, sir, because Doyle called the Scotsman 'Mr Tyler'.'

'Well done, Sergeant!'

'Thank you, sir.'

'Did Timken tell you anything else about them?'

'Only that Tyler said they planned to return to London later that night, sir,' replied Talbot.

'This all fits, Sergeant.'

'What's next, sir?' asked Cooper.

'We put out an all stations request to find and arrest Doyle and Tyler on suspicion of murder, Sergeant,' replied Hadley as Brackley entered the office and said 'the Commissioner wishes to see you immediately, sir.'

'Very well, Mr Brackley,' replied Hadley and as he stood up from his desk, Devaux said 'Jim, tell the Commissioner that we are catching the train to Stirling tonight.'

CHAPTER 12

The Commissioner was studying the paperwork on his desk and did not look up when Hadley entered the office. The Chief Inspector sat pale and pensive before glancing at Hadley.

'You'd better sit down, Inspector,' said the Commissioner.

'Thank you, sir.'

'I am very relieved that the Porter's have been found alive, Hadley.'

'Yes, I am too, sir, as I did fear the worst.'

'I must confess that I shared your fears. Now it appears from your report and this telegraph from Inspector MacKay that Sinclair has probably disappeared with Murphy, so we can only assume from this information is that they know where the relic is hidden and have gone to retrieve it.'

'I believe that is the case, sir.'

The Commissioner studied the report for a few moments then asked 'have you any thoughts on the whereabouts of the murderers, Hadley?'

'Sergeant Talbot has just returned from Oxford and was able to trace the suspects to a farrier on the day of Pennington's murder and has discovered their names, sir.'

'Well that's a positive move forward,' said the Commissioner and Bell looked relieved.

'Yes, sir, the suspects are a Scotsman called 'Tyler' and his companion is named 'Doyle',' said Hadley.

'Do you believe that they were responsible for the attack on Major Fielding outside his home?'

'I think that's very probable, sir.'

'And have you any idea where are they now, Inspector?'

'They told the farrier that they were going back to London that night, sir.'

'Excellent... so put out a telegraph to all stations giving the details and requesting their immediate arrest!'

'I was just about to do that when you sent for me, sir.'

'Well go and get to it, Hadley.'

'Yes, sir, oh... there is one more thing that I think you should know, sir.'

'And what's that?'

'Captain Devaux asked me to tell you that he and Sergeant Rousseau are catching a train to Scotland tonight, sir.'

'What!' shrieked the Commissioner and Bell's jaw dropped in absolute horror.

'Sir, they're…'

'I heard what you said Hadley! Did you know about this Chief Inspector?'

'No sir, not at all, sir,' replied Bell anxiously before continuing 'as I told you, sir, these French are so unruly and undisciplined…'

'How do they know about Murphy and Sinclair, Hadley?' interrupted the great one.

'I read out the telegraph from Mackay, sir and they must…'

'Hadley!'

'I'm sorry, sir.'

'Oh dear God Almighty! What a mess this is' said the Commissioner as his side whiskers bristled.

'You've let us down badly this time, Hadley,' said Bell reproachfully.

'I know, sir, but…'

'There are no 'buts', Inspector!' roared the Commissioner.

'No, sir.'

'What we need now, gentlemen, is urgent action!' he exclaimed as he banged his fist on the desk.

'Yes of course you're right as always, sir,' said Bell.

'We must not let these Frenchmen steal the Grail from under our very noses!'

'No indeed not, sir,' said Bell.

'The secret letter that Devaux brought from Paris was requesting our assistance in recovering the Holy Grail for them! Would you believe the damned nerve of these French!' thundered the Commissioner.

'An unmitigated cheek, sir, but not unexpected in my view as they are our natural enemies,' said Bell haughtily.

'It would be an unbearable disgrace that her Majesty, the Archbishop of Canterbury and the Prime Minister along with the whole country, could never forgive or forget if we failed in our duty to recover the Grail,' said the great one as he shook his head.

'You're absolutely right, sir,' said Bell.

'So Hadley... you accompany them to Scotland with your Sergeants whilst Hanson and Mercer can lead the hunt for the killers in London,' said the Commissioner and Hadley nodded as Bell's mouth opened in amazement.

'Very good, sir.'

'And when the Grail is found, do not let these Frenchmen get their hands on it under any circumstances.'

'No, sir.'

'Bring it safely back to me, Hadley.'

'Yes, sir, I will.'

'Her Majesty, along with the government and the country will be expecting us to do our duty Hadley, so you must not let them down.'

'I won't, sir.'

'Good, now go to it, Inspector and keep me well informed,' said the Commissioner.

Hadley raced downstairs to his office to find Hanson and Mercer talking to the French officers whilst Cooper and Talbot were busy writing reports.

'Your attention if you please, gentlemen!' he called and there was silence before he continued 'I've just come from the Commissioner and he has given direct orders that I, along with Cooper and Talbot, should accompany Captain Devaux to Stirling whilst Inspector's Hanson and Mercer lead the search for the murder suspects here.'

'Ah, très bien, Jim!' exclaimed Devaux.

'You're all off to Scotland?' asked Hanson in surprise.

'We are.'

'When?' asked Mercer.

'Tonight.'

'Blimmin' heck! Things move fast around here,' said Mercer.

'They do indeed. What time is the train, Marcel?' asked Hadley.

'It leaves from Kings Cross at ten o'clock, mon ami.'

'Right... Sergeants, please go home now and pack your things... and make sure you bring plenty of warm clothes with you,' said Hadley.

'Very good, sir,' they replied in chorus.

113

After they had left the office Hadley composed a telegraph message for Inspector MacKay informing him of their arrival the next morning in Stirling. Hanson and Mercer looked surprised by the turn of events, whilst the French officers could hardly hide their pleasure at the prospect of having their friends join them in the search for the Grail.

George took the message up to the telegraph office and on his return made a pot of tea for them. When Big Ben struck four o'clock, Hadley checked his fob watch. He had six hours left to write up the full report on Talbot's inquiries in Oxford, draw expenses for the trip, go home and get packed, organise a late meal for them all before setting off to Kings Cross in time to buy the tickets and catch the train. That was plenty of time if nothing else occurred to waylay him.

Whilst Hadley wrote his report, Hanson and Mercer went up to the Chief's office to discuss with him their next moves in the search for the murderers in London. After drawing sufficient expenses for the trip, Hadley went to see the canteen manager to organise a meal before they left for Stirling. Having ensured that they would enjoy hot food before the long night journey, Hadley went home to pack. Alice was pleasantly surprised to see her husband so early for once but when he explained why he was there, she was not pleased.

'Surely you're not going all the way up to Scotland tonight, Jim?' she asked.

'Yes, dear, I am.'

'What on earth for?'

'It's an important investigation dear and I have to go to follow up lines of inquiry.'

'Well can't they send someone else?' she asked.

'Not really, but I should be back in a day or two… so please don't worry.'

'What about having something to eat before you go?'

'I've arranged a meal in the canteen for us all, dear.'

'Who's 'us', Jim?'

'Cooper, Talbot and the French officers from Paris.'

'French officers from Paris?'

'Yes, dear,'

'Well, I just wonder what this is all about, but I suppose I'd better not ask,' she said.

'Quite so, my dear, just help me pack please.'

It was just after seven o'clock when Hadley arrived back at the Yard. Cooper and Talbot were already there with their portmanteaus and in busy conversation with the French officers. There was an air of excitement in the office and Hadley was pleased that morale was high and he had such reliable officers with him in what could be very dangerous circumstances. If they recovered the Grail he wondered how he could persuade Devaux to leave the relic in England for scientific examination, to confirm its authenticity, before the wrangle between the Government and the French authorities started on its rightful ownership. With the Church on both sides of the Channel making demands on their respective Governments for its retention it would be much more than a cause célèbre. The Pope would also be making demands on behalf of the Catholic Church for the relic to be taken to Rome, which would probably lead to major disagreements between all three. Hadley was glad that he was not a politician and all he had to do was discover where the Grail was hidden and bring it back to the Commissioner.

The detectives sat and with the aid of a map, made plans for the search of likely hiding places around Stirling. As Big Ben struck eight o'clock Hadley said 'Time for our evening meal, gentlemen.'

'Bon, so where are you taking us, mon ami?'

'Some bijou café where the girls are pretty or maybe one of your noisy pubs where the food is good, Monsieur?' asked Rousseau with a smile.

'Neither I'm afraid,' replied Hadley with a chuckle.

'Where then, mon ami?' asked Devaux.

'Our canteen downstairs!'

'Mon Dieu! This will be an experience to forget!' said Devaux and Hadley smiled.

The canteen manager had put their table in a corner behind screens which brought a slight smile to the Frenchman's faces.

'So this is how the British detectives entertain guests at Scotland Yard,' said Devaux as he sat down.

'It is, Marcel,' replied Hadley with a grin.

'In the corner behind screens!'

'It's for your privacy, Marcel.'

'Mon Dieu! You English have a lot to learn about entertaining from us, mon ami!'

'I'm sure we have.'

'Well, I hope the food is good, Jim, because I do not want to travel overnight on one of your slow trains with nothing inside me.'

'I'm sure you'll enjoy what I've chosen for you, Marcel,' said Hadley.

'Mon Dieu! You mean to say I have no choice?'

'None whatever.'

'This is barbaric!' exclaimed Devaux as the waitress appeared with bowls of French onion soup which pleased him a little. After his first taste, Devaux looked at Rousseau and said with a smile 'at least they almost know how to make proper soup, Michel.'

'Oui, mon Captain.'

The main course was steak and kidney pie with mash and peas, all covered in thick gravy and it was delicious. For dessert they had jam roly-poly with custard followed by coffee. When they had finished the meal Hadley asked 'so how was that gentlemen?'

'It was very good, sir,' replied Cooper, Talbot nodded and said 'delicious, sir.'

'Good... and what did you think, Marcel?'

'Well, it was much better than I expected, mon ami.'

'That's praise indeed coming from you,' said Hadley with a grin and his Sergeants laughed.

As they made their way upstairs to the office to collect their bags, Devaux said to Hadley 'before we leave, Jim, I must send a telegraph to Paris.'

'Very well... if you write it out, Cooper will take it up for you and it will be sent immediately.'

'Très bien.'

'May I ask what's in the message, Marcel?'

'Oui, I am just going to tell my Commissioner that we are going to Scotland with you, mon ami,' replied Devaux.

'Anything else?'

'Non, nothing… he will know that you are now helping us in the search for the relic.'

'Which is what he wanted all along.'

'Oui, it is mon ami.'

Devaux sat at Cooper's desk and wrote out a short message in French, which he then read out in English for the benefit of Hadley and the Sergeants. As he promised, the message was quite straightforward, stating that they were about to leave London on the ten o'clock train to Stirling with Hadley and his Sergeants.

When Cooper returned from the telegraph office, they all went down stairs to the waiting Police coach which took them at the trot through the gloomy, gas lit, cobbled streets to Kings Cross station.

After purchasing their tickets, the detectives crossed the concourse to platform six where the express to Edinburgh was waiting for the passengers to board. Hadley glanced at the huge clock in the concourse, took out his fob watch and confirmed the time. It was half past nine exactly and in half an hour they would be on their way to Edinburgh, the time of arrival was six fifteen the next morning. They would then catch a local train out to Stirling which should arrive at about eight o'clock.

They found an empty compartment and made themselves comfortable for the long journey. The Sergeants started reading the papers they had bought at the kiosk whilst Hadley sat and gazed out of the window at the passengers hurrying to board the train. He wondered what lay ahead, there were many un-answered questions and the responsibility lay heavily on his mind. The Commissioner's words kept coming back that the whole country would look to him to do his duty. He could only pray that he would not disappoint them.

At ten o'clock precisely, guards blew their whistles and waved flags as doors slammed shut, the locomotive belched steam and the couplings clinked before the train slowly pulled away from platform six. They were on their way to Stirling and Hadley felt a dreadful foreboding descend upon him. He looked at Devaux sitting opposite, who smiled and said 'now that we are on our way, mon ami, you can tell me your orders.'

'Orders?'

'Oui, are you coming with us to see that we don't run away with the Grail, or are you concentrating on investigating the murders?'

'Both, Marcel,' Hadley replied and Devaux laughed.

'Let me tell you, mon ami, we will always be friends but my duty comes first in this instance...'

'So does mine,' interrupted Hadley firmly and the Sergeants quickly put down their papers to pay attention.

'The Grail belongs to France! So I will make sure that when we find it I will take it back to Paris,' said Devaux in a menacing tone.

'You may do so, Marcel' began Hadley and Devaux smiled before Hadley continued 'after it has been examined by our experts and permission granted by Her Majesty's Government for you to take it...'

'Non! It is ours, so French experts will examine it in Paris, mon ami!'

'We will see, Marcel.'

'Oui, mon ami, we will, but I promise you that it will be very difficult for you to stop us!'

'Well, we have to find it first... so this argument is somewhat premature,' said Hadley with a smile.

'Oui, that is true, so we can fight over it then.'

'We can,' said Hadley before he gazed out of the window at the moonlit countryside flashing by. Devaux's attitude was now another problem for him to deal with and he did not relish some difficult stand-off when the Grail was discovered. He was certain that the French officers would do anything to ensure that they took the holy relic back with them to Paris and this could lead to a very ugly confrontation.

It was almost midnight when the train made its first stop at Peterborough. Hadley glanced at his fob watch and thought that he should try and get some sleep for the last six hours of the journey. He looked at Talbot, Cooper and Rousseau, who were asleep, then Devaux who was still awake.

'Mon ami, let us hope that we find the relic quickly and come to an agreement that will suit everybody,' said Devaux in a whisper.

'Yes let's… now I suggest we try and get some sleep, Marcel.'

Hadley slept soundly and was only woken by the slamming of carriage doors when the train stopped at York. He fell asleep again and was not disturbed when it stopped at Darlington or Newcastle.

Cooper shook him awake when the train was slowing for its arrival at Edinburgh.

'Morning, sir, we're nearly there.'

'Morning, Sergeant,' he replied and thought 'now another part of this dangerous adventure begins.'

CHAPTER 13

Leaving the train, the detectives made their way across the concourse to a tea room where they enjoyed a light breakfast of hot tea with toast and marmalade. Feeling refreshed they were ready for the journey out to Stirling on the local train. It departed from Edinburgh at seven o'clock and slowly made its' way westwards, running beside the grey, rolling Firth of Forth and stopping at every station. After Falkirk it speeded up slightly and Hadley was relieved when at last the train pulled into the station.

'I hope that someone is here to meet us, gentlemen,' said Hadley as they strode along the platform towards the ticket barrier.

'I'm sure there will be, sir,' said Cooper as he spotted two tall men standing beyond the barrier. When Hadley led the way passed the ticket inspector onto the concourse one of the men moved forward and said 'Inspector Hadley?'

'Yes.'

'Good morning, sir... gentlemen, I'm Inspector Ross Mackay and this is Sergeant Melrose.'

'Ah, good morning Inspector, Sergeant, thank you for meeting us,' said Hadley as he shook hands with MacKay and nodded at Melrose.

'Not at all, sir, it's not often that we get visits from Scotland Yard officers accompanied by Gendarmes from Paris,' said MacKay with a smile.

'No, I suppose not,' said Hadley before he introduced all the officers and MacKay shook hands with them.

'Now let's get you away to the station where we can discuss matters over hot drinks,' said MacKay. They followed him out of the train station to two Police coaches. MacKay, Hadley and Devaux boarded the first coach whilst the Sergeants climbed aboard the second.

As the first coach rattled along the cobbled streets MacKay looked hard at Hadley and asked 'now, sir may I know what this is all about?'

'Of course, Inspector, we're investigating three recent murders and two of the victims have connections to Father Sinclair along with another priest called Murphy,' replied Hadley.

'I see… so, why are you here, Captain?' asked MacKay.

'We are studying Scotland Yard's methods of detection, Monsieur Inspector,' replied Devaux with a smile.

'Are you now… how very interesting,' said MacKay and by his tone they knew he did not believe that for a moment.

'Have you called again at Father Sinclair's house to see if he's returned?' asked Hadley.

'No, I thought it best to wait for you, Inspector,' replied MacKay.

'Quite so,' said Hadley and they remained silent for the rest of the short journey to the Police station.

Over cups of coffee laced with a 'wee dram' to keep out the cold, Hadley briefed MacKay on the details of the investigation. He told him that he intended to question Sinclair's housekeeper, Mrs Murray, and then to search his home for any clue that would lead him to Sinclair.

'Well, we'll have to get a search warrant organised in that case,' said MacKay.

'There's no time for that, Inspector.'

'With all due respect sir, we prefer to do things by the law up here,' said MacKay firmly.

'I'm sure you do, but I have the authority from the Commissioner to conduct my investigations as quickly as possible,' said Hadley.

'If that's the case then I'm beginning to think there's more to this investigation than you're telling me, sir,' said MacKay and Devaux glanced anxiously at Hadley.

'You may think what you wish, Inspector. Now I suggest that we make our way to Sinclair's house,' replied Hadley.

The detectives set off in the two coaches to Father Sinclair's house situated on the Falkirk Road. Although the day was bright with watery sunshine the house appeared dark and gloomy when they arrived. Mrs Murray opened the door and smiled at MacKay but became anxious when she saw the number of Police officers standing with him.

'Good morning, Mrs Murray.'

'Good morning, sir.'

'Has Father Sinclair returned by any chance?' asked MacKay.

'No, sir, and I'm not expecting him back yet.'

'May we come in?'

'May I ask what for, sir?'

'These officers are from London and wish to speak to you and search the house,' replied MacKay.

'Why?... Father Sinclair is not here, sir and I told you before that he would be away for a few days on church business.'

'Mrs Murray, I'm Inspector Hadley from Scotland Yard and I have reason to believe that Father Sinclair may be in great personal danger, so...'

'Oh, Mary mother of God!' she interrupted.

'So I would urge you to assist us, madam,' said Hadley firmly.

'Yes, yes of course, sir, please come in.'

'Thank you.'

Mrs Murray stood back and allowed them to enter the musty hallway then led them into a spacious, oak panelled study.

'Do you have any idea where Father Sinclair has gone to, Mrs Murray?' asked Hadley.

'No, sir, he didn't say.'

'Before we begin the search for anything that may give a clue to Father Sinclair's whereabouts, please tell me all you know about the day he left, Mrs Murray,' said Hadley.

'Well, sir, I really can't say much...'

'Tell me about the other priest who went off with Father Sinclair.'

She looked anxious and began wringing her hands before saying 'I don't think that he was expected, sir, because when I opened the door and showed him in here, Father Sinclair looked surprised to see him.'

'Did Father Sinclair know this priest?'

'I don't know, sir.'

'What happened next?'

'I was dismissed and left them alone until Father Sinclair rang the bell and told me that he was going away on important church business for a few days, sir.'

'Please think once again, do you have any idea where they might have gone?'

'No, sir, and it wasn't my place to ask,' she replied.

'Quite so, Mrs Murray... did Father Sinclair look at all concerned before he left?'

'No, sir, he seemed to be his normal kindly self.'

'Has he had any other unexpected visitors in the last few weeks?'

'Only one that I can think of, sir.'

'And who was that?'

'He was up from London, a quiet man who said he'd just left the army, sir, he stayed overnight then went out with Father Sinclair early the next morning and I never saw him again,' she replied.

'Do you know his name?' asked Hadley his eyes bright with anticipation.

'No, sir, although I thought I heard the Father call him 'William' when they were having dinner together,' she replied.

'Thank you Mrs Murray, you've been very helpful.'

'What do you think has happened to Father Sinclair?' she asked anxiously.

'I can't say for certain, Mrs Murray, but be assured we will find him before anything untoward occurs,' replied Hadley.

'Oh, I pray that you do, sir.'

'We'll now begin the search of his papers to see what we can discover,' said Hadley.

'Very good, sir, I know he has a diary that he keeps locked in the top drawer of his desk, which might be helpful.'

'Thank you, Mrs Murray... Right gentlemen, let's begin,' said Hadley.

Cooper produced his stainless steel instruments from their leather wallet and proceeded to unpick the locked drawer whilst Hadley went through the papers on the untidy desk. MacKay and Melrose looked on, slightly bemused, whilst Talbot started rummaging through the paperwork on a nearby bureau. The French officers searched through the books piled up on the shelves on the opposite wall with Mrs Murray anxiously glancing at them all.

Within minutes Cooper opened the desk drawer, removed the diary and handed it to Hadley.

'Now let's see what we have here, Sergeant,' said Hadley as he opened the diary at the 1st of April and began to read the entries from then on. There was nothing of significance until the 30th when there was written 'William Porter... 6 p.m.'

'Ah, here it is... Sinclair was expecting Porter, so I wonder where they went to the next day,' Hadley mused.

'Perhaps Mrs Murray knows, sir.'

'Yes... Mrs Murray, do you know where Father Sinclair went with his visitor from London?'

'No, sir, but I presumed that they went to Saint Mary's Church, sir,' she replied.

'When the Father returned alone did he say anything about his guest?'

'No, sir.'

'What time did he get back?'

'About seven o'clock, sir and he just asked for his dinner at eight as usual,' she replied.

'Here's something I think you should look at, sir,' said Talbot as he picked up a letter from a pile on the bureau and handed it to Hadley. It was from Pennington and read *'Dear Father Sinclair, I am very interested in your recent discovery of church records regarding a relic of some historical importance. I originally believed that this relic may have been taken to the Toulouse area from Scotland by Guillame de Rieux, a Knight Templar, after the death of King Philip but I am now certain that it remains hidden in Scotland. Perhaps you would kindly give me further information that I may follow up here at Oxford before I journey to Stirling, yours truly. Professor Horace Pennington.'*

'Well, this tie's in nicely with the letters from Sinclair we found in Pennington's study, Sergeant.'

'Indeed it does, sir. Do you think Sinclair wrote back to him with some important information and the Professor was on his way here?'

'Possibly, Sergeant, but remember the last letter was warning the Professor of danger.'

'Yes, it was... so perhaps Murphy received the same information but got here before Pennington was murdered, sir,' said Cooper.

'If that's the case then it puts Murphy high up on our suspects list, sir,' said Talbot.

'It does indeed, Sergeant.'

124

'Have you found anything interesting, sir?' asked MacKay with a smile.

'Yes, I think this is all beginning to make sense, Inspector,' replied Hadley.

'So are you any nearer discovering where Father Sinclair has gone with his guest?' asked MacKay.

'I'm afraid not, but I'm sure that we'll find something amongst his papers that will give us a lead,' replied Hadley.

'Then you must continue your search, sir,' said MacKay in a slightly patronising tone.

'That we will, Inspector,' replied Hadley.

Within half an hour the detectives had looked through all the papers, letters and diary entries they could find, but there was nothing that gave any lead to where Sinclair had gone with Murphy. Hadley wanted to discuss the investigation with his colleagues without MacKay or Melrose present so he decided on a little ruse.

'Well, I think we're finished here for the moment, gentlemen, so perhaps we can go to Saint Mary's now,' said Hadley.

'Right, sir,' said Cooper.

'I presume you wish to continue the search for clues there, Inspector?' asked MacKay.

'Yes indeed, so will you kindly take us to the church?'

'Of course, sir.'

'And on the way perhaps you could suggest a suitable hotel where we can stay?'

'Yes... I believe that 'The Falkirk' would be the best for you,' replied MacKay.

'Excellent, I think we should go to the hotel and book in on our way to Saint Mary's,' said Hadley.

'As you wish, sir.'

MacKay was becoming more and more suspicious of the real motives behind the investigation but he remained silent until the coach pulled up outside 'The Falkirk' hotel.

'Here we are, gentlemen, I'm sure you'll be fine and cosy here,' said MacKay.

'Thank you.'

'And how long do you plan to stay?'

'Until we find Father Sinclair,' replied Hadley and MacKay gave a nod. Whilst Hadley, Devaux and the Sergeants made their way into the warm and welcoming hotel reception, MacKay went to speak to Melrose in the other coach.

Hadley booked rooms for the next two days with the option of further accommodation should the need arise. After they had all signed the register, Hadley led them into the empty lounge where a roaring log fire lit up the room.

'Now, gentlemen, I fear this is going to get very tricky from now on as MacKay obviously smells a rat,' said Hadley.

'What is this rat, mon ami?' asked Devaux and Hadley smiled then replied 'it means he is suspicious of us.'

'Why?'

'Because we're up here with you investigating two murders linked to Sinclair, Marcel.'

'Moi, mon ami?' asked Devaux in surprise.

'Yes, he's no fool and I think somehow he knows about the French connection to the case and he's trying to discover what it is, so when we go to the church we must be careful that we discuss nothing that might give him a lead to our real purpose,' said Hadley.

'Very good, sir,' said Cooper and Talbot nodded.

'Our lips are sealed, mon ami,' said Devaux.

'Right, gentlemen, let's go and see if we can find something at the church that will lead us to these priests,' said Hadley.

MacKay said nothing during the journey to Saint Mary's church, which was situated almost on the outskirts of the city. This silence concerned Hadley and he occasionally glanced across at Devaux who pulled a face, raised his eyebrows before gazing out of the window.

When they arrived at the church MacKay said 'I hope that we find something here that will lead us to Father Sinclair, sir.'

'So do I, Inspector,' replied Hadley.

'Otherwise it will have been a waste of your valuable time coming up from Scotland Yard, let alone the French officers coming all the way from Paris for nothing,' said MacKay with a curious smile.

'It will indeed.'

Mackay and Melrose led the way into Saint Mary's and proceeded to the vestry where two elderly ladies were busy tidying the room. MacKay announced himself to the women and asked if they knew where Father Sinclair had gone. They looked anxiously at each other before replying that they had no idea but asked questions about the reason for MacKay's inquiry. He was able to placate them and then the detectives searched through all the papers they could find but discovered nothing of any significance. Hadley began to feel frustrated and wondered how he could proceed next in the investigation. As they left the church, MacKay said to Hadley 'may I have a wee word with you in private, sir?'

'By all means,' replied Hadley. MacKay nodded and led him a away from the others into the churchyard, stopping by a large granite headstone.

MacKay looked Hadley in the eye and said 'this is all very puzzling to me, sir.'

'Why is that, Inspector?'

'Because I keep asking myself, why would a Scotland Yard detective with two Sergeants accompanied by a French Captain and his Sergeant come all the way up here just to question a priest who has vague connections with two murdered people? So I have to think that there's more to this investigation than you're telling me, sir.'

'Well, Inspector…'

'After sending your telegraph message, you could have left me to question Sinclair and prepare a report for you, which is the normal practice,' interrupted MacKay.

'I realise that, but on this occasion there were special circumstances that made the Commissioner take the decision to send me…'

'Is that so, sir?'

'Yes and I hasten to add that it is no reflection whatever on your competence,' said Hadley with a smile.

'I'm relieved to hear it, so what are these 'special circumstances'?' asked MacKay and Hadley took a deep breath and replied 'it concerns the blackmail of prominent church people, Inspector.'

MacKay looked shocked and said 'I knew that it was something of that nature, so can you tell me anymore, sir?'

'Yes, provided you keep everything I say confidential and discuss it with no one,' said Hadley.

'You have my word, sir.'

'Very well... there are two clergy involved, the Bishop of London, Lord Stillwell and the Archbishop of Canterbury.'

'Good heavens!'

'And the victim William Porter, who as you know was linked to Sinclair, was attempting to blackmail these important clergy just before he was murdered,' said Hadley.

'This is terrible,' said MacKay shaking his head.

'It is and now you understand why we've come here to find Sinclair and question him.'

'I do, sir, but what about the French officers?'

'I can't say much more at the moment but I can tell you that part of the blackmail plot was initiated in France and discovered by the French authorities,' replied Hadley.

'This is truly awful, sir.'

'Yes it is, and I must rely on your co-operation to find Sinclair and Murphy as quickly as possible,' said Hadley firmly, hoping that he had persuaded MacKay with part of the truth.

'You may count on me, sir.'

'Thank you, Inspector.'

They had just moved away from the headstone to join the others when a dog cart, driven by a Constable, pulled up outside the church.

'Hello, I wonder what this is all about,' said MacKay under his breath as the Constable hurried toward him.

'Inspector MacKay, sir, we've just had a report that the body of priest has been found!'

CHAPTER 14

Hadley looked at MacKay who had gone quite pale before he asked the Constable 'has the body been identified yet?'

'No, sir.'

'Where was it found, Constable?' asked MacKay.

'On the heath at Bannockburn sir.'

'How far away is that?' asked Hadley.

'About three miles,' replied MacKay.

'Who discovered him?'

'A gentleman walking his dog, sir... he's still at the station giving a statement.'

'Where is the body now?' asked Hadley.

'It's been taken to the Infirmary, sir,' replied the Constable.

Hadley looked at MacKay and said 'then I suggest we collect Mrs Murray and take her to the Infirmary to identify the priest.'

'This is a terrible shock, sir and she'll be mightily distressed if it is Father Sinclair,' said MacKay shaking his head.

'I'm sure she will... but let's make haste because if he has been murdered then we have no time to lose in finding his killer,'

'Yes, sir, you're quite right,' said MacKay haltingly, visibly shaken by the news.

Hadley informed the others of the events and after briefing Cooper and Talbot, ordered them to their coach. He asked MacKay to send all the Sergeants on to the Infirmary to start making background inquiries whilst he, Devaux and MacKay went to break the dreadful news to Mrs Murray.

The coaches set off at the trot in different directions and Hadley's mind was now in a whirl. He wondered for a moment if Sinclair had murdered Murphy or was it the other way around? He thought that the killer was much more likely to be Murphy and he knew if that was the case then Mrs Murray would be able to give a good description of this elusive and mysterious priest. Then on the other hand, he reasoned that the murder could have been committed by others unknown or possibly Tyler and Doyle.

MacKay broke the news as gently as he could to Mrs Murray who immediately burst into tears. The detectives assured her that if the victim was Father Sinclair then his killer would be quickly hunted down and brought to justice. When she had composed herself they set off to the Infirmary.

After introductions to Doctor Macpherson at the mortuary, Mrs Murray waited in his office with an attendant whilst the Doctor led the detectives to a marble slab at the end of the white tiled dissecting room. The Sergeants were already grouped round the naked body and stood back when the senior officers approached.

'So how did he die, Doctor?' asked Hadley.

'First indications are that he was strangled, Inspector, you can see the bruising around the neck here,' said Macpherson as he pointed to the marks.

'How long has he been dead, Doctor?'

'I can't be too precise at the moment but I would say about 12 hours,' replied Macpherson and Hadley took out his fob watch and noted that it was just after eleven o'clock.

'So around this time last night,' said Hadley.

'Yes... and once I have carried out my examination I may be able to be more accurate,' said Macpherson. Hadley remained silent for a few moments before saying 'now I'd like to examine his personal effects, Doctor.'

'Nothing at all was found on the body when it arrived here, Inspector.'

'Nothing?' asked Hadley in a surprised tone.

'No, it appeared to have been stripped of anything that could give a clue to his identity.'

Hadley glanced at the others who raised their eyebrows looking surprised as he was and he asked MacKay 'did your men search the body at the crime scene, Inspector?'

'I'm sure they must have, but I will have to confirm that when we return to the station,' replied MacKay, Hadley nodded and said 'let's hope they've found something.'

'Doctor, we'd like Mrs Murray to identify the body so would you kindly arrange for it to be suitably covered?' asked MacKay.

'Yes of course, Inspector.'

The detectives returned to the office whilst an attendant prepared the body for Mrs Murray to view. Hadley was sure it was Sinclair and he knew that the housekeeper would be distraught and unlikely to be much help into the murder investigation until she had composed herself. It seemed an age before Macpherson arrived back in the office and said that they could now view the body. Hadley, MacKay and Macpherson led Mrs Murray to the slab and when they were ready, the Doctor uncovered the face of the priest. Mrs Murray looked down at the pale, marble features and burst into tears.

'Mrs Murray, I'm so sorry, we know this is very difficult for you but please try to compose yourself,' said Hadley calmly and she nodded before clasping her handkerchief to her face.

'Can you identify this person?' Hadley asked gently and she mumbled something which they did not understand.

'Pardon, Mrs Murray?'

'I said it's not him... it's the other one,' she said through her handkerchief.

'It's not Father Sinclair?' asked Hadley in surprise, she shook her head and whispered 'no, sir.'

'Is it Father Murphy?' asked MacKay and she nodded and replied 'yes, sir.'

'Are you absolutely sure, Mrs Murray?' asked Hadley.

'Yes I am, sir,' she replied and the detectives glanced at each other.

'Well I'm sure you must be relieved Mrs Murray,' said MacKay.

'I am, sir, but now I wonder what has happened to dear Father Sinclair.'

'We'll find out to be sure,' said MacKay with a smile.

'Mother of God, he may be lying dead somewhere out in the hills like this poor man here,' she said and began to cry again. They escorted her back to the office and MacKay offered her soothing platitudes whilst Hadley felt wrong footed over this unexpected turn of events. Was Sinclair lying dead in the hills after being murdered by Tyler and Doyle or was someone else guilty or did Sinclair kill Murphy? This investigation was getting darker by the minute.

Hadley briefed the others whilst MacKay made arrangements with Melrose to take Mrs Murray home. MacKay thanked

Macpherson for his help before they left the Infirmary and made their way back to the Police station. On arrival, MacKay questioned the attending officers at Bannockburn who said they had searched the body before calling for an ambulance, but found nothing.

Mr Balfour, who had discovered the body, was with the Duty Sergeant when the detectives arrived and Hadley was keen to question him. When the elderly Scotsman had finished giving a statement he and his dog were shown into the interview room and sat for a few moments before Hadley, MacKay and Cooper arrived.

After introductions, Hadley said 'please give us all the details of when you discovered the body, sir, and leave nothing out.'

'It's a sad business that it is, sir,' said Balfour slowly shaking his head.

'It is indeed and any help you can give us will be appreciated,' said Hadley.

'Well, I've given a statement to the Sergeant, is that not good enough for you?' asked Balfour.

'It's very helpful, sir, but I'd just like to hear it once again in case there is something that may come to light,' replied Hadley.

Balfour sighed, paused for a moment then said 'I was walking my dog, Angus, here' and he glanced down at the Highland Terrier at his feet then continued 'across Bannockburn heath when I saw what I thought was a wee bundle of rags by some bushes. Angus hurried over and started to bark, which is unusual as he's normally a quiet wee animal, you know.'

'What time was this, sir?' asked Hadley.

'About half past eight.'

'Please continue, sir.'

'Well, I went over to see what Angus was making such a fuss about and then I saw that it was a man laying there, Inspector,' said Balfour as he began to shake his head again and remained silent.

'And what happened next?' asked Hadley, becoming a little impatient with the elderly Scotsman.

'I thought he was asleep for the moment... then saw that his eyes were open and I knew he was dead, so I called Angus away and came here to report it,' replied Balfour.

'Did you see anybody nearby, strangers for instance?'

'No, there was no one to be seen, but I usually meet Mr McFee about nine o'clock when he takes his dog for a walk, Inspector,' replied Balfour.

'How agreeable... now did you notice anything at all near the body?'

'No, sir, nothing... there was only a wee scrap of paper nearby which I picked up.'

'Did you give it to the officers?'

'No.'

'Where is it now, sir?'

'Here, still in my pocket, but it's of no consequence,' replied Balfour as he took out a crumpled piece of paper and handed it to Hadley. There were just three words written in capital letters, Doune, Drummond and Culcreuch. Hadley was convinced that Murphy's killer had found this when he stripped the body then discarded it or dropped it accidentally before leaving the scene. He handed the paper to MacKay and asked 'do these names mean anything to you, Inspector?'

'Yes, Doune is a small village close by, but there's only a ruined castles at Drummond and Culcreuch,' replied MacKay, Hadley's eyes lit up 'now that is interesting' he said, as his mind raced with the probability that the Grail was hidden at one of these places.

'Why is that, sir?' asked MacKay but Hadley ignored the question and asked him 'is there also a castle at Doune?'

'Ay, there is,' replied MacKay.

'Then I've a feeling that's where we'll find Sinclair... if he's still alive,' said Hadley before he looked at Balfour, smiled and said 'thank you for all your help, sir.'

After Balfour left the room with his dog, MacKay asked Hadley 'do you suspect Sinclair of Murphy's murder?'

'At the moment I believe it is a strong possibility.'

'And what would be the motive, sir?'

'I'm not sure and only time will tell, Inspector.'

In MacKay's office Hadley briefed the officers and the implications of the Grail's hiding place were not lost on his

Sergeants or the Frenchmen.

'So, gentlemen, I suggest we split up into three parties and search these places for Father Sinclair,' said Hadley.

MacKay nodded and said 'right... if Sergeant Melrose comes with me to Doune then you and your men can go to Drummond and Culcreuch, sir.'

'That's agreed, Inspector... Cooper, you and Talbot go to Culcreuch.'

'Very good, sir.'

'And Captain Devaux and Sergeant Rousseau will come with me to Drummond,' said Hadley and Devaux nodded then smiled knowing that Hadley wanted to stay close to him just in case he discovered the Grail.

'Although the castles are not too far away, I'll arrange to take some lunch with us,' said MacKay.

It was just after two o'clock when the three coaches set off to their various destinations. Doune is west of Dunblane and only ten miles from Stirling so MacKay expected to be there in about an hour's time. During the journey he discussed the investigation with Melrose who was very suspicious of the Scotland Yard detectives and their reasons for being there. MacKay did his best to alleviate Melrose's concerns but was sure that his Sergeant remained to be convinced.

Cooper and Talbot were quite pleased to be on their own and chatted enthusiastically about the case, hoping that they would find Sinclair and the Grail at Culcreuch Castle.

'What a turn up for the book it would be, Bill, if we arrested Sinclair and found it,' said Cooper.

'You could just imagine old Bell's face,' said Talbot before he laughed.

'And the Commissioner's!'

'I bet his old side whiskers would be twitching something horrible,' said Talbot with a grin.

'Without a doubt, but I'm sure whatever we find, all the praise will have to go to the guvnor,' said Cooper.

'It was ever thus, Bob,' said Talbot with a sigh.

They arrived at Culcreuch castle as the light was beginning to fade and the old ruin looked dark and mysterious in the evening gloom.

'Searching this place will take some time,' said Talbot as they stepped down from the coach.

'That it will and I can see us coming back tomorrow,' said Cooper.

Talbot asked the driver for a torch but he did not carry one so could only offer one of the coach's acetylene lamps.

'Then that'll have to do,' said Talbot. The lamp was removed from its bracket, lit and handed to Talbot.

'If we're not back in about two hours you'll have to come and search for us,' said Cooper to the driver.

'Very good, sir.'

Drummond Castle was the farthest away from Stirling being to the north by about eighteen miles and to the west of Muthill. Hadley and the French officers were keen to get there as quickly as possible before the night closed in. Searching ruined castles in the dark was not a prospect that any of them fancied but they knew it had to be done.

'So we have only a one in three chance of finding Sinclair and the relic, mon ami,' said Devaux as the coach made good progress towards Drummond.

'Yes, I'm afraid so.'

'I do not like the odds, in fact I do not like any of this,' said Devaux anxiously.

'Neither do I, Marcel.'

The Frenchman remained quiet for a few minutes before he asked 'do you think Sinclair murdered Murphy, mon ami?'

'I think it is highly likely.'

'But why?'

'I've no idea... perhaps there was some jealous rivalry over the ownership of the Grail...'

'Ah, it will be just like us when we find it!' interrupted Devaux and Hadley smiled before replying 'I think we're too professional for that, Marcel,' but Devaux's remark concerned him a little.

It was just after five o'clock when they reached Drummond Castle in the fading light. As they stepped down from the coach Devaux said 'I think this is going to be very difficult, mon ami.'

'Nothing worthwhile is ever easy, Marcel,' replied Hadley and the Frenchman shrugged his shoulders before striding off towards the ruined gatehouse with Rousseau. Hadley said to the driver 'we'll return when it gets too dark to continue our search, Constable.'

'Right you are, sir.'

The French officers had reached the gatehouse by the time Hadley caught up with them.

'I suggest we split up and meet back here in an hour, Marcel,' said Hadley as he took out his fob watch.

'Très bien, Jim,' replied Devaux as he and Rousseau took out their watches.

'So let's make it back here by a quarter past six... by then I think it will probably be too dark to carry on safely,' said Hadley as he glanced up at the crumbling ruins.

'Mon Dieu...if we don't find Sinclair or the relic now it means we'll have to come back tomorrow!' exclaimed Devaux.

'It will... so that's all the more reason why we should start searching quickly, Marcel.'

Devaux headed for the main hall of the castle whilst Rousseau made his way towards roofless buildings attached to the outer wall of the fortress. Hadley looked about before deciding to search a large round tower situated on the other side of the wide courtyard. He reached the arched doorway into the tower and looked about the gloomy interior before making his way up the worn, spiral staircase. He was slightly nervous and felt in his coat pocket for his .45 calibre revolver and was comforted by its presence. The stairs became steeper and narrower the further he climbed and the sound of his footsteps on the granite stairs seemed unusually loud to him. Suddenly he heard an eerie howling sound which made the hairs on the back of his neck stand up as it seemed quite unnatural. His nerves were now jangling and he drew his revolver just in case there was something untoward facing him as he climbed higher around the tower. He remembered that it is said that all Scottish castles are haunted... but as he didn't believe in ghosts he was unconcerned. He thought, however, it was all well and good to have that firm conviction in busy Whitechapel... but it felt a touch different in a ruined Scottish castle when it was getting darker by the minute. As he took further steps slowly upwards, the eerie sound became louder then died away before becoming louder once more. He slipped off the .45's safety catch and pulled back the hammer with his thumb so he was ready to fire... just in case. After taking a few more steps he saw an arched doorway into a large room to his left. The sound was emanating from in there and he stepped boldly into the room. He glanced about and immediately realised that it was wind noise he heard as it came through the narrow window openings either side of the room. In the gloom he noticed a wooden table close to the open fireplace and on it was the body of a man.

CHAPTER 15

Hadley approached the corpse after glancing about him for anything untoward. The room was quite empty except for the body on the wooden table, which gave his nerves some relief. He carefully lowered the hammer on his .45, slipped the safety catch on and placed the revolver back in his coat pocket. The noise of the wind persisted and the howling was an unwelcome distraction to his concentration. He looked down at the pale face and wondered if it was Sinclair. He touched the forehead and surmised that the person had not been dead long as the cold skin moved gently under his fingers. He could not see any injuries to the face or neck and there was no trace of blood around the body. He looked at the clothes but they were not priestly garments and gave no clue as to the identity of the man. He searched the pockets in the top coat and then the jacket but he found nothing and assumed it was not Sinclair. He wondered if this person was connected in some way to the investigation or had anything to do with the murder of Murphy and the disappearance of Sinclair. His suspicions were aroused by the fact that the body had been stripped of anything which could identify it. He decided to call out for the French officer's assistance and then get the body away to Stirling.

Hadley went to the narrow window and glanced down at the courtyard below before he shouted out their names several times in the wind but there was no response. He had no alternative but to go and find them so he hurried down the spiral staircase and out into the courtyard before making his way across to the great hall in search of Devaux. There was no sign of the Frenchman in the vast, roofless, granite building and Hadley called out his name loudly several times. The only sound was the howling of the wind which was now becoming stronger as the dark night closed in. Hadley looked about him and noticed two arched doorways either side of the far wall leading from the hall. He hurried to the nearest and called out Devaux's name but there was no response. At the other he called again and heard a muffled reply half drowned out by the noise of the wind. He called again before striding into the long, dark corridor that led away from the hall.

'Where the hell are you, Marcel?' he shouted in the echoing corridor.

'Here, mon ami, here, I'm down here!' called Devaux.

Hadley came to the end of the passageway and found another arched doorway with narrow stairs leading down.

'Have you found something?'

'Non, mon ami.'

By the tone of the reply Hadley became concerned and called out 'Marcel, are you alright?'

'Non, mon ami, I'm not!'

'Oh bloody hell,' whispered Hadley as he hurried down the steps and when he reached the last one, called out 'where are you?'

'I'm here, mon ami!' replied Devaux before a flickering light emanated from behind a pillar.

Hadley found Devaux sitting on the stone floor, leaning against the pillar, holding a match in one hand and nursing his ankle with the other.

'What have you done for heaven's sake?' asked Hadley as the match flickered and died, plunging them into darkness.

'I fell down the last step and twisted my ankle, mon ami,' replied Devaux as he struck another match.

'Oh dear God.'

'If you help me, I'm sure I can get back to the coach,' said Devaux.

'Right, let's get you up, Marcel.'

Hadley placed his arm around Devaux and helped him to his feet. The Frenchman let out a cry of pain as he tried to stand on his damaged ankle.

'Mon Dieu, I think this is very bad, mon ami,' whispered Devaux as the match flickered out.

'It can't be helped, Marcel, put your arm around my shoulder and just hop on one foot towards the steps.'

'It is a catastrophe, Jim.'

'It bloody well is.'

In the darkness they struggled slowly up the stairs to the corridor and as they reached the archway to the hall they heard Rousseau calling above the noise of the wind.

When Hadley saw him at the far end of the hall he shouted

'here! Over here, Sergeant!' Rousseau hurried towards them and as he came close Devaux said 'you're just in time to save your Captain, mon ami!'

'What has happened to you?'

'I've twisted my ankle, so help me get to the coach before something else happens to me in this cruel, dangerous place,' said Devaux.

'Mon Dieu! I knew this would end badly, mon Captain... I never wanted us to come here because I knew something bad would happen,' said Rousseau as he supported Devaux. They made their way back across the courtyard, through the gatehouse and down to the waiting coach. When the Constable saw them he jumped down and ran to give assistance.

'Captain Devaux has twisted his ankle, so take him and Sergeant Rousseau back to Muthill and find a Doctor,' said Hadley.

'There's no Doctor in Muthill, sir, the nearest will be up at Crieff,' said the Constable.

'Well take the Captain there then.'

'Very good, sir.'

'Then round up some men and come back with a cart as quick as you can,' said Hadley.

'Yes, sir.'

'Why do you need men and a cart, mon ami?' asked Devaux as they helped him into the coach.

'I found a body in the tower...'

'Mon Dieu! Is it Sinclair?'

'I don't think so.'

'Who is it then?'

'I don't know, but hopefully we'll find out when we get the body back to Stirling,' replied Hadley.

'This is a terrible nightmare, mon ami,' said Devaux as Rousseau climbed in and sat next to him.

'I must admit it seems that way at the moment, Marcel.'

'And it is a catastrophe for the investigation that I am injured,' said Devaux.

'It certainly is,' said Hadley before he asked the driver 'Constable, do you have a spare lamp?'

'Yes, sir,' he replied with a nod and went to the luggage

pannier fixed to the rear of the coach.

'Why do you want a lamp, mon ami?'

'To see with.'

'But surely you're not staying here... are you?' asked Devaux in surprise.

'I am.'

'Why, mon ami?'

'To continue the search and see if any unexpected visitors arrive,' replied Hadley.

'Mon Dieu! It is a dangerous place and I think you are very foolish,' said Devaux.

'Possibly, but I have my duty to perform.'

'Then Rousseau will stay with you, mon ami.'

'I think you need him more than I do, Marcel.'

'Mon Dieu! You English!' exclaimed Devaux and Hadley smiled as he closed the coach door.

The Constable lit the acetylene lamp and handed it to Hadley before he climbed back up to his seat.

'I will be back with help as quick as I can, sir,' he said as he slapped the reins and urged the horses to walk on.

'Thank you, Constable.'

Hadley stood and gave a wave as he watched the coach pull away and disappear into the gathering dusk. He turned and looked at the ruined castle for a moment, drew in a deep breath and headed back towards the gatehouse, holding on firmly to the flickering acetylene lamp.

He decided to explore the cellar where he had found Devaux before returning to the tower to search for clues that might give a lead to the identity of the body. By the time he reached the great hall it had started to rain and he hurried to the archway that led into the closed corridor. The lamp flickered and gave a ghostly intermittent light with fleeting shadows as he strode towards the archway that led down to the cellar. He became a little anxious, felt for his .45 and drew it from his coat pocket when he reached the steps.

The cellar was quite expansive and had supporting pillars every so often along its length, which gave dancing shadows on the stone floor as he passed by. Hadley thought it could have been used for food storage or possibly a dungeon in former times. He shivered at the thought of tormented souls suffering excruciating pain in this dark place before they died at the hands of their captors. He made his way to the far end where there was a stout wooden door that appeared as if it had not been opened for many years. He tried to open it but knew instinctively that it would take some force to make it yield. He made a note to return at a later date and force it open to reveal any secrets that might lie beyond.

When he was satisfied with his search of the cellar he returned to the entrance to the roofless hall where the rain was now pouring down heavily onto the flagstones. He waited for a few minutes and decided that it was not going to ease so he made a dash for the tower at the far end of the courtyard. By the time he reached the arched entrance his coat was soaked through and he cursed under his breath for being so stupid. He climbed the narrow spiral stair case to the room where the body lay, he did not enter but instead carried on up the stairs. Around the next full spiral there was an entrance to another room and this time he was surprised to see signs of habitation illuminated in the flickering light of his lamp. He stepped into the room and looked about, whoever was living there had boarded up the windows with planks of wood and hung thick blankets over the planks. There was a table with two wooden chairs by the fireplace, which had the remains of a log fire in it and a large, thick patch of straw on the floor, half covered with blankets. A bottle of whiskey stood on the table, with only a few drams left at the bottom, along with two cracked cups, plates, spoons, some knives, half a loaf of bread and an oil lamp. In the fire hearth were two blackened cooking pots, the larger one had some form of gruel in the bottom whilst the other had the remains of a stew.

He searched the room carefully but found nothing of any significance. He discovered some dry kindling wood with a pile of logs by the side of the fireplace and proceeded to light a fire. When it was burning brightly, he took off his coat and placed on the back of one of the chairs to dry off. He sat warming himself in front of the roaring logs and wondered if the men living here were connected to the murder investigation and the search for the Grail. He thought it was more than a strong possibility that desperate men were involved and he hoped that the Constable would return sooner rather than later. He glanced at his fob watch, noted that it was just after eight o'clock and reasoned it would be at least two hours before the Constable would arrive back.

He decided to search the room with the body once again and took his revolver from his topcoat before picking up his acetylene lamp and making for the stairs. As he descended, the howling of the wind increased making him feel even more anxious. Entering the room he looked carefully about, aided by the lamp light, and went across to the corpse on the table. He studied the pale face and thought that man was about forty years old. He searched the pockets once again but found nothing. He looked for a makers label in the topcoat and found that it had been made by Jeeves and Fortescue of Regent Street, London. In the jacket was a similar label, so whoever was before him on the table, he could assume with some confidence originally came from London. The two burning questions uppermost in his mind were… who was he and how did he die? He undid the waistcoat and opened the shirt but found no injuries to the chest or stomach. He examined the neck carefully but could see no sign of bruising. It was a mystery which would have to remain so until the body could be examined by Doctor Macpherson at the Infirmary in Stirling. The one thing now certain in Hadley's mind was that this man was somehow connected to the hunt for the Holy Grail and possibly implicated in the murder of Murphy and the disappearance of Sinclair.

Returning to the room upstairs, he sat by the fire feeling hungry and longing for one of Alice's hot beef stews with dumplings and pearl barley or Vera's tasty steak and kidney pie with mash covered with thick gravy, followed by a pint or two of stout. He tried to forget about the food and began to think logically about the case so far. It was a relief that Devaux was no longer in a position where he could prove troublesome when or if the Grail was discovered but on the other hand he would miss the Frenchman's input to the investigation. Hadley believed that Tyler and Doyle had murdered the Porter brothers, kidnapped their parents, killed Pennington and attacked Major Fielding. He wondered if they were still in London and if Hanson and Mercer had any success in finding them.

Sinclair was the prime suspect for the murder of Murphy and Hadley thought that this cruel act might have been brought about by jealous rivalry. It stood to reason that whoever discovered the Grail and took it to Rome would be rewarded beyond a priest's wildest dreams by a grateful Pope. That heavenly prospect was certainly worth killing for in some people's minds.

The minutes ticked slowly by and he wondered how Cooper and Talbot were faring at Culcreuch Castle, he hoped that they were having more success in the search for Sinclair and the Grail than he had so far at Drummond. His thoughts then turned to MacKay and Melrose at Doune. If they found Sinclair would he tell them about the Grail? Hadley was worrying about that when the room suddenly began to shake and he heard a rumbling sound followed by an almighty crashing noise that made him jump. He leapt up, grabbed his revolver and lamp then headed for the stairs. He hurried down to the next floor and looked in at the corpse on the table. All seemed well and undisturbed in the room so he quickly descended to the entrance to the tower and saw outside in the pouring rain, piles of granite blocks intermingled with bricks that had fallen from the battlements of the tower. The wind had at last toppled the highest part of the castle and Hadley was immediately concerned about the rest of the tower's structure. Devaux was right when he said it was a dangerous place. He came to the decision that it was unsafe to remain in the tower and somehow he had to bring the body down and take it elsewhere. The thought of carrying a dead body did not appeal to him but it had to be done, so he quickly retraced his steps to the top floor, put on his topcoat and descended to the room with the mysterious corpse.

He looked down at the serene, pale face and said 'sorry about this my friend but we have to move you somewhere safe until help arrives.' He attempted to lift the body by its shoulders but rigor mortis had set in making the whole corpse rigid. He had no option but to place his hands under the arms and drag it off the table. The feet drummed as they hit the floor and Hadley dragged the body towards the doorway wondering how he would manage the spiral stairs backwards. He had to be very careful as he descended because one slip could result in a similar accident to Devaux's. If he fell it was likely that the dead body would land on top of him and he knew the weight would entrap him until help arrived. He stepped back slowly, found his footing and then dragged the body after him before moving his lamp down to the next step. This was going to be laborious but he knew it had to be done. He proceeded slowly and carefully, step after step, repeating the process of moving the lamp, finding his footing and dragging the body after him.

It seemed an age before he reached the final step and stopped for breath once the body was stretched out on the flagstone floor. He went to the arched doorway and looked out through the rain at the fallen debris and wondered where he could take the body. The only place that sprang to mind was the corridor off the great hall but that would mean dragging the body over the fallen masonry and all the way across the courtyard. He was not sure he could manage it and wondered if he should take a chance and stay where he was until the Constable arrived with help. He looked at his fob watch, saw it was almost ten o'clock and thought that he had not long to wait for assistance, so decided to stay in the tower and hope that it remained standing.

Within minutes he saw, through the gatehouse, a coach pull up on the road and he felt relieved that help was at hand. Two figures climbed down from the coach and started to make their way up into the castle. One carried a lamp and as they got closer Hadley could see that they were not Policemen, he became concerned as they passed through the gatehouse and made their way across the courtyard in the direction of the tower. He knew that they might be the suspects in the investigation who had been living in the tower, so he stood back from the entrance, drew his revolver, slipped off the safety catch, pulled back the hammer until it clicked and waited for their arrival.

CHAPTER 16

As the Sergeants approached the crumbling gatehouse of Culcreuch Castle in the strengthening wind they agreed that Cooper would search the exposed part of the ruin whilst Talbot with his lamp would go into the dark interior.

'I don't think we've even got a couple of hours before it gets dark, Bill,' said Cooper glancing up at the grey, cloudy sky.

'If you're right it'll mean a trip back here tomorrow morning,' said Talbot.

'That's no bad thing.'

'Well I'm sure if we found Sinclair here it would be enough for the moment.'

'True, so let's go to it, Bill and I'll meet you back here in… say an hour,' said Cooper looking at his fob watch.

'Right,' said Talbot with a nod as he glanced at his watch.

Cooper headed for the roofless buildings clustered around the far battlement wall whilst Talbot made for the arched entrance to the great hall. Most of the roof had collapsed into a pile of debris at the far end and Talbot stood in the entrance looking around for doorways off the desolate building. As the wind howled about the structure he noticed two archways in the wall opposite to where he was standing. He strode to the nearest one, stopped when he reached it and held the lamp up to see into the darkness beyond. He could make out a short narrow corridor that led to another doorway then nothing. He drew his revolver and walked cautiously along the corridor to the doorway and in the flickering light saw steps leading down into an inky darkness. He descended the steps carefully until he reached the last one then stopped, gazed into the darkness ahead for a moment before stepping down to the flagstone floor and continued along slowly. The lamp shone just a small flickering pool of light in front of him so he could only make out vague shapes ahead. He noticed pillars either side and suddenly he came to the end wall where there was a door. He stopped and listened for a moment, sure that he had heard a sound beyond and he became quite anxious. He slipped off the safety catch on his .45 and pulled back the hammer before he reached for the door handle. As he did so the door was suddenly flung open by a tall man coming out of the room. He carried a lamp and looked as shocked as Talbot, who jumped instinctively as the man demanded 'who the bloody hell are you?' but before he could answer, another man appeared in the doorway.

They looked at each other for a split second as Talbot replied 'I'm a Police officer...' but before he could say anything more, the tall man grabbed the barrel of his revolver and twisted it upwards. Talbot instinctively pulled the trigger, the muzzle flash lit up the cellar and the bullet shot off into the darkness. Talbot dropped his lamp and lashed out at the man with his clenched fist, catching him on the side of his face, the man staggered slightly dropping his lamp as he lunged at Talbot with his free hand. Talbot was unable to wrest his revolver from the man's strong grip but knew he had to hold on to it because he feared for his life if he lost the weapon. The other man moved forward quickly, grabbing Talbot around his neck and twisting the Sergeant down to the stone floor, he fell on top of him, knocking him breathless. The man, who still held onto the revolver clutched in Talbot's hand, gave a mighty kick to the Sergeant's head, which rendered him unconscious. The man relieved him of the revolver and they dragged the unconscious officer into the room, where another man sat chained up to one of the pillars.

Talbot was searched and they found his warrant card in his wallet before he was similarly chained, still unconscious, to the pillar with the other prisoner.

'He's a bloody Bobbie right enough,' said the tall man gazing at the card in the lamplight.

'And from Scotland Yard,' added the other.

'He'll not be alone, that's for sure.'

'What do we do now?'

'Have a look about the place to see who else is here,' replied the tall man.

'And then what?'

'Lock them all up in here if we have to... it'll not be long before we find what we're looking for and then we can be away.'

The two men left the prisoners in the dark and locked the door behind them before making their way cautiously back up to the great hall. The tall man had taken the Sergeant's revolver knowing that it would enable him to force anyone else they found in the castle back to the room at gunpoint.

Cooper had searched the open buildings for any sign of Sinclair or a likely hiding place of the Grail. He found nothing amongst the piles of fallen stones and ruined archways and made his way back towards the gatehouse in the ever increasing wind. It was beginning to rain and the light was fading rapidly when he reached the shelter of the gatehouse. He glanced at his pocket watch and noted that the hour was almost up. He looked about for Talbot and began to get impatient as the rain started to fall more heavily. He glanced at the coach standing in the road and gave a wave to the Constable sitting in the driver's seat. He waved back and Cooper decided that, for all intents and purposes, the day was over. He knew that it was useless to call for Talbot in the wind so he left the shelter of the gatehouse and ran to the hall in search of his colleague. He reached the archway entrance just as the two men appeared from the doorway opposite but Cooper did not see them in the gloomy interior as his attention was immediately drawn to the other end of the hall. Several black rooks were screeching and flapping about amongst the debris of the roof which distracted him long enough for the two men to get close and one to call out to him.

'Hands up, my Bobbie boy,' said the tall man, pointing Talbot's revolver at Cooper's head.

'Oh bloody hell!' exclaimed Cooper in total surprise.

'I said hands up!' shouted the man angrily and Cooper hesitantly raised his hands.

'Who are you?'

'Never mind about that laddie... search him!'

Cooper's mind was racing as to the whereabouts of Talbot while other man relieved him of his revolver and wallet.

'Right... now come with us,' said the tall man waving the revolver at him.

The two men stood either side of Cooper, pointing revolvers at his body before guiding him towards the doorway opposite that led down to the cellar.

Cooper realised with dreadful certainty that these men had

already captured Talbot as it was unlikely that they would possess an identical revolver to his. Cooper's heart sank when they made their way down the narrow stairs towards the cellar and he wondered what Hadley would do in these circumstances. By the time they reached the locked cellar, Talbot had regained consciousness and looked up as they entered the room. When Cooper saw him chained to the pillar he gasped and asked 'are you alright, Bill?' Talbot nodded and mumbled 'I'll live.'

'Don't count on it, laddie,' said the tall man as he placed the lamp on the table while the other one chained Cooper to the pillar alongside Talbot. In the pale flickering light, Cooper could see the gash on the side of Talbot's head and the blood that had trickled down his face. He felt angry and disappointed with himself that he had fallen so easily into the hands of these criminals.

'Listen to me you villains...' Cooper began.

'Save your breath, laddie!' interrupted the tall man.

'We're from Scotland Yard and there are more armed officers outside...'

'As I said, save your breath, we know all about you!'

'Then you'll know that it is only a matter of time...'

'Before you're dead if you're not very careful, laddie!'

'If you kill us you'll both hang... I promise you!'

'Perhaps, but if you keep on, you and your cronies will all be dead by then, so it'll be too late for you to have the pleasure of seeing us swing,' said the tall man with a grin.

'If you harm us then you'd better pray that our guvnor doesn't find you before the others get here,' said Talbot.

'Now is that so?'

'Oh yes.'

'Well I hope he's quicker on his feet than you two hopeless loons!'

'He is and you'll find that out to your cost in due course,' said Talbot.

'We'll see about that,' replied the man before he turned to his compatriot and said 'let's go and see if we can find any others lurking about.' The man nodded, took the lamp from the table and followed the tall man out of the room leaving the prisoners in total darkness. After the door slammed shut they heard the key turn in the lock. They sat in silence for a few moments gathering their thoughts. Cooper was sure he knew who the other prisoner was but asked 'may we know who you are, sir?'

'Yes, my son, I'm Father Sinclair... a Catholic priest from Stirling,' replied Sinclair in a whisper.

'I thought so... I'm Sergeant Cooper and my colleague is Sergeant Talbot... we're from Scotland Yard.'

'I'm very glad you're here... but what a terrible situation this is,' said Sinclair.

'It is... but we'll get out of it somehow.'

'I pray God that we do.'

'Now we've been looking for you...'

'Have you, my son?'

'Yes, so tell us why you're here, Father.'

'It's a long and unpleasant story,' said Sinclair in a whisper.

'Well it'll help our investigations if you tell us,' said Cooper but the priest remained silent for some while until Cooper prompted him again to tell why he was there.

Sinclair replied 'several days ago, Father Murphy, a priest from London, came to see me regarding some church history that he was interested in and whilst he was with me at Saint Mary's searching through the records, these two men came into the vestry and said that they were on an important mission.'

'Did they say what their mission was?' asked Cooper.

'Only that it was in connection with the Catholic Faith and told us that it involved the search for some medieval relic at a nearby castle,' replied Sinclair.

'Then what happened?'

'After I asked them some questions about the castle, I studied a map carefully and decided that there were three castles in the area that might be suitable for their search,' replied Sinclair.

'Please go on, Father.'

'They appeared quite satisfied, so I wrote the names down on a piece of paper for them.'

'Did they leave then?'

'Yes, but came back the next day.'

'What for?'

'They said that if I would go with them to Culcreuch Castle, which is where we are now, to help in the search for this relic, they would make a generous donation to the church for my time, and so, foolishly, I agreed.'

Cooper knew the priest was not telling the truth and asked 'do you know where Father Murphy is now?'

'Yes, he went back to London,' replied Sinclair.

'When was that?'

'The same day these men came to ask for my help.'

'Did you see Father Murphy actually board the train?'

'No… but we dropped him off at the station on our way here, so I presumed he was going back to London as he said,' replied Sinclair.

'Well I'm afraid he didn't catch the train,' said Cooper quietly.

'Is Father Murphy still in Stirling then?' asked Sinclair.

'Yes he is,' replied Cooper.

'Do you know where he is, Sergeant?'

'Yes he's at the Infirmary… I'm sorry to tell you Father, that he was found murdered at Bannockburn,' replied Cooper.

'Oh, may Almighty God have mercy on us!'

'I hope he does.'

'These terrible men must have killed him!'

'I believe that they are the most likely suspects… but why have they chained you up, Father?'

'I have no idea, my son… no idea at all and it was a complete shock when they brought me down here.'

'Surely they must have given you a reason,' said Cooper.

'Well they didn't… they are very violent and desperate men who threaten to kill anyone who gets in their way, as you have already seen for yourselves,' said Sinclair.

'Yes indeed we have,' mumbled Talbot.

'Are there really more Police outside who can come and rescue us?' asked Sinclair.

'I'm afraid there's only one Constable… he's the coach driver and unarmed,' replied Cooper.

'Oh dear God… I fear that there is no hope for us.'

'There's always hope, Father.'

'Then I will pray silently for our deliverance and the departed soul of poor Father Murphy,' said Sinclair.

'Please do, while we think of how we can get out of these chains,' said Cooper.

'Have you any ideas then?' asked Talbot.

'Well... there's a couple of padlocks round the side which seem to hold everything together, so if I can get to them I might have a chance of picking the locks,' replied Cooper.

'What with?'

'I've still got my little wallet of special tools,' replied Cooper.

'But you can't see anything,' said Talbot.

'I know Bill... but I can feel... if I can get my hand free to reach my tools.'

'Then go to it as quick as you like, Bob... before those bastards get back!'

The chains that bound them all to the pillar were tightly wrapped around their torso's which left their lower arms free. When Cooper struggled to release his right arm it caused the others pain but he persevered until he managed, by breathing out, to squeeze his hand free. He reached for his small wallet in his jacket inside pocket, which had fortunately been missed when he was searched. In the darkness he felt for the smallest pick and attempted to reach the padlocks around his side of the pillar. No matter how he tried he could only just touch the nearest padlock with outstretched fingers.

'I can't reach... so can we try to move the chains around?'

'We can have a go, but I think it'll be impossible,' said Talbot.

'Well let's try shall we?'

'Of course... so which way, Bob?'

'If we all pull from our left on three it should do it,' replied Cooper before he counted down. They pulled together but the chains did not move and Talbot said 'I think it's all a waste of time because these chains are probably fixed to the pillar at the back.'

'Then I'll try again to reach the padlocks,' said Cooper but he knew it was a forlorn hope. Once again his fingers could only just touch the first padlock and after a few more futile attempts he said with a sigh 'I'm afraid it's no good, I can't reach it.'

'Well at least you tried,' said Talbot.

'Yes you did, so bless you my son,' said Sinclair

They sat in silence for a few minutes, each deep in thought, when they suddenly heard the sounds of movement outside. The door was unlocked and flung open to reveal the Constable before he was pushed into the room by the tall man holding a revolver in one hand and a lamp in the other.

'Another one for the pot!' he said with a hideous chuckle.

They all looked at the battered and bleeding face of the young Policeman as he was forced towards them by the other man.

'Now once we've got this last loon chained up, we'll be leaving you all for awhile,' said the tall man.

'May God forgive you,' said Sinclair but the men made no reply.

The padlocks were unlocked and the chains unravelled whilst the tall man stood close and pointed the revolver menacingly at the prisoners. They all knew that one false move would ensure that he would shoot them dead without any hesitation. The Constable was made to sit next to Talbot which moved Cooper round towards the padlocks. The chains were replaced tightly and the man grinned as he relocked the padlocks.

'All done now,' he said as he stood back with his hands on his hips.

'Good, we'll be away then,' said the tall man.

The men left quickly, leaving the prisoners once again in complete darkness and after they heard the key turn in the door lock, Talbot said 'I hope you can reach those bloody padlocks now, Bob!'

'Oh yes!' replied Cooper with glee and Sinclair said 'thank the good Lord!'

'It's the Constable who has saved us,' said Talbot.

'Have I, sir?'

'Indeed you have… now all breathe out so I can free my hand,' said Cooper, they did as asked and he felt the chains loosen a little. He managed to free his hand and recover his wallet that he had quickly hidden from the villains. He worked with his smallest pick on the first padlock and within a few moments it sprung open with a click.

'Done it!' he exclaimed.

'I'll see you get a medal for this,' said Talbot.

'A pint of stout would do nicely at the moment, Bill,' said Cooper as he started to unpick the second padlock.

'Ah, yes… I could manage one right now,' said Talbot as the padlock was opened.

Cooper hurriedly released the chains and soon they were free.

153

'Now let's see if we can find a light of some sort,' said Cooper.

'I've got a match, sir,' said the Constable.

'Good man,' said Cooper as the Constable struck his match and the flickering light lit up the room. Cooper went to the table where he found the remnants of a candle amongst the other debris. The candle was lit and they grouped around the table.

'Now because we don't know where these blackguards have gone, we'll have to be careful when we leave here,' said Cooper.

'Right, I suggest that I go ahead and find out if it's all clear,' said Talbot.

'Agreed... once we get away from the castle I think we should stop at the nearest habitation for help and sustenance,' said Cooper.

'That's a good idea, Bob, we all need something hot inside us before trying to get back to Stirling tonight,' said Talbot.

Cooper set to work on the door lock with his steel instruments and soon it was opened. Talbot led the way, holding the fluttering candle, until they reached the archway into the great hall. He left Cooper holding the candle and moved quickly across the hall to the outer doorway, paused and looked about then waved to them. They joined him and he said above the wind noise 'I think they've left.'

'Good, and let's hope they haven't taken our coach,' said Cooper. They hurried through the pouring rain to the gatehouse and paused to shelter for a moment but they looked for the coach in vain.

'The bastards have taken it,' said Talbot.

'Which now means a long walk in the dark for us,' said Cooper.

'Oh dear God,' said Sinclair.

'We'd better get on with it then,' said Talbot.

'Never truer words spoken,' said Cooper before he turned to the Constable and asked 'where's the nearest place?'

'That'll be Fintry, sir.'

'And how far is it?'

'About a mile or so, sir.'

'Right... well lead on Constable and we'll follow you.'

CHAPTER 17

Hadley remained in the shadows of the dark entrance to the tower and became more anxious as the men approached. When they got closer he raised his revolver and was just about to call out a challenge to them when he heard a rumbling noise above the wind and more masonry crashed down from the ruined battlements. The men jumped back in alarm and shouted something which he could not hear. They looked at the debris before them and then up at the top of the tower before the taller man holding the lamp spoke to the other, who nodded. They carried on speaking for a few moments before they turned and made their way back to the waiting coach. Hadley breathed a sigh of relief and thought whoever they were they would be certain to return in daylight.

He sat on the last step and waited patiently, listening to the wind driven rain pouring down and occasionally glancing at the corpse nearby, then at his fob watch. From his position he could see out to the gatehouse and he became anxious when he eventually saw a coach pull up in the road in case it was the strangers returning. His anxiety turned to heartfelt relief when he saw it was the Constable carrying a lamp and approaching with several men.

'Thank God,' he murmured before standing at the doorway and shouting 'I'm over here Constable! Over here!'

The Constable looked in his direction, gave a wave and hurried towards the tower with four men following. They quickly skirted the fallen debris from the battlements and as the Constable stepped through the archway into the tower he asked 'are you alright, sir?'

'Yes, thank you... and I'm very glad to see you all,' replied Hadley when the men entered and gave him a nod.

'Right, sir, now let's get you away from here before the whole place collapses,' said the Constable.

'Yes... and I think it is only a matter of time before it does,' said Hadley. The men clustered around the body looking down at it and Hadley said 'he's rigid now so he should be easy to lift.'

'Aye, sir,' said one of the men before they bent down and lifted the corpse by its clothes. Hadley and the Constable led the way out to the coach and the covered wagon that had been brought to retrieve the body. Before they set off in convoy Hadley asked the Constable 'how is the Captain?'

'I took him and his Sergeant to the Doctor in Crieff, sir, but after he'd been examined, the Doctor bandaged his ankle and said he'd have to take the Captain to the Infirmary in Stirling for further treatment.'

'It would appear to be a serious injury then,' said Hadley.

'I believe so, sir.'

'It's a terrible set-back for the Captain.'

'Indeed, sir.'

'Right... let's get under way to Stirling Infirmary and deliver our corpse to the mortuary then find out how Captain Devaux is faring,' said Hadley as he boarded the coach.

On the slow journey in the rain Hadley went through every facet of the investigation and came to the conclusion that there was no hope of any immediate arrests followed by a quick and final close to the inquiry. He believed Sinclair was still missing and he thought probably dead by now, the Grail remained hidden, possibly somewhere amongst the ruins of one of three castles and that was tantamount to looking for one needle in three haystacks. The killers of the Porter brothers, Professor Pennington and Father Murphy remained at large, so he felt more than usually burdened by the complexity of this case. He wondered how Cooper and Talbot were faring at Culcreuch, perhaps they had found Sinclair alive, which would give a new lead to the direction of the investigation. His thoughts turned to MacKay and Melrose at Doune, but doubted if they had enjoyed any success. He planned that as soon as they all arrived back at Stirling, depending on what they reported, he would lead a force of armed officers to all three castles in search of the two strangers that had come to Drummond. He would also telegraph the Yard to see if Hanson and Mercer had found the suspects who had kidnapped the Porter's and visited Oxford, if they had not been arrested in London then it was possible that they were the strangers at Drummond.

The coach arrived at Stirling Infirmary and Hadley went immediately to see Doctor Macpherson in his office. After explaining the situation, two mortuary attendants were sent to remove the corpse from the wagon.

'I could find no injuries when I looked, Doctor, so I would be obliged if you could discover the cause of death as quickly as possible,' said Hadley.

'What's the hurry, Inspector?'

'I believe I saw the murder suspects when they came back to Drummond Castle and it is important that I know how this man died before I can charge them with his murder,' replied Hadley.

'Have you arrested them?'

'No, but we soon will... I assure you.'

Hadley left the morgue and went in search of Devaux and Rousseau. After making inquiries at reception, he was directed to Nightingale ward, where he found Devaux with Rousseau at his bedside. The Frenchmen were all smiles when they saw Hadley approach.

'Ah mon brave, I knew you would come soon,' said Devaux.

'Of course, Marcel, you didn't think for a moment I'd leave you at the mercy of all these pretty nurses.'

'Oh, mon ami, it's not the nurses who are merciless... it's the matron!' said Devaux, Hadley laughed and said 'oh dear.'

'I call her Madam Guillotine, mon ami.'

'Well as long as she doesn't chop off your head... I'm sure you'll be alright.'

'Ah, do not joke mon ami, I am seriously injured and the Doctor says my ankle will take time to heal,' said Devaux.

'How long, Marcel?' asked Hadley in a concerned tone.

'He says about a week before I can leave... that is if everything goes well... but I will not be able to walk so I will need to be in a wheelchair,' replied Devaux.

'Oh dear God,' said Hadley.

'It is a catastrophe, Jim.'

'I agree, Marcel.'

'So, mon ami, tell me what did you discover at the castle?'

'Well in the tower I found signs that someone was living there and other than the mysterious corpse, nothing else I'm afraid,' replied Hadley.

'First tell me about the dead man, have you no clue as to who he is?'

157

'I could find nothing on the body, it had been stripped... all I discovered was the makers label in the clothes.'

'And who were they?'

'Jeeves and Fortescue of Regent Street in London.'

'Ah... a possible lead to his identity, mon ami.'

'Yes, I'm going to ask MacKay if he has a photographer who can take a picture of the man so that I can send it down to the Yard and ask Hanson to take it to the outfitters and see if they recognise him,' said Hadley.

'Très bien... How did he die, Jim?'

'That I don't know... there were no obvious wounds when I examined the body, which is with Macpherson now... I am waiting for his report.'

'Bon, so what about the person living in the tower?'

'I think there were two men living there, judging by the things I found...'

'Mon Dieu! Two men you say,' interrupted Devaux.

'Yes and when I was waiting for the Constable to come back, they arrived and approached the tower but just then the wind blew some masonry down from the battlements, which stopped them from coming any further.'

'Mon Dieu! You have had two lucky escapes in that dangerous place, Jim!'

'Indeed I have.'

'So are you going back there tomorrow?'

'I am, because I think these two may be our suspects from London,' replied Hadley.

'Then Rousseau will go with you, mon ami.'

'Good, I need all the help I can get, Marcel.'

'Bon... and as I am now so terribly injured, he will be in charge of the French search for the relic.'

'Yes of course, that's understandable.'

'Do you know if the others have found Sinclair?' asked Devaux.

'No, I've not been to the station yet... I came straight here with the corpse and to see you, Marcel,' replied Hadley with a smile.

'You are very kind, mon ami but you may not be so considerate when we take the relic back to Paris.'

'We'll wait and see about that,' replied Hadley.

'Oui. Now, Rousseau will go to the station with you so he can telegraph Paris with a report on my accident and he can tell me later what's been happening, because I need to know everything, Jim.'

'Of course, Marcel.'

After leaving Devaux, Hadley found the duty Doctor and asked about his friend's injury.

'He has a severely sprained ankle, Inspector and all being well he should be able to leave hospital as soon as the swelling has gone down,' said the Doctor.

'So it's not broken then?'

'No, it's just a sprain with extensive bruising,' replied the Doctor.

'Thank heavens for that.'

'Indeed... but some of the nurses will be sad to see him go as he has quite a charming way with them,' said the Doctor with a smile, Hadley nodded and said 'oh don't I know.'

The Doctor hurried away, Rousseau grinned and said 'mon Captain sometimes exaggerates a little... he likes a lot of attention, Monsieur Inspector.'

When the officers arrived back at the Police station, Hadley was concerned to learn that Cooper and Talbot had not returned from Culcreuch Castle.

'I'm sure they'll be back soon, sir,' said MacKay.

'I hope so, Inspector because I don't fancy organising a search party tonight,' said Hadley.

'It'll not come to that, sir.'

'Well don't be too sure as we have had some adventures at Drummond,' said Hadley.

'Oh really, sir, what has happened?'

'Captain Devaux has been injured...'

'Oh mercy me... is it serious?' interrupted MacKay.

'Thankfully no, but he'll be in the Infirmary for a few days with a sprained ankle,' replied Hadley.

'Oh dear, oh dear.'

'And I found a corpse in the tower at Drummond...'

'Good heavens!' interrupted MacKay.

'Two men are living rough there and I suspect them of murdering the man I found,' said Hadley.

'Is it Sinclair, sir?'

'No, I'm sure it's not the priest.'

'How do you know?'

'The body had been stripped of all identity but his clothes were made by London outfitter's. I intend to post a photograph of the dead man to the Yard and request one of our officers to take it to the shop to see if they recognise the deceased,' said Hadley.

'That's a good idea, sir.'

'So have you a photographer who can take his picture at the morgue tonight?' asked Hadley.

'I'm sure we can arrange that for you, sir.'

'Thank you, now how did you get on at Doune?'

'We found no trace of Father Sinclair or anybody who knew him… we searched the castle but found nothing of any interest in the ruins I'm afraid, sir,' replied MacKay.

'Well that's a shame… so we can only hope that Cooper and Talbot have discovered something which will give a positive lead to his whereabouts,' said Hadley.

By the time the party of escapees from Culcreuch Castle had reached the outskirts of Fintry they were wet through and very cold. The Constable knocked at the first substantial house on the outskirts of the village and it was eventually opened by a large bearded man holding a lantern.

'Aye?' he asked suspiciously.

'We're Police Officers from Stirling …'

'Well what do you want with me, Laddie?' interrupted the man.

'We've been held up at the castle by two men…'

'Who is it, Angus?' came a woman's voice.

'It's the Police from Stirling…'

'What do they want?' she asked as she suddenly appeared beside the man.

'May we just come in and shelter for awhile?' asked Cooper, she looked at them in turn and replied 'oh aye, you look fair to middlin' half deed.'

'I'm not so sure, woman…' said the bearded man.

'Och, Angus, cannie no see the state they're in?'

'Listen to me, Flora…' he began but she pushed him aside and said 'come in by the fire.'

'Oh thank you, madam,' said Cooper with relief.

They followed her into a large, warm room where a log fire was roaring in the open fireplace. Two young women stood up when they entered and Cooper gave them a smile.

'Now let's get those wet clothes of you… Mary, take their coats and hang them up in the scullery to dry,' said the woman.

'Yes, Ma.'

'And Fiona, you get the stew from the kitchen.'

'Yes, Ma,' replied Fiona before she left the room, whilst Mary waited for their coats.

'And pour a wee dram for our guests, Angus,' said Flora as she put her hands on her hips and glared at her husband. He shook his head slowly and went to a cupboard in the corner, opened it, brought out a large bottle of clear liquid and five glasses. He placed the glasses on the table, poured out the whiskey and handed them a glass each.

'I only usually give this to special visitors,' said Angus in a dour tone as he raised his glass then swallowed the whiskey in one gulp.

'I'm sure you do… so thank you, sir,' said Cooper as the others raised their glasses. They almost choked on the strong spirit, Talbot coughed whilst Cooper went red in the face before giving a gasp but the Constable and Sinclair managed to drink it down. Angus smiled and said 'it's a good dram for keeping 'oot the cold.'

'It certainly is,' said Talbot in a hoarse whisper.

'Now sit by the fire and you'll have some hot stew,' said Flora.

'Thank you, madam,' said Cooper.

'And you're not from Stirling are you?' she asked.

'No, we're both from London,' replied Cooper, nodding at Talbot.

'All the way up from London… do you hear that, Angus?'

'And what are you doing up at the castle?' asked Angus.

'We were searching for Father Sinclair here, who had been kidnapped by two men,' replied Cooper.

'Aye, I'm no surprised, there's no end of marauders here about.'

'And they stole our coach,' said Talbot.

'Well you're safe now, so have some food to keep you going,' said Flora as she ladled out hot stew into bowls.

When they had finished eating, Cooper thanked Flora and said to Angus 'we need to get back to Stirling tonight... so could you take us?'

'Nay, laddie, I've no horse even,' Angus replied.

'Do you know anybody who could help?'

'Aye, there's Robbie McGregor, he's a pony and trap... but it would be a fearful journey down to Stirling on such a night as this,' replied Angus.

'You're welcome to stay here 'til morning,' said Flora.

'That's very kind of you, but we must get back tonight no matter what,' said Cooper and the girls looked disappointed.

'Well I'll away and ask McGregor for you,' said Angus.

'Thank you.'

After the Scotsman had left the house Cooper said to Flora 'I can't thank you enough for your kindness tonight, madam.'

'Och away with you, I'd help anybody on such a night,' she replied.

'Even Policemen!' said Talbot and they laughed.

'Aye, so I would,' she said with a smile.

'Well, we're very grateful to you and your family,' said Cooper with a smile and Mary and Fiona blushed slightly.

'Och... it's nae bother... now you say you're from London?' asked Flora.

'Yes, Scotland Yard.'

'You're a long way from your home then.'

'We are indeed.'

'So tell us... what's London like?'

'It's very busy, noisy and full of foreigners,' replied Talbot.

'Then I'll make it my business not ever to go there,' she said and they smiled.

'Very wise,' said Cooper.

'Are all the ladies always in fine dresses?' asked Mary.

'Only a very few I'm afraid,' replied Cooper as the images of Agnes and Florrie along with the other streetwalkers came to mind.

'But are they all beautiful?' asked Fiona.

'No… they're not,' replied Cooper.

'Precious few in my experience,' added Talbot with a sniff and the women looked pleased.

Mary and Fiona carried on asking questions about London whilst Flora smiled and listened to the answers until Angus returned to the house.

'McGregor says he'll take you.'

'That's good news, thank you, sir,' said Cooper.

'So have wee dram afore you go to keep the cold out,' said Angus.

'That would be very agreeable.'

CHAPTER 18

was becoming more and more concerned about the safety of his Sergeants as the time went on. He was about to ask MacKay to provide men and a coach to go up to Culcreuch Castle to search for them when McGregor arrived in the yard with the escapees huddled together in his open trap. The Duty Sergeant alerted Hadley and MacKay and they hurried down with Rousseau to meet the officers. Cooper introduced Sinclair, much to Hadley's relief.

'I'm glad that you've been found safe, Father,' said Hadley.

'Yes, Inspector, and it's all thanks to your men, who were very brave and resourceful,' replied Sinclair.

'...er,' said Hadley whilst MacKay ... our coach, Constable?'

...risoners, sir...'

...alarm.

...d if Mr McGregor here hadn't br... we'd still be in Fintry,' replied Cooper.

'Good heavens!'

'Let's all go inside and get those wet clothes off you before you report what's happened,' said Hadley, leading them up to MacKay's office. After changing into dry clothes from the stores, they sat by the fire drinking mugs of hot tea laced with a dram. Hadley and MacKay thanked McGregor for his help and Hadley gave the surprised Scotsman two guineas.

'That's very generous of you, sir,' said McGregor.

'Not at all, Mr McGregor, we're very grateful to you for bringing Father Sinclair and our officer's back safely,' said Hadley.

'Do you want to stay here for the night, Mr McGregor?' asked MacKay.

'No thank you kindly, sir, I'll be away home after I've finished me tea,' replied McGregor with a smile.

The Sergeants thanked McGregor and waited until he had left

before giving the Inspectors their account of what happened at Culcreuch Castle. Hadley sat in stony faced silence whilst MacKay interrupted with gasps of surprise as the events were described in detail. When Cooper and Talbot had finished, Hadley paused for a moment weighing up the situation before saying 'and now we've got two viscous murderers running loose armed with Police revolvers.'

'I am very sorry about that, sir,' said Cooper.

'And so am I, sir,' added Talbot.

'It can't be helped... now, Father I suggest that you stay here in our protective custody until we apprehend these men,' said Hadley.

'I can't do that, Inspector...'

'Why not?' interrupted Hadley.

'I have my duties to attend to, I mean, I can't be away from my people,' replied Sinclair.

'I think that you do not fully understand how near you came to death, Father...'

'When the good Lord sends for me, I will go willingly to him and that will be not a minute before or after he decides, Inspector,' said Sinclair.

'Very well, Father, now I have some questions before you leave,' said Hadley in a firm tone.

'I will answer them truthfully, my son.'

'I would expect nothing less, Father.'

'Quite so.'

Hadley waited a few moments to gather his thoughts before asking 'did Father Murphy contact you before he arrived?'

'No, it was a complete surprise when he came to see me, Inspector.'

'Do you know what he was looking for in your church records?'

'Not exactly.'

'Well he must have said something to you so perhaps you could tell me what that was.'

'He only said that he was tracing the history of some Knights Templar's when they arrived in Scotland in the fourteenth century,' replied Sinclair.

'Is that all?'

'He claimed that our Catholic Church helped them to settle and in return they gave many religious relics which he wished to trace... it was for a book he was writing with a learned Professor of history,' replied Sinclair.

'That would be Professor Pennington at Oxford.'

'Yes... do you know him?' asked Sinclair.

'Unfortunately we are investigating his cruel murder...'

'Oh, dear God no!' whispered Sinclair.

'I'm afraid so, Father.'

'It must have been those two men who held us prisoners who committed this evil act,' said Sinclair firmly.

'They are the prime suspects at the moment.'

'May God forgive them for that and the murder of dear Father Murphy, a more pious, generous and kinder man never existed.'

'I'm sure... now what did he find in your records, Father?'

'Only obscure references to various relics that were held in safe keeping at castles, Inspector.'

'And when these two men arrived they persuaded you to go to Culcreuch Castle after you had given them the names of three castles. Why didn't Father Murphy go with you to search for these relics?'

'He told me that he had sufficient information for the time being to help the Professor,' replied Sinclair and Hadley remained silent for a few moments, which seemed to unsettle the priest.

'We have letters from you that contained information linking the French Catholic Church authorities with a search for a particular relic, Father,' said Hadley.

'I think that you must be mistaken, my son.'

'There's no mistake Father, and furthermore, you advised Professor Pennington that he was in danger and urged him to come up to Stirling.'

'I... I... was just aware of something untoward...'

'So tell me, what imminent danger faced the Professor?'

'I was unsure, Inspector,' replied Sinclair hesitantly.

'You were unsure Father? That seems a little vague to me so perhaps you'd like to cast your mind back and tell me precisely what the danger was and who threatened it?'

'I really can't remember, I really can't... it's all been too much for me to cope with... being held prisoner by those awful men...

you can see I'm an old man…'

'Yes… and you are an old man who knows more than he's telling us!'

'Inspector I think you go too far!'

'I have to remind you that I'm investigating several murders that have direct links with you!'

'That may be so but I have not murdered anyone…'

'In your diary you noted on the 30th of April that William Porter was expected at 6.00 pm and we know from Mrs Murray that he stayed overnight before you both went out the next day and you returned alone…'

'You have no right to read my private diary!'

'Oh yes I have… now where did you go?'

'We went to Saint Mary's…'

'What for?'

'He wished to make a confession.'

'And of course you cannot disclose that to me,' said Hadley.

'I cannot, Inspector.'

'It seems strange to me that William Porter should travel all the way to Stirling to confess to you.'

'You may think what you wish, Inspector.'

'I think it is more likely there was another reason for his visit after he warned Professor Pennington that he was in danger,' said Hadley and the priest looked surprised.

'I cannot comment because I do not know what he…'

'Tell me about the holy relic that you referred to in your letter,' interrupted Hadley firmly.

Sinclair looked uncertain when Hadley remained silent, waiting for his answer. The room went eerily quiet and the Sergeants glanced at each other in anticipation of the reply.

It seemed as if Sinclair had to gather his thoughts before he blurted out 'it is a cross, a large golden cross, studded with precious stones… depicting our Lord's suffering.'

'Presumably it was brought to Scotland by the Knights?'

'Yes, the church records state that there were several relics but the most glorious was the cross,' replied Sinclair.

'And do you have any idea where this holy cross may be hidden, Father?'

'I believe that is either at Drummond or Culcreuch Castle,

Inspector.'

'Did the two men refer to this relic?'

'No, they just said that they were searching for a holy relic of immense value to the Catholic Church and so I assumed it was the cross,' replied Sinclair.

'Why did they chain you up, Father?'

'I have no idea, no idea at all, my son.'

'But what did they say when they made you a prisoner?'

'I really cannot remember... it was all too horrible to contemplate... my memory is a blank,' replied Sinclair, shaking his head.

Hadley remained silent once again and after a few moments MacKay said to him 'I think Father Sinclair has endured enough for one day, so if you're agreeable, sir, I suggest that I arrange for him to be taken home.'

'Yes, by all means, Inspector,' replied Hadley and the priest looked relieved.

After thanking Cooper and Talbot for saving him, Sinclair left the office with the Constable who was assigned to drive him home. Rousseau excused himself and made his way to the Infirmary to brief Devaux on the events of the day.

Hadley asked MacKay 'well, what do you make of that, Inspector?'

'I think Father Sinclair is hiding something, that's for sure,' replied MacKay with a sigh.

'Indeed he is and I will want to question him further tomorrow.'

'Very good, sir.'

'I think we've all had enough excitement today so I suggest we meet here in the morning before we search Drummond and Culcreuch for these two men,' said Hadley.

The detectives arrived too late for dinner at the Falkirk Hotel but the cook was persuaded to prepare some broth and ham sandwiches for them. They sat by a roaring log fire in the lounge and were discussing the investigation, over their late supper, when Rousseau joined them. He reported that Devaux was very comfortable and enjoying the attention of the nurses, which brought a smile to them all. After a glass of stout they retired to their rooms for the night but Hadley lay awake for some while worrying about every aspect of the investigation. He felt certain that it would end violently and he prayed that none of his officers were caught up in it and injured... or worse.

At the Police station the next morning the first thing Hadley did was to send a telegraph message to Chief Inspector Bell reporting the events of the previous day and the murder of Murphy. He advised Bell that he was posting a photograph of the corpse found at Drummond for Hanson to take to Jeeves and Fortescue to ascertain the identity. He also asked if Hanson had found the two suspects, Doyle and Tyler, as he suspected that they could be the men in Scotland.

MacKay showed Hadley the photograph and he was impressed by its clarity and good likeness to the deceased.

'I just hope that the outfitters can recognise their customer,' said Hadley.

'Oh I'm sure they will, sir,' said Cooper and Talbot nodded.

Hadley quickly wrote a note to Bell and addressed an envelope before placing the sepia tint photo in it.

'Would you arrange for somebody to post this for me, Inspector?'

'Yes of course,' replied MacKay.

'Right gentlemen... we have work to do. Inspector MacKay, will you allow my Sergeants to sign out revolvers to replace those taken by the suspects?'

'Yes, sir.'

'Then we will split into two parties to search Drummond and Culcreuch for these men.'

'And our coach,' added MacKay.

'Of course, Inspector. Now, do not hesitate to use your weapons if any of you are threatened by these men because they are dangerous and desperate,' said Hadley firmly and they all nodded murmuring 'right, sir.'

Within twenty minutes, Hadley, Cooper, Talbot and Rousseau now fully armed, left Stirling in a closed coach heading to Drummond whilst MacKay, Melrose and two Constables set off for Culcreuch.

As the coach rattled along, Hadley wondered if any more of the tower had been dislodged overnight. He hoped it was safe enough to enter and search the top room where the men had been living. With any luck they might have returned there and could be arrested without further ado. The detectives discussed the investigation and Hadley listened carefully to his Sergeant's opinions regarding Father Sinclair. Rousseau also made his feelings known and as expected defended the priest's account of what had occurred.

'I believe that he has only told us half truths... many answers he gave were unconvincing, Sergeant,' said Hadley to Rousseau.

'Bien sûr, but he has a duty to protect his position, Monsieur Inspector, and you must remember that he is an old man who has suffered at the hands of these villains and may be confused.'

'That's very true, but I do have some lingering suspicions about him and perhaps when we talk to him later he may be able to satisfy me,' said Hadley, Rousseau nodded and smiled.

'Do you think that he knows about the Grail, sir?' asked Cooper.

'I think he must know, Sergeant, and of course he wants to keep that from us,' replied Hadley.

'And my guess is that he knows it's hidden at either Drummond or Culcreuch and he will search for it as soon as he can,' said Talbot.

'You may be right, Sergeant.'

'He'll wait until we've arrested the two suspects then make his move in comparative safety,' said Talbot.

'I'm sure he will.'

'What a prize it would be if he can find the Grail and take it to Rome, why he'd be a Cardinal before Christmas!' said Talbot.

'Without a doubt, Sergeant.'

They fell silent after they reached Muthill and Hadley felt more than a little anxious as they approached the ruins of Drummond Castle.

'We're nearly there, gentlemen, so from now on be on your guard at all times,' said Hadley, they nodded and chorused 'yes, sir.'

When the coach stopped the detectives climbed down and looked about in the bright morning sun.

'Cooper you're with me.'

'Right, sir.'

'We'll search the tower whilst Talbot and Rousseau search the hall and the cellars.'

'Very good, sir,' said Talbot.

'You'll need a lamp, Sergeant.'

'Yes, sir.'

'And don't hesitate to shoot these villains down if they make any move to resist arrest!' said Hadley as he drew his revolver and slipped off the safety catch. The Sergeants all did the same and followed Hadley up through the ruined gatehouse to the castle courtyard.

CHAPTER 19

Hadley stopped and surveyed the fallen masonry at the base of the tower before looking up at the crumbling battlements.

'It was all too damned close for comfort when this lot fell down last night, Sergeant.'

'I'm sure it was, sir.'

'Let's hope the bloody place doesn't fall down whilst we're in it!'

'Hope always springs eternal, sir, especially so for a Policeman,' replied Cooper and Hadley chuckled before stepping round the debris and entering the tower. They climbed the spiral staircase cautiously, listening for any sound from the rooms above. When they reached the first room, where Hadley discovered the corpse, they stopped and peered in to ensure that no one was there before proceeding upwards to the room above. Hadley drew the hammer back on his revolver as they neared the doorway. He stepped quickly into the room and glanced about before lowering the hammer back to its former position.

Cooper followed him, looked about and said 'blimey, sir, it looks like a real home from home in here.'

'It does, Sergeant and whoever is living here must have been doing so for awhile,' said Hadley as Cooper inspected the room.

'Do you think that it's Doyle and Tyler, sir?'

'If Hanson and Mercer have not arrested them in London then it's more than a strong possibility, Sergeant.'

'Blimey, sir, they get about and no mistake.'

'That's true, and we should know tonight when we get back to Stirling as I asked the Chief to let me know if they've been successful,' said Hadley.

A careful search of the room indicated that the men living there had returned after Hadley had left the tower the previous night. The fire was still warm and the pot with the stew had been placed on the table along with a loaf of bread.

'If they are not found here in the castle, I think we only have to wait for them to return, Sergeant.'

'Then we'll have them, sir.'

'We will, now I'll warn the others while you tell the driver to get the coach off the road and hide it somewhere it can't be seen... then we'll search the whole castle as quick as we can.'

The detectives hurried out of the tower and whilst Cooper went to speak to the driver, Hadley strode across to the hall and down the stairs to where Talbot and Rousseau were searching.

When Hadley caught up with them in the cellar they were in front of the old door that he had previously decided to force open.

'Right, gentlemen, we've searched the tower and it appears that our friends have not abandoned it so we will catch them if they return... but just in case they're still here in the castle, we'll have a quick search before we wait for them.'

'Oh yes, sir, then we'll have them and no mistake!' said Talbot.

'Quite so.'

They returned to the ruined hall where they met Cooper hurrying towards them. He said to Hadley 'the driver has taken the coach to a place where he knows it can't be seen from the road, sir.'

'Good.'

'And when we want him, I only have to give a blast on my whistle, sir.'

'Right, Sergeant... now we'll search all the buildings as quickly as possible then we'll meet at the gatehouse to watch for the suspects,' said Hadley and they all nodded.

'And if any of you find these villains just fire your weapon to alert the rest of us,' said Hadley.

'Oui, Monsieur,' said Rousseau.

'They'll not get away from me this time, sir,' said Talbot.

'Me neither, I want my revolver back!' said Cooper.

'So do I,' added Talbot.

Hadley smiled and said 'then go to it gentlemen!'

The castle was more extensive than Hadley first imagined when he quickly made his way through the ruined out buildings butted against the battlement walls. He found a small tower that formed part of the battlements, went inside and up the spiral staircase then out onto the walkway along the casements. The view across the rolling hills was superb and he stood for a few moments in the sunshine enjoying the glorious panorama before him. Suddenly he was aware of Cooper calling to him 'are you alright up there, sir?'

Hadley turned and looked down at Cooper standing below.

'Yes, I'm fine thank you, Sergeant… just enjoying the view!'

'Well mind you don't fall, sir.'

'I'll watch my step!' Hadley called back and Cooper nodded before turning away.

The casements led to another small watch tower which Hadley entered and climbed just the few steps up to the top. Through the arched lookout he could see the road back to Muthill and coming towards the castle was a coach being driven at speed. He waited for a few moments until he could see plainly that the driver was a Policeman. He hurriedly left the lookout and retraced his steps along the casements, down the tower then out through the gatehouse to meet the coach. Hadley stood in the road when the coach pulled up and looked at the breathless driver.

'Inspector Hadley, sir, please come as quick as you can…'

'What's the matter, Constable?'

'Inspector MacKay and Sergeant Melrose need help, sir…'

'Why?'

'They found two men at Culcreuch, sir, and when they tried to arrest them… one of the men shot Sergeant Melrose and Constable McKenzie, sir.'

'Good God Almighty!… Are they dead?'

'No sir, but Sergeant Melrose is badly wounded, I think McKenzie is alright.'

'Have you been back to Stirling to get more help?' asked Hadley.

'Yes, sir, Inspector MacKay told me to alert the Duty Sergeant and then come and get you, sir.'

'Right, turn the coach around, Constable and we'll be with you in a minute!' said Hadley before he stepped back and drew his revolver and fired a shot into the air. By the time the coach was turned, all the Sergeants were with Hadley, who explained what had happened. Cooper blew his whistle for the coach in hiding and waited for it to appear before he joined the others on the first coach.

The two coaches set off in convoy at a fast trot back towards Muthill and the road south to Culcreuch Castle.

'This is what I feared the most, gentlemen,' said Hadley in the swaying coach.

'Well at least we know where these villains are, sir,' said Cooper.

'Yes, but at what a terrible cost, Sergeant.'

'And they won't get away now, sir,' said Talbot

'I hope not!'

They remained silent each deep in thought at what they were about to face until the coach began to slow down.

'I think something is wrong, sir,' said Cooper.

'I expect the driver is giving the horses a rest for a mile or two,' said Hadley.

'I think I can smell burning, sir,' said Talbot as the coach slowed even more.

'Mon Dieu! So can I, Monsieur.'

'Well we don't need anything to go wrong now!' said Hadley as the coach finally stopped. The smell of burning invaded the interior and when the driver opened the door they could see the smoke wafting in.

'I'm afraid we've run a bearing on one of the front wheels, sir,' said the Constable.

'That's a damned nuisance! We'll have to use the other coach,' said Hadley.

'Lucky we had it, sir,' said Talbot and Hadley nodded before they disembarked and stood for a moment looking at the smouldering bearing.

'I'll follow on when it's cooled down and I can pack it with fresh grease, sir,' said the driver.

'Very good, Constable, I've a feeling that we'll need all the help we can muster,' said Hadley as he climbed aboard the second coach followed by the Sergeants.

The journey to Culcreuch Castle seemed to take an age but when they arrived and disembarked they were struck by the total silence. They looked about, drew their revolvers and hastily made for the gatehouse where they stopped and listened for a moment.

'There's no blimmin' sound at all, sir,' said Cooper.

'No there isn't.'

'Perhaps the officers came from Stirling, arrested the villains and have taken the wounded to the Infirmary, sir,' said Talbot.

'That's possible, Sergeant but I think we should search the place just in case,' said Hadley.

'Right, sir.'

'Cooper... you come with me and Rousseau, you go with Talbot to search the hall and outbuildings,' said Hadley before striding off towards the tower.

Hadley quickly climbed the spiral staircase and as they neared the top he heard a sound. He turned to Cooper and put his finger to his lips then slipped off the safety catch of his revolver and drew the hammer back before proceeding quietly up the few remaining steps to an arched doorway. Hadley stepped into the room and was ready to open fire on the occupants but to his surprise he saw MacKay sitting on a chair pointing his revolver at him.

'Oh thank God you're here, Inspector,' said MacKay with a sigh as he lowered his weapon.

'I only wish that we would have been here sooner,' replied Hadley glancing down at Melrose, lying in a pool of blood on the floor with McKenzie attending to him.

'When we tried to arrest those murdering villains they made their escape after shooting Melrose and McKenzie,' said MacKay.

'They won't get far and we'll see them in custody soon,' said Hadley.

'I pray that you're right, sir.'

'Sergeant, give a hand to the Constable,' said Hadley.

'Yes, sir,' said Cooper before kneeling down to assist McKenzie in staunching the blood from Melrose's wounded shoulder.

'I'm surprised that your officers from Stirling are not here yet,' said Hadley.

'So am I, sir,' said MacKay.

'Let's hope that nothing untoward has happened to them,' said Hadley as the sound of a Police whistle echoed round the castle.

'I think they've just arrived,' said MacKay with a smile.

'Thank heavens for that... Sergeant, nip down and let everybody know where we are,' said Hadley.

'Right, sir.'

Within minutes the room was full of Police, including Talbot and Rousseau. Melrose was quickly carried down to the coach and

McKenzie followed, assisted by a colleague.

The coach was sent off at the gallop to the Infirmary taking the wounded officers and an armed Constable, Hadley and MacKay discussed the plan of action to arrest the villains.

'They can't have got far, Inspector.'

'Possibly not, but I didn't see which way they went and they could hide in the hills for days and we'd never find them,' said MacKay.

'Well, we must make the attempt however difficult,' said Hadley.

'Yes of course... I think it unlikely that they went back towards Stirling because I sent my Constable to get help and alert you, these villains knew that, so they wouldn't take the chance of being caught on the road by my officers,' said MacKay.

'That's logical, so where do you propose that we commence the search?' asked Hadley.

'They could have taken the road south to Lennoxtown or the road to Killearn in the west, so I suggest we split up and I'll go to Lennoxtown whilst you go west, sir,' replied MacKay.

'Right... and we'll meet back in Stirling later,' said Hadley.

Hadley and his Sergeants climbed aboard the coach and after MacKay gave instructions to the driver, it set off at a fast pace towards Killearn.

Hadley was in a grim mood, the result of the men being shot, he blamed himself for not challenging the suspects when they arrived at Drummond Castle. He looked anxiously at his Sergeants and said 'gentlemen, when we find these villains, whatever you do... do not hesitate to shoot them down if they make one false move!'

'Oh, we won't, sir,' said Cooper.

'They'll be dead before they hit the floor, sir,' said Talbot.

'Oui, bien sûr, Monsieur Inspector.'

Hadley nodded and looked out at the passing countryside. It was very beautiful and quite rugged, which worried him as he remembered what MacKay had said about the men disappearing into the hills making it nigh impossible to find them. He wondered about the Grail and if the villains had already discovered it. He surmised that they would be heading back to London to deliver it up to the Catholic hierarchy if they had and in which case, they would be long gone by the time he or MacKay reached their destinations. He also reasoned that perhaps someone else may be behind the search for the Grail and had employed the two murderous thugs to find it. He was still deep in thought when the coach pulled into Killearn.

Inquiries were made by the Sergeants at the farrier, blacksmith and the pub, but no one had seen a coach passing that morning. Reporting back to Hadley he said 'right, we'll retrace our steps and take the first road we come to that leads up into the hills.'

The driver was instructed, so he turned the coach around and headed back towards Culcreuch. The first turning was to the north and led them to the village of Boquhan but inquiries there confirmed that no coach had passed that day. The next turning was at Fintry, also to the north to Balafark and again the Sergeants were met with the same response. They retraced their steps to Fintry and on to Gonachan where the road forked and ran south to Lennoxtown.

'We can only hope that Inspector MacKay has caught up with them because they obviously have not made their escape to Killearn or anywhere else along the way,' said Hadley in a frustrated tone.

'What now, sir?' asked Cooper.

'I think we'd better head back to Stirling,' replied Hadley with a sigh.

'Perhaps the villains went to Stirling, sir and took the chance of meeting the officers coming out,' said Cooper.

'You could be right, Sergeant.'

'And if they were challenged we know that the bastards wouldn't hesitate to shoot the Police officers, sir,' said Talbot angrily.

'You're quite correct, Sergeant, so let's get back quickly just in case they're paying a visit to Father Sinclair or catching a train to London with the relic!'

'Mon Dieu!' exclaimed Rousseau.

'Do you think they've found it, sir?' asked Cooper.

'It's a possibility… we'll never know unless we find them!'

After giving the driver his instructions, the coach and horses were driven at the gallop to Stirling with Hadley explaining his next moves to his men.

'Sergeant Talbot, when we get to the railway station I want you and Rousseau to search for the suspects and check the train times to Edinburgh as our murderous friends may be there waiting to make their escape to London.'

'Very good, sir.'

'Cooper and I will go to Father Sinclair's house and place him in protective custody whether he likes it or not,' said Hadley firmly.

'Quite right, sir, we don't want another dead priest on our hands,' said Cooper.

'Indeed not and when we've taken him to the Police station we'll come and join you, Sergeant,' said Hadley.

'Right you are, sir,' said Talbot.

'Of course this may be all quite un-necessary if Inspector MacKay and his men have caught the villains,' said Hadley.

'Let's hope so, sir,' said Cooper.

'Oui, then all we have to do is find the Grail, Inspector,' said Rousseau.

'I hadn't forgotten, Sergeant,' replied Hadley with a smile.

After they left Talbot and Rousseau at the railway station the detectives hurried to Sinclair's house where Mrs Murray opened the door to them.

'Good afternoon, Mrs Murray... is Father Sinclair at home?' asked Hadley with a smile.

'No, sir, he's not,' she replied.

'Do you know where he is?' asked Hadley anxiously, fearing the worst.

'Yes, sir, he's gone to London.'

'London?' Hadley asked in surprise.

'Yes, sir, he left first thing this morning,' she replied.

'Do you know where in London?'

'No, sir, all he said to me was that he'd be going down there on Church business and would be back in a day or two but if there was any change, he'd write me a note,' she replied with a smile.

'Was he alone?'

'Oh yes, quite alone, sir.'

'Thank you Mrs Murray.'

'Was there anything else, sir?'

'No, nothing.'

'Can I give him a message when he returns, sir?'

'No thank you.'

When Hadley climbed back in the coach he said angrily 'if only we'd insisted that he remained in protective custody, Sergeant.'

'That's hindsight, sir.'

'Don't remind me... now heaven only knows what he's up to in London!'

'Do you think he has the Grail, sir?'

'I really don't know, Sergeant, but I am very suspicious of this priest and I think he still has a lot of questions to answer.'

They returned to the railway station just after five o'clock and found Talbot and Rousseau in the concourse.

'There's been no sign of them, sir,' said Talbot.

'Somehow I'm not surprised Sergeant and we now have Sinclair to add to our list of people who have mysteriously disappeared,' said Hadley.

'Blimey!' exclaimed Talbot.

'Mon Dieu, this is very worrying, Monsieur Inspector.'

'It is, Sergeant.'

'So do you know where he's gone, sir?'

'According to Mrs Murray he's gone to London.'

'London, sir... who with?'

'He travelled alone first thing this morning.'

'Well stone the blimmin' crows!' said Talbot.

'I couldn't have put it better myself, Sergeant,' grinned Hadley.

'What now, sir?' asked Cooper.

'We'll go back to the Police station to see if Inspector MacKay has returned... and I'd like you to stay here Sergeant until we return with officers to relieve you,' said Hadley.

'Very good, sir,' said Talbot.

'Then I think we all could do with some tea and something to eat...it's been a long day!' said Hadley.

On arrival at the Police station the detectives were pleased to see that MacKay and his men had returned. In the office Mackay said 'we didn't find any sign of them and no one at Lennoxtown had seen a passing coach this morning.'

'We went to Killearn then retraced our steps and ventured up the roads off into the hills with no luck, so they must have come back to Stirling,' said Hadley.

'Then we'll plan a widespread search for them right now... I've already cancelled all leave and called in men who are off duty,' said MacKay.

'Very good, Inspector... now we have also called at Sinclair's house to bring him into custody but Mrs Murray informed us that he left for London this morning,' said Hadley.

'London you say... well this is a wee bit suspicious don't you think, sir?'

'I do indeed... any word on your wounded officers?' asked Hadley in a concerned tone.

'I'm afraid that Melrose is in a critical state and awaiting surgery whilst McKenzie has only suffered a flesh wound and is expected to be released from the Infirmary tomorrow,' replied MacKay.

'I'm extremely sorry that your men have been injured in this way,' said Hadley.

'Thank you, sir, but risk is part of our job and we all understand that when we join the force,' said MacKay as a Constable entered and said 'sorry to disturb you, sir, but this telegraph just came in for Inspector Hadley.'

The buff envelope was handed to Hadley who opened it and read the message out loud *'Hadley, must advise you that suspects Tyler and Doyle are still at large. Await your speedy return with the relic. When photograph arrives will commence inquiries regarding the identity of the deceased male found at Drummond Castle. Bell'*

There followed a moments silence before MacKay asked Hadley 'I suppose this relic is the cross that Sinclair spoke of, sir?'

Hadley cleared his throat and replied 'we are not absolutely sure about that, so I don't want to comment further, but it forms part of the blackmail of our clergy that I told you about previously.'

'I see,' said MacKay slowly.

'It is now obvious that Tyler and Doyle are not in London but here, searching for this relic,' said Hadley.

'In that case we must find them and recover this relic... whatever it is,' said MacKay.

'Indeed we must.'

CHAPTER 20

Hadley sent a telegraph message to Bell informing him that Sinclair had left for London that morning and requesting that he be found and held for questioning. It was six o'clock when Hadley and Cooper returned to the railway station with two Constables to relieve Talbot and Rousseau. MacKay had given instructions to the Constables to remain at the station until the last train to Edinburgh had departed. Hadley thought it possible that the suspects had already left Stirling, provided they had the Grail, but if they were still in hiding they could attempt to escape by train in the morning.

The detectives stopped for a quick tea and a sandwich at the concourse tea room before making their way back to the Police station, whilst Rousseau went off to report to Inspector Devaux.

In the office, Hadley and MacKay discussed the planned search for the suspects until everything was organised for the rest of the night and the next day.

'If we haven't found them by this time tomorrow, I think we can safely assume they left Stirling before we returned this afternoon,' said Hadley.

'I'm afraid I have to agree with you, sir,' said MacKay as he slowly shook his head.

'Which would mean they've eluded us, probably recovered the relic and are now on the way to London with it.'

'Will you follow on tomorrow, sir?' asked MacKay.

'No, I intend to remain until we are absolutely sure of what has happened,' replied Hadley.

'That's very good to hear because I have the matter of Murphy's murder to investigate and I would appreciate your help,' said MacKay.

'You have it, Inspector.'

It was just before eight o'clock when the weary detectives arrived at the Falkirk Hotel and found Rousseau in the bar. He bought them each a pint of stout and informed Hadley that Devaux was due to be discharged from the Infirmary tomorrow afternoon.

'Well that's good news to end the day with, Sergeant,' said

Hadley with a smile.

'Bien sûr, Monsieur.'

'Will he be in a wheelchair, Michel?' asked Talbot.

'Non, he says he can manage with a stick,' replied Rousseau with a smile.

'So his injury wasn't as bad as he made out after all,' said Cooper.

'I don't think so, mon ami.'

Hadley smiled and said 'the Captain likes attention… especially from the ladies…shall we go in and have some dinner?'

The menu was limited but they settled on wild mushroom soup followed by tender Angus beef with the season's vegetables, for dessert they had apple pie with cream, followed by the cheese board. The meal was delicious and they relaxed, taking their time to recover from the hectic day. Later in the lounge they enjoyed a brandy in front of the roaring log fire and discussed the plans for the next day. Hadley outlined his proposed lines of inquiry to find the suspects if they were still in Scotland, as well as discovering the hiding place of the Grail. Before he went up to his room his last words to them were 'from now on, gentlemen, I think it is going to be difficult and even more dangerous.'

When the detectives arrived at the office the next morning MacKay was already there, he informed them that his men had not seen the suspects at the railway station last night. He confirmed that armed Constables were now on duty there and would apprehend anybody fitting the descriptions of the suspects.

'Very good, I just hope that they haven't left Stirling yet,' said Hadley.

'Indeed, sir, but you can be sure we'll catch them if they're still here,' said MacKay.

'Let's hope so.'

'I've detailed three parties of armed officers to make inquiries at all the hotels and lodgings in the area for these villains, sir,' said MacKay.

'Good, now I intend to visit Drummond and Culreuch again this morning to search for the relic,' said Hadley.

'Is that your top priority, sir?' asked MacKay in surprise.

'I believe so, because if the suspects have not recovered it, they will obviously continue their search at the castles and then we will have them,' replied Hadley.

'I must confess that I do not share your confidence, sir,' said MacKay.

'Well I agree it's a long shot, but with you and your men searching Stirling for them it is better that we go up to the castles in case the suspects have remained in the hills close by.'

'Really, sir?'

'I think so, because it stands to reason that they will not leave until they have found the relic, which we know from Sinclair is probably hidden at one of these ruined castles,' replied Hadley.

'As you wish, sir… and whilst you're there, please look out for our missing coach,' said MacKay.

'I certainly will, Inspector.'

Within half an hour Hadley and his Sergeants had set off in a coach to Drummond Castle. The two hour journey was pleasant in the weak, misty sunshine and they discussed the investigation for most of the way. Hadley was keen to force open the door in the cellar and determined to make it his first priority on arrival. When they passed through Muthill Hadley noticed the blacksmith standing outside his forge with hands on his hips looking hard at them as they went by before glancing up the road towards Crieff. He put it to the back of his mind for the moment but thought it was worth stopping to make an inquiry when they returned from Drummond.

On arrival at the castle, Hadley instructed the driver to take the coach through the gatehouse into the courtyard so it could not be seen from the road and asked Rousseau to keep watch for any unexpected visitors from the lookout in the battlement tower. After leaving the coach, Hadley led the way through the great hall and down to the cellar holding an acetylene lamp with Talbot and Cooper carrying a steel bar and wooden beam taken from the coach pannier. When they reached the door at the far end Hadley examined it in the flickering light and said 'I think the only way to open this is with brute force, gentlemen.'

'There is a keyhole, sir, so let me try first,' said Cooper.

'Carry on then, Sergeant.'

Cooper produced his wallet, selected the largest pick and began to work at the lock. Within minutes they heard the tumblers click one by one and Cooper said 'I think it's unlocked now, sir.'

'Well done, Sergeant, now let's see if we can push the door open.'

'It doesn't look like it's been opened for years, sir,' said Talbot.

'I'm sure you're right, Sergeant, which makes me think that we may not find anything of interest immediately behind it,' said Hadley.

'Why is that, sir?' asked Talbot.

'Because Porter told Lord Stillwell that he had seen the Grail and he obviously didn't go through here... but it might lead us to another entrance into the castle,' replied Hadley before he pushed with his shoulder at the door. It did not move an inch so Cooper and Talbot joined him and on the count of three they heaved, the door creaked loudly and gave a little on its rusty hinges.

'Keep pushing!' said Hadley between gasps and they did, which forced it open enough for them to pass through into the narrow corridor beyond. Hadley drew his revolver and cautiously led the way with the lamp. At the end of the corridor were some steps leading down into an inky blackness and Hadley stopped for a moment trying to see what was before him in the flickering light.

'I wonder how far it goes down, sir,' said Cooper, peering over Hadley's shoulder.

'Well there's only one way to find out, Sergeant.'

'Take it steady, sir, we don't want you to end up in the Infirmary with the Captain,' said Talbot.

'No indeed not,' replied Hadley as he placed his revolver back in his coat pocket before stretching out his hand to steady himself against the cold stone wall and stepping down into the narrow, dimly lit void. The stone steps were worn and uneven which caused him some anxiety but he eventually reached the last one safely and stepped down onto flagstones. He held the lamp up high and saw that he was in a small cellar with another door at the far end. The Sergeants joined him and Cooper said 'this place just seems to go on and on, sir.'

'Yes it does, Sergeant and it's what I expected.'

'Look, sir...there's some boxes over there,' said Talbot

pointing to three, iron bound chests that were in the far corner.

'Now they look interesting,' said Hadley before he quickly strode across and peered at them in the light. Cooper bent down and lifted the lid of the largest chest and they saw that it was empty. Talbot opened the other two which were also empty.

'Do you think that the Grail was here, sir?' asked Cooper.

'I don't know, Sergeant, but if we can get beyond this door it might give us a clue,' replied Hadley.

'How is that, sir?' asked Talbot.

'If we find that it leads to somewhere out of the castle,' replied Hadley.

They made their way to the door which, when Hadley tried the rusty handle, opened quite easily to reveal another dark corridor beyond. Hadley led the way and as he did so he felt a cool draught on his face.

'I think this probably leads us out into fresh air,' he said.

After a few yards the stone floor finished and they found themselves walking on earth. The walls had crumbled in various places and tumbled down to form mounds of debris, which they climbed over with care. The corridor meandered several times until it eventually straightened out and Hadley could feel the draught of cool air becoming stronger. He saw a small pinprick of light in the distance and said 'I think we're nearly at the end!'

As they made their way quickly towards the light, they came upon pools of muddy water which splashed over their shoes when they stepped through them. Hadley was becoming excited as he got closer to the exit from the castle and through which he could now see bright blue sky. At last he reached the small opening, there were several steep steps leading up to it which Hadley climbed with ease. Stepping out into daylight through a narrow space between two huge granite blocks of stone set in a rocky outcrop, he breathed in a deep breath of the crystal clear air, looked around at the rolling scenery and then down at the footprints in the soft earth leading to and from the entrance. When the Sergeants had joined him Hadley said 'we can see that someone has been here recently by the numerous footprints so I think that we can safely assume what's taken place.'

'Without any doubt, sir,' said Cooper.

'Do you think the Grail was hidden in one of those chests, sir?'

asked Talbot.

'Yes I do… and there are two possibilities, either Sinclair brought Porter here and showed it to him before hiding it somewhere else then taking it to London, or Doyle and Tyler persuaded Sinclair, on pain of death, to tell them where it was hidden and they have been here and escaped with it back to London,' replied Hadley.

'So it's back to London for us, sir,' said Cooper.

'Only after I've made a few more inquiries, Sergeant… and remember, I've telegraphed the Chief requesting Sinclair's arrest when he arrives in London and MacKay is continuing the search for Doyle and Tyler here whilst Hanson and Mercer are doing the same in London, so with any luck we should catch them all before long.'

'So our list of suspects for all the murders now consists of Sinclair, Doyle and Tyler, sir,' said Cooper.

'Yes, I believe that is so, Sergeant.'

'Are we going to Culcreuch Castle, sir?' asked Talbot.

'I'm not sure that's necessary now, Sergeant.'

'In that case, sir, perhaps we've time to stop for some lunch at Muthill on our way back to Stirling?' asked Talbot.

'Why not?... Providing we don't spend too long in the pub,' replied Hadley.

'Perish the very thought, sir,' said Talbot with a smile and Cooper laughed.

Walking around the outcrop of rock they saw the ruins of Drummond Castle about a quarter of a mile away. They hurried towards the Castle and Rousseau was very surprised to see them as they approached and he waved from the lookout. Hadley explained everything to Rousseau as the detectives set off in the coach to Muthill. On the short journey, Hadley told his Sergeants that he wanted to speak to the blacksmith.

'Do you think he saw something unusual, sir?' asked Cooper.

'I'm not sure… but he did look perplexed when he noticed us,' replied Hadley.

'Perhaps he hadn't seen so many Police before, sir,' said Talbot.

'Or Police coaches, Sergeant!'

'He saw the stolen coach!' exclaimed Cooper.

'Possibly, Sergeant.'

When they reached Muthill the driver pulled up outside the forge and the detectives disembarked, going in to find the blacksmith. He was hammering a piece of red hot steel against his anvil and never missed a stroke when he looked up at them.

'Good day, sir,' said Hadley with a smile.

'Good day.'

'We're Police officers from Stirling.'

'Oh, aye.'

'When we passed earlier I noticed that you glanced at our coach before you looked up the road towards Crieff,' said Hadley.

'Aye, I did.'

'Did you see anything unusual, sir?'

'Aye, I did,' the blacksmith replied as he continued hammering the steel into shape.

'And what was that?' asked Hadley. The blacksmith stopped working the steel and shoved it back into the glowing coals.

'I was a might surprised to see another Police coach just now and I wondered what was going on,' said the blacksmith.

'Tell me... was the first coach you saw being driven by a Policeman?'

'No, the driver was a man in ordinary clothes,' he replied.

'Did you see any passengers?'

'Oh aye, there was one fella inside.'

'Have you seen them around here before?'

'No, but as we never see any Police at Muthill... I di'na ken what they would look like.'

'I see.'

'Ah mean, how do I know that you're Police? You're travelling in a coach marked 'Police' but you're not in uniform, so you could be marauders for all I ken,' he said before taking the red hot steel out of the coals and hammering it once again.

'Quite true, sir and thank you for your help,' said Hadley with a smile.

They left the forge and as Hadley gave instructions to the driver to make haste up to Crieff, they quickly boarded the coach. On the journey Hadley cursed himself for not speaking to the blacksmith first thing, as by now the fugitives in the stolen coach had a two hour head start. He told his Sergeants that he had learned a lesson not to delay an inquiry into anything remotely suspicious.

'Do you suspect that it's Tyler and Doyle in the coach, sir?' asked Cooper.

'Yes... at least I hope so, because that means they're still here looking for the Grail,' replied Hadley.

'And this time we'll catch the bastards!' said Talbot.

On the road to Crieff there was only one small turning off that led to the village of Balloch which they passed unnoticed. They remained silent until the coach trotted into the outskirts of Crieff and pulled up. The driver jumped down, opened the door and asked 'where to, sir?'

'Find a blacksmith or a farrier and stop at the first pub, someone must have seen the coach this morning,' replied Hadley and the driver nodded. The detectives looked out of the open windows as the coach trundled along towards the centre of the town but they saw no one. The driver stopped outside a blacksmiths and while Talbot and Rousseau ran into the forge to make inquiries, Hadley and Cooper strode across to the pub opposite. Just as they were about to enter they heard a noise of a trotting horse and Hadley glanced up to see an open trap hurrying by with a figure seated in the back that he instantly recognised. Their eyes met for a split second before Father Sinclair turned his head away.

CHAPTER 21

Hadley glanced at Cooper and said 'did you see who that was, Sergeant?'

'I did, sir.'

'Find the others quickly,' said Hadley before he rushed back across the street and shouted to the Police driver 'turn about! Turn about... quickly man!'

By the time the coach was turned in the narrow street, Talbot and Rousseau had been found and were about to board with Cooper. Hadley jumped up and sat next to the driver, ordering him to follow the fast disappearing trap at the gallop. The chestnut mares reared up at the crack of the whip and when accompanied by shouts from the driver took off at some speed, with the coach swaying alarmingly for several hundred yards down the road towards Stirling. Hadley's mind was in turmoil. Sinclair had lied to Mrs Murray about his trip to London and seeing him brazenly ride by in Crieff put him at the top of Hadley's list of suspects for intense questioning regarding the murder of Murphy. Sinclair had to explain many incriminating facts and Hadley was determined that the priest would not escape from him again.

The coach was slowly gaining on the trap, which was about half a mile ahead, but Hadley could hardly contain his impatience. He was tempted to urge the driver to increase speed but he could see that the sweating mares were racing along as fast as they could on the uneven road. It seemed an age before the coach was within shouting distance of the trap and as it drew near, Sinclair turned and looked back for an instant before saying something to his driver who also turned around.

'Pull over! Pull over! Pull over damn you!' shouted Hadley and waved his left arm towards the nearside of the road. The trap slowed to a walk as the Police coach pulled alongside and Hadley shouted at the pale faced driver 'stop immediately!' The trap was brought to a halt and Hadley jumped down as the Sergeants scrambled out of the coach and Talbot went forward to hold the bridle of the trap horse.

'Father Sinclair, you're under arrest!' said Hadley firmly.

'In God's name...what for, my son?'

'Come on, out you get,' said Hadley as he opened the door at the rear of the trap.

The priest slowly climbed down from the trap and Cooper held the door of the coach open for him to enter. When he was seated Hadley looked in at the priest and said 'you're under arrest on suspicion of murder…'

'Of whom may I ask?'

'Father Murphy,' replied Hadley.

'This is monstrous!'

'You may think so but you will be questioned at length when we get back to Stirling and meanwhile anything you say will be taken down and used in evidence against you,' said Hadley.

'I protest my innocence…'

'Protest all you like,' replied Hadley dismissively and turning to the Sergeants said 'gentlemen, get aboard and keep Father Sinclair company... and don't let him out of your sight when we stop!'

'Right, sir,' said Cooper.

Hadley climbed up, sat beside the driver and said 'now let's resume our journey back to Crieff.'

The coach was turned slowly around before beginning its way back at the trot and leaving the trap driver in a state of shock.

Despite inquiries at the blacksmith, two pubs and the farrier's, no one had seen a Police coach pass by that morning. On Hadley's instructions the coach proceeded northwards out of Crieff to where the road forked. The driver stopped the horses and asked Hadley 'which way now, sir?'

Hadley looked at the signpost to Perth, which was to the east and Aberfeldy to the north.

'I think we should follow the road to Perth to start with, driver.'

'To start with, sir?'

'Yes, then we'll return here and take the road up to Aberfeldy.'

'If I may say so, sir, it would be a might foolish to travel all the way to Perth and then journey up towards Aberfeldy so late in the day… its wild country up in the Highlands and the horses are tired.'

Hadley realised the sense of what the driver had said and

replied 'very well, Constable, let's just go a few miles along the road to Perth and see if we can find the coach, then we can return to Stirling.'

'Very good, sir,' said the relieved driver.

When they reached the village of Forbrae, Hadley ordered the driver to stop and turn round whilst he and the Sergeants made inquiries at the pub. Again, no one had seen a Police coach passing and Hadley was now convinced that the suspects had taken it up beyond Aberfeldy to the Highlands. He determined to return to Stirling and arrange a search party for the following day.

On the journey back they passed through Crieff and the coach trundled by the small un-noticed turning to Balloch before it reached Muthill.

It was late afternoon when the coach pulled into the Police station yard at Stirling. The weary detectives entered the building with Father Sinclair who was taken to the interview room and served a cup of tea whilst a Constable remained on watch outside. The Duty Sergeant told Hadley that MacKay was still out searching for the suspects. The detectives went to the small canteen in search of food and were saved from starvation by mugs of hot tea and ham sandwiches. When they had finished eating and were just about to leave the Duty Sergeant came in with a brown envelope which he handed to Hadley.

'This just came in for you from London, sir.'

Hadley opened the telegraph and read aloud *'Hadley, murder victim recognised by the manager at Jeeves and Fortescue. Identified as Captain Hugo Sefton of 4th Hussars and confirmed by Colonel Pickering and Captain Davenport. Pickering states that Sefton was on leave in Scotland, deer shooting. Next of kin being advised. No sign of Sinclair, Doyle or Tyler yet. Advise when you intend to return. Bell'*

'Well what do you make of that, sir?' asked Cooper.

'I'm not yet sure, Sergeant.'

'It's a bit of a coincidence that Major Fielding is in the same Regiment, sir,' said Talbot.

'Yes it is... and you know I don't like coincidences.'

'Perhaps Doyle and Tyler were working for Sefton, sir.'

'That's a possibility, Sergeant.'

'So who killed him and why?' asked Cooper.

'Perhaps they did,' said Talbot.

'But why would they want to murder him?' persisted Cooper.

'It could be that he found the relic, they killed him for it so they could have the reward money promised to Porter by Lord Stillwell,' said Talbot.

'But how would they know?' asked Cooper.

'Perhaps Porter told them when they tortured him,' replied Talbot.

'That's a possibility, Sergeant, but we don't yet know the cause of Sefton's death... he may have died of natural causes.' Hadley had just finished speaking when MacKay entered with Devaux, who smiled as he limped in and banged his walking stick on the floor for attention.

'Bonjour mes amis, bonjour!'

'Oh, mon Captain!' exclaimed Rousseau as he stood up to embrace his superior.

'It's good to see you, Marcel,' said Hadley with a smile.

'Merci, Jim, how have you all been managing without me?'

'Quite well thank you,' replied Hadley with a chuckle.

'I am glad to hear it... I think... mon ami.'

'But we couldn't go much further without you, Marcel,' said Hadley with a smile.

'Of course not, but now I'm here, we can make some real progress!' said Devaux and they all laughed except MacKay, who said solemnly 'if you've finished here, gentlemen, I suggest we now go up to my office to discuss matters.' Hadley guessed he was not a happy man and replied 'yes of course, Inspector.'

When they were all settled in MacKay's office Hadley asked 'first of all, what news of Melrose?'

'He's out of danger after the operation but the Doctor says his recovery will be slow,' replied MacKay.

'And what about McKenzie?'

'He was discharged this morning and is at home recovering.'

'Well that's good to hear,' said Hadley.

'Ay it is, but I have to report that there's no sign of the suspects in Stirling,' said MacKay with a shake of his head.

'I think they've been seen up at Muthill,' said Hadley and MacKay looked surprised.

'Who saw them?'

'A blacksmith saw the Police coach with two men aboard travelling up the road to Crieff,' replied Hadley.

'Did you follow, sir?'

'We did, but we were unable to find them and I suspect that they've gone north to the Highlands,' replied Hadley.

'If that's the case, we'll never find them,' said MacKay.

'I'm determined that we will... because we arrested Sinclair in Crieff and he may know where they are...'

'You found him there?'

'Yes... he's in the interview room now and I'm about to question him,' said Hadley.

'It will be very interesting to hear what he has to say,' said MacKay.

'Also, I've just received a telegraph from the Yard saying that the corpse at Drummond has been identified as Captain Sefton of the 4th Hussars,' said Hadley.

'Well at least we know who he is now,' said MacKay before opening a folder on his desk and continuing 'I've received the autopsy report from Doctor Macpherson and it states that the cause of death was a broken neck, the third and fourth vertebrae had been violently wrenched apart.'

'So he was brutally murdered,' said Hadley.

'Indeed he was.'

'And the prime suspects are Doyle and Tyler, who we know are still here somewhere,' said Hadley.

'What do you propose we do next, sir?' asked MacKay.

'Interview Sinclair and hold him in custody whilst we search for the other two tomorrow,' replied Hadley.

'Right, after we've questioned Sinclair, I'll organise my men into armed parties and we'll set off to Crieff and the Highlands first thing,' said MacKay.

Father Sinclair looked quite composed when Hadley, Cooper, Devaux and MacKay entered the interview room. The detectives sat at the table opposite the priest and Cooper produced his notebook. Hadley cleared his throat and began 'Father Sinclair, you are in very serious trouble and under caution, so you would do well to answer my questions truthfully.'

'I always speak the truth, my son.'

'I'm pleased to hear it.'

'It is one of God's precious gifts to me.'

'What were you doing in Crieff?' asked Hadley.

'When you saw me, I had just visited a dear friend who is seriously ill and I was returning to Stirling,' Sinclair replied.

'Mrs Murray informed us that you left for London this morning.'

'Yes that's quite true... and after seeing my ailing friend I intended to catch the twelve o'clock train to Edinburgh and then the express to London.'

'How long did you plan to stay in London?'

'Just a few days.'

'Who were you going to see?'

'Our Holy Father, Cardinal Freeman in Westminster.'

'Where's your luggage?'

'I sent it on ahead, Inspector,' Sinclair replied with a grin. Hadley did not believe him at first but then wondered if he had found the Grail and sent it to London. He was concerned, waited a moment before dismissing it as improbable and asked 'what is your friend's name and address in Crieff?'

'Gregory Burns... he lives at twelve, Fintry Road, Inspector... and if you decide to call upon him, please remember that he is an old, sick person with a wandering mind and failing memory who is near to his death.' Hadley thought it was very convenient for Sinclair to have a witness who suffered with loss of memory.

'I will need to verify your visit to Mr Burns and will bear in mind your concern for his health,' replied Hadley.

'Thank you, my son.'

'Now, do you know the whereabouts of the two men who imprisoned you at Culcreuch Castle?'

'No Inspector, I do not... why do you ask?'

'They were seen driving a stolen Police coach through Muthill towards Crieff this morning.'

'May God preserve us,' whispered Sinclair.

'Did you notice anything untoward on your journey?'

'No, I did not, Inspector,' replied Sinclair. Hadley gathered his

196

thoughts for a moment and said 'now we come to the serious matter of Father Murphy's murder.'

Sinclair glared at Hadley and said 'well it is quite obvious that the two villains who kidnapped me and held me in chains with your Sergeants are the perpetrators of that monstrous crime, Inspector!'

'Indeed they are suspects… but so are you!'

'Why in God's name?' asked Sinclair angrily.

'Because you were the last person to see him alive and you have a motive,' replied Hadley.

'Neither assertion is true… I was with the two villains when we left Father Murphy at the train station… besides, what reason on God's earth would I have for murdering a brother priest?'

'I don't believe that you took Murphy to the station because he was already dead…'

'Not true!' interrupted Sinclair.

'And your motive for his killing was the holy relic…'

'This is quite ridiculous!'

'I think that he arrived un-expectedly at your house with news that your church records held some information regarding the hiding place of the relic…'

'But why would I wish to murder him?'

'Because if you found the relic you wanted all the fame and glory for yourself…'

'Not so!'

'It is obvious that it would undoubtedly bring you high praise from within the Catholic Church and an audience with the Pope.'

'Do you really think that I have the holy relic, Inspector?'

'Yes… or you know where it is hidden,' replied Hadley.

'This is absolute nonsense!'

'Nevertheless, I'm holding you in custody on suspicion of the unlawful murder of Father Murphy,' said Hadley.

'This is a travesty!' shouted Sinclair angrily.

'You will be held pending further inquiries,' said Hadley firmly before he stood up and led the others from the room. Sinclair, loudly protesting his innocence, was taken to a cell by the Duty Sergeant.

The detectives returned to MacKay's office where they discussed the investigation at length. MacKay was somewhat relieved to have had the responsibility of charging Sinclair with murder lifted from his shoulders. He reasoned that if a senior officer from Scotland Yard had made the charge, he would be exonerated from any blame that would ensue if Sinclair was subsequently proved innocent.

Hadley sent a short telegraph to Bell saying that he had arrested Sinclair at Crieff and suspected that Doyle and Tyler were still in Scotland. His return to London would depend on changing circumstances.

With the aid of several maps of the area, the detectives meticulously planned their search pattern for the following day. It was decided that four coaches would be used, Hadley, Cooper, Talbot and one Constable would set off to Culcreuch, then on to Drummond. Devaux and Rousseau, with two Constables, would travel up to Muthill and Crieff, making inquiries, whilst MacKay, Sergeant McDuff with two Constables would travel up to Aberfeldy. Sergeant Dundee with three Constables would journey along the road to Perth before returning to assist MacKay in his search of the Highlands.

Hadley looked serious when he said 'gentlemen, we must not fail in our duty to find Doyle and Tyler tomorrow.'

'We will succeed for certain, mon ami,' said Devaux and the others nodded but MacKay asked 'what if we don't find them, sir?'

'We'll just keep on looking until we do, Inspector,' replied Hadley firmly.

The detectives arrived at the Falkirk Hotel after seven o'clock and went straight to the bar where Devaux ordered the drinks and charged it to his room. After they had said 'cheers' and taken a sip, Devaux smiled saying 'well mes amis, what a day you've all had.'

'A busy one to be sure but I fancy that tomorrow will be even busier,' said Hadley

'Realistically Jim, what chance have we got of finding these two men?' asked Devaux and Hadley sighed before he replied 'I think it will be difficult, Marcel... but someone, somewhere must have seen the Police coach and we have to find out who in order to give us a positive lead.'

'MacKay seems a little uncertain, Jim.'

'That's to be expected in the circumstances... as you know he's had two of his men shot and his Sergeant is seriously wounded, so he realises that Doyle and Tyler are very violent, desperate men who will be difficult to find.'

'But I'm sure we can do it, mon ami.'

'Let's hope so.'

'What about the relic?'

'Its' whereabouts remains a mystery for the moment but I'm sure that once we have our suspects in custody we might find out from them where it's hidden,' replied Hadley.

'If they haven't got it with them, sir,' said Cooper.

'Quite so, Sergeant.'

'Ah, then tomorrow we shall find out,' said Devaux.

'Indeed we shall, now let's go into dinner,' said Hadley.

During the lengthy meal of roast lamb followed by sultana pudding, Devaux kept them all very amused with stories of his stay in hospital with the pretty nurses and the matron... Madame Guillotine. Despite the Frenchman's good humour, Hadley was in a sombre mood when he went to his room as he knew the enormity of the task that lay before them the next day.

CHAPTER 22

The next morning four coaches set off from the station yard at eight o'clock and there was an air of excitement and anticipation amongst the officers. The coach carrying Hadley and his men turned westwards on the road to Culcreuch Castle while the other three made their way in convoy north towards Crieff, Perth and Aberfeldy.

Hadley remained deep in thought whilst gazing out at the landscape during most of the two hour journey to Culcreuch. His Sergeants chatted amiably with Constable Elgin, who soon relaxed in their company whilst being acutely aware of Hadley's presence.

Hadley cleared his mind of a myriad of 'what if's?' in the investigation, came back to the task in hand and said 'when we arrive, gentlemen the first thing I want to see is the cellar where you were held captive.'

'Right, sir,' replied Cooper.

'I must admit that I didn't know how we were going to get out of there, sir,' said Talbot.

'Ah, you must thank providence for that, Sergeant... and Cooper's unfailing, natural ability to pick locks, which has always worried me slightly,' said Hadley with a smile. The Sergeants grinned and Talbot nodded as Cooper asked 'what do you think the chances are of finding Doyle and Tyler there, sir?'

'I really don't know, but unless we look we'll never know, Sergeant.'

'Well if we do find them I'm more than ready to shoot them down if they resist arrest!' said Talbot firmly.

'Quite right, Sergeant.'

'They'll not get away this time, sir,' said Talbot.

'Indeed not... but what about you Constable, are you ready to shoot?' asked Hadley and the young officer paled slightly before replying 'if I have to, sir.'

'Very good, but I don't think it will be necessary as Sergeant Talbot is my heavy artillery and is always ready to open fire on villains!' said Hadley with a smile.

'That you can be sure of,' said Cooper with a grin as the coach came to a halt outside the Castle.

'We will keep together at all times whilst we search the place for the suspects and anything that might lead us to the relic,' said Hadley.

'Very good, sir' chorused the officers as they climbed down from the coach. At Talbot's request, the driver produced an acetylene lamp from the coach pannier, lit it and handed it to him. The officers followed Hadley to the gatehouse, Talbot led the way to the ruined hall and down the steps to the dark cellar. The door into the room where they were held captive was locked but Cooper produced his picks and soon the lock clicked open. Hadley assumed nobody was in there but just in case, he drew his revolver, slipped off the safety catch and opened the door slowly, Talbot held the lamp up high behind him. The room was empty except for the table, chairs and chains around the pillar.

'They must have been back here since we escaped, sir,' said Cooper.

'What makes you so sure, Sergeant?'

'Because I didn't lock the door behind us when we left, sir.'

'Of course,' said Hadley before he stepped into the room and began looking around for any clues. They spent the next ten minutes searching for anything that might give a lead to where the suspects were or the hiding place of the Grail, but they found nothing.

'Let's quickly search outside then get away to Drummond,' said Hadley.

'I think we may have more luck there, sir,' said Cooper.

'I do hope so, Sergeant,' replied Hadley as he led them out of the room.

An hour later, after a fruitless search of the ruins, they left Culcreuch Castle and began the long journey up to Drummond. They stopped for lunch and to rest the horses when they reached Dunblane two hours later. After half an hour they were refreshed and eager to get to Drummond. The coach left the inn at the trot but the fourteen miles north to Muthill seemed to take forever and Hadley was concerned at the time the journey was taking. He was determined to look beyond the castle at the surrounding area for any signs of the suspects. He remembered, when gazing out of the lookout tower, seeing a cluster of houses about a mile or so away which were half hidden by a dip in the landscape and decided that he would make inquiries there after searching the ruins. He did not know that the place was called Balloch and two coaches were hidden in Mr Campbell's derelict barn.

It was nearly four o'clock when the coach pulled up outside Drummond Castle and the detectives quickly disembarked and made their way into the courtyard where Hadley stopped for a moment to look up at the crumbling tower.

'Well it doesn't appear that any more of the place has fallen down recently,' he said.

'I think you had a lucky escape the other night, sir,' said Cooper.

'Yes… and always remember, Sergeant, it's better to be lucky than rich,' replied Hadley with a grin. Suddenly there came the sound of a raised voice from within the tower.

'By God... there's someone in there!' exclaimed Hadley before he made a dash for the arched entrance. The others followed, drew their revolvers and hurried up the spiral steps after Hadley. Their noisy approach alerted the people in the tower and more raised voices were heard before there was silence. Hadley drew his revolver and made ready to fire before glancing in at the first room where he had discovered the body of Sefton. No one was there so he hurried up the narrow steps to the next room where he strode in ready to fire and to his amazement saw Major Fielding sitting at the table.

'Bloody hell! It's you, Inspector!' shouted Fielding.

'It is indeed, Major,' said Hadley as he lowered his weapon.

'Well what the devil are you doing here?' asked Fielding as he stood up.

'I might ask you the same question, sir,' replied Hadley as his officers crowded into the room.

'I see you've brought your meddlesome army with you, Inspector!'

'I have, sir, now who were you talking too?'

'I don't know who they are… besides it's none of your business!' replied Fielding firmly.

'They must have escaped further up, sir,' said Cooper.

'Then find them!'

202

'Right, sir,' replied Cooper hurrying out with Talbot and Elgin.

'So Major, I'll ask you once again… what are you doing here?'

'If you must know I'm here on leave to do a little hunting, Inspector.'

'Like Captain Sefton?'

'How do you know about him?' queried Fielding.

'Because I found his body here,' replied Hadley, Fielding's jaw dropped open and he whispered 'oh my God, I wondered where he was.'

'So in the circumstances Major, I'm taking you in for further questioning….' Hadley was interrupted by the sound of two shots from above and he whirled round, raced from the room and up the steps to an open door that led out onto the battlements. He saw Cooper, lying on the flagstones with blood pouring from a wound in his side being attended to by Elgin, while Talbot was in hot pursuit of two men running along the casemates.

'Oh dear God, Sergeant!' exclaimed Hadley as he knelt down beside him.

'I'm alright for the moment sir… you get after those bastards!'

'Oh that I will, Sergeant!'

Hadley leapt up and raced after Talbot who had closed the gap between himself and the men as they ran along the battlement wall. Suddenly Talbot went down on one knee, took careful aim and fired two shots. Hadley saw one of the men tumble to the ground whilst the other carried on running. Talbot sprinted passed the wounded man, who was screaming and quivering with pain and closed once again on the remaining gunman. When Hadley reached the wounded man he glanced down and said 'I just hope you live long enough to face the hangman my friend' before he picked up the dropped Police revolver and raced after Talbot.

Hadley saw the fugitive gunman stop, turn and fire two shots at Talbot. The bullets whistled through the air over Hadley's head as he instinctively ducked down and Talbot took up the firing position once more before firing two shots. The gunman staggered back as the bullets tore into his chest, he dropped the revolver and stumbled against the battlement, which suddenly gave way. Hadley looked on in disbelief as the man plummeted over the wall amongst the falling debris, his arms and legs flailing about in all directions like a marionette whose strings had been cut. His body hit the ground more than a hundred feet below and he lay open mouthed with eyes staring up towards the ruined battlement. Hadley joined Talbot by the ragged gap in the wall and gazed down at the dead gunman.

'Well done, Sergeant.'

'Thank you, sir... I'm afraid they left me no alternative... I had to shoot them.'

'You did indeed... now let's take care of Cooper.'

'Right, sir,' replied Talbot as he bent down to pick up the Police revolver.

Retracing their steps along the casemates to where the wounded gunman lay and Hadley asked him his name but all he said in a whisper was 'for God's sake help me.'

'Your name!' shouted Hadley.

'It's... it's Doyle, Charlie Doyle.'

'And your deceased friends name is?'

'Oh God, don't say he's dead.'

'I'm afraid so... but that's the price you villains have to pay when you break the law and defy the Police,' said Hadley. Doyle remained silent for a moment and replied 'he's called Tyler, Jack Tyler.'

'Right... we'll try and get you to a Doctor as soon as we can,' said Hadley before he strode off to attend to Cooper leaving Talbot with Doyle.

Hadley knelt once again at Cooper's side and said 'we'll get you away to the Doctor in Crieff, Sergeant.'

'Thank you, sir.'

'Can you move at all?'

'I think so, sir, it's just knocked the wind out of me for the moment,' replied Cooper. Hadley nodded but was concerned at the amount of blood leaking through the handkerchief that Elgin was holding to the wound.

'Constable, run down and ask our driver to come and help us.'

'Yes, sir,' replied Elgin as Hadley took over and pressed his hand on the blood stained handkerchief. Cooper was looking very pale and Hadley became increasingly concerned about the seriousness of the injury to his young officer.

'You do seem to be in the habit of getting hurt these days... I

204

must try and break you of it,' said Hadley with a smile.

'Yes sir… but it was my own silly fault this time.'

'How so?'

'When we challenged them, they pulled their weapons and threatened us… but I attempted to rush them and the tall man fired, sir.'

'Ah, there's a lesson for you, Sergeant, always obey orders. I told you repeatedly that if they resisted arrest, shoot them!' said Hadley.

'Yes you did, sir.'

'I'm pleased to tell you that it's all over now… Talbot brought them down, Doyle is wounded but Tyler is dead,' said Hadley as he was suddenly aware of Fielding standing in the doorway of the tower.

'Can I be of any assistance, Inspector?' asked Fielding.

'In a moment, sir, if you would be so kind,' replied Hadley.

'Yes of course, how can I help?'

'I've sent for our driver so we can get my Sergeant down to the coach and if you can give Sergeant Talbot help to carry the other man, I'd be obliged.'

'Of course, Inspector… but there were two of them, so what's happened to the other person?'

'I'm afraid he's dead,' replied Hadley.

'Oh dear, what a shame, violent death is such a waste,' said Fielding shaking his head.

'Were they working for you, sir?'

'Good heavens no Inspector, I'd never seen either of them before… it seems they were just living here, for what reason I know not, and I came up to see what was going on when I heard their voices… they were arguing loudly,' replied Fielding but Hadley did not believe a word of it.

'Didn't you recognise them as the men who attacked you in London, sir?'

'No Inspector.'

Hadley waited for a moment then asked 'why are you here in the castle?'

'I told you, I'm up here deer hunting and the tower gives a fine view over the landscape,' replied Fielding.

'I didn't notice you carrying a rifle.'

'Quite right, you didn't… because I was just reconnoitring the area, Inspector.'

'And how did you get here, sir?'

'I walked out from Muthill.'

'Before that?'

'I had a trap bring me down to Muthill from Crieff, where I'm staying presently,' replied Fielding. At that moment Elgin and the driver appeared and immediately hurried to Hadley's side.

They lifted Cooper gently to his feet and half carried him, with some difficulty, down the spiral steps and out to the coach. Talbot assisted by Fielding followed on with Doyle, who was now in a serious state through loss of blood. When the wounded men were safely in the coach the others climbed aboard and the driver set the horses off at a gallop to Crieff.

Fortunately Doctor Andrews was still conducting his afternoon surgery when they arrived and soon the wounded men were being attended by the Doctor and his nurse. Ten minutes later, Andrews came out and said to Hadley 'I've bandaged them as best I can, Inspector, but they need urgent attention at the Stirling Infirmary, they've both lost a lot of blood and I'm particularly concerned about the condition of the older man.'

'Thank you Doctor, I'll get them there as fast as I can.'

'I'll come with you just in case they need my attention on the journey,' said Andrews.

'Thank you.'

When the wounded were back on the coach Hadley said to Talbot 'Sergeant, stay here with Elgin, hire a trap and retrieve the body of Tyler, then bring it down to Stirling.'

'Very good, sir, but will you be alright on your own with Fielding?'

'Don't worry about that, Sergeant… The mood I'm in I'm just as likely to shoot him as not and he knows it!'

On the journey, Doctor Andrews gave both wounded men an injection of morphine to ease their pain and Hadley became increasingly worried about Cooper. He was relieved when the coach pulled into the Infirmary just after six o'clock. Attendants were quickly summoned by Andrews, the men were placed on stretchers and carried into casualty where two duty Doctors, assisted by Andrews, immediately began treatment. Hadley paced up and down outside in the corridor waiting for news of Cooper whilst Fielding sat on a bench seat looking unperturbed. It seemed an age before the Doctor attending to Cooper came out with Andrews and said to Hadley 'he's going to be alright, Inspector, the wound to his side did not injure any vital organs.'

'Thank God for that,' said Hadley with a relieved sigh.

'Your Sergeant is a very fit young man and I'm sure that he will recover quickly.'

'He'll be fine in a few days, Inspector,' added Andrews

'I'm very glad to hear it, may I see him now?'

'Only for a few minutes, Inspector then we'll get him up to the ward,' replied the Doctor and Hadley nodded.

Cooper managed a smile when Hadley entered the room and the two nurses who were busy tidying up, stopped and left them alone.

'How are you feeling now?'

'A lot better thank you, sir, and pleased to be out of the coach.'

'Yes, I'm sure… it did seem to be a long journey.'

'Will you let my wife know that I'll be stuck in here for awhile, sir?'

'Of course, Sergeant, but according to the Doctors you're fit and will recover quickly so I'm sure your stay in hospital will not be long,' said Hadley with a smile.

'Let's hope so, sir.'

At that moment a matron with two nurses suddenly appeared and said 'come along now… it's time for you to go up to the ward.'

'Yes matron,' said Cooper and Hadley smiled knowing his Sergeant was in good hands.

'I'll come and see you later.'

'Thank you, sir.'

Hadley waited in the corridor for the Doctor treating Doyle to appear and inform him of the gunman's condition. When the Doctor eventually came out he looked concerned and said 'I'm afraid that he's in a very poor state, Inspector and I think it's unlikely that he will live long.'

'I'm sorry to hear that, Doctor... may I see him now?'

'I don't see why not... but I must warn you that he's semi-conscious at the moment.'

'I'll bear that in mind.'

'If you would Inspector, and I want you to know that we've done everything possible for him and it is only a matter of time to see if he recovers,' said the Doctor.

'I'm sure you have... so thank you, Doctor.'

Hadley went into the cubicle and stood for a moment looking at the pale face of Doyle while a nurse tidied away blood stained bandages into a bag before leaving. As Hadley came close to him he opened his eyes and tried to smile.

'Take it easy my friend,' said Hadley quietly.

'Your old boy certainly did it for me, guvnor,' whispered Doyle.

'I'm afraid he did.'

'I deserved it and no mistake.'

'Yes I think you did... but before I leave you in peace, I just want to ask you a few questions,' said Hadley gently and Doyle nodded slowly.

'Were you employed by Major Fielding?'

'Yes, guvnor... he asked Tyler and me to get involved in some caper looking for a relic... and the money was good so I couldn't turn it down,' whispered Doyle.

'Do you know what it was?'

'No... Tyler knew... but he wouldn't tell me.'

Hadley waited for a few moments before he asked 'did Tyler murder the Porter brothers, Sefton and the Professor?'

Doyle's eyes glazed over and his eyelids quivered before he gave a slight nod and slipped into unconsciousness. Hadley quickly left the bedside, found a nurse in the corridor and said 'I think the patient in there needs some attention, nurse.'

'Yes, sir,' she said and hurried into the cubicle.

Hadley looked hard at Fielding sitting on the bench seat and said 'now, Major, if you're quite ready, we'll go to the Police station for what I believe will be a very long interview.'

208

CHAPTER 23

When the coach carrying the French officers passed through Muthill and arrived in Crieff, Devaux instructed the driver to stop at number twelve Fintry Road.

'Let's see what Monsieur Burns can tell us about Father Sinclair's visit, Sergeant,' said Devaux as the coach turned off the main road.

'If he can remember, mon Captain.'

'Ah oui, we shall soon see.'

As the coach pulled up outside the small house, Devaux said to the two Constables 'we will only be a few minutes so you may stay here and wait, mes amis.'

'Very good, sir,' said Redman and Allan nodded. They were impressed with the French officer's good nature and kind concern towards them since they first met and boarded the coach at Stirling Police station.

Rousseau knocked on the door and eventually it was opened by an elderly woman who looked quizzically at them in turn.

'Ay, and what do you want?'

'We're Police officers, madam, and we would like to have a word with Monsieur Burns if you please,' said Devaux with a smile.

'He's at his bed for now… and a might poorly I have to say.'

'We only want a moment of his time, madam,' Devaux persisted.

'What's this about?' she asked.

'Are you Madam Burns?'

'Ay, I am so,' she replied.

'Then perhaps you can help us,' said Devaux with a smile.

'You're not from these parts are you?'

'Non Madam, I'm Captain Devaux from Paris.'

'You've come a long way to talk to my husband then,' she said with a slight chuckle.

'Oui, I have indeed.'

'So it must be important!'

'It is. Did a priest called Father Sinclair visit your husband recently?'

'Oh ay, that he did… it was on his way back from the Priory…'

'The Priory?' interrupted Devaux his eyes bright with anticipation.

'Ay… the Priory.'

'And what Priory is that, Madam?'

'It's Inchaffray Priory… just off the road to Perth… not more than five miles away,' she replied with a smile.

'Merci beaucoup, Madam Burns you've been very helpful,' said Devaux with a broad smile.

'Why thank you,' she said with a smile, bobbed a quick curtsey and asked 'is that all, sir?'

'Oui madam.'

'Will you no' be coming back again to see ma husband?'

'I'm afraid not, Madam,' replied Devaux with a smile. The officers turned and made their way back to the coach but before they boarded, Devaux whispered to Rousseau in French 'I'm sure that is where Sinclair must have hidden it, mon ami, and all we have to do now is make a plan to get it!'

'What kind of plan, mon Captain?'

'I don't know yet, but I will think of something!' replied Devaux before giving instructions to the driver to stop in the town centre before taking them to the Priory at Inchaffray.

When the driver pulled the horses up, Devaux asked the Constables to begin making inquiries in the town regarding the two suspects and the missing coach whilst he and Rousseau went on to the Priory to confirm Mrs Burn's account of events. Redman and Alan nodded and climbed down from the coach which then hurried on out to the Perth Road. Just over five miles along the road from Crieff there was a turning to the right that was sign posted to 'Inchaffray Abbey.'

The medieval building stood at the end of a long, tree lined drive and looked impressive in the sunshine. Devaux believed that success was imminent and felt excited when the coach swung round and stopped outside the iron studded door. The French officers climbed down and steadied themselves before Rousseau pulled the large bell handle by the side of the door. They heard it ring deep inside the building and waited for some while before the small, cross barred hatch in the door opened and a pale young face stared out.

'Good morning, Monsieur, may we see the Abbot?' said Devaux with a smile.

'Who are you, sir?'

'We are French Police Officers on very important business,' replied Devaux and he produced his warrant card and held it up for the young man to see. He hesitated for a moment then said 'please come in.' The bolts were drawn back and the door opened to allow them to step into the interior of the Priory.

'Please follow me' said the monk before leading them down a short corridor to a room.

'Please wait in here, gentlemen.'

'Merci, Monsieur.'

The room was quite spacious but was only furnished with a long table with four chairs at either side and one large chair at its head. The detectives sat down and waited in silence, each deep in thought for awhile before Devaux looked at Rousseau and said 'I think this is the moment we've been waiting for, mon ami.'

'Please God,' whispered Rousseau as they heard footsteps outside in the corridor, the door opened and the Abbot appeared, followed by the young monk.

'Good morning, my sons,' said the tall, august looking man as the detectives stood up.

'Good morning, Monsieur Abbot.'

'I understand that you wish to speak to me on an important matter,' said the Abbot as he sat at the head of the table and they resumed their seats whilst the monk stood behind the Abbot's chair.

'Oui, Monsieur.'

'Please continue.'

'I am Captain Marcel Devaux and this is Sergeant Rousseau, we are Gendarme Officers from Paris' said Devaux with a smile as he showed the Abbot his warrant card with its sepia tint photograph. Rousseau followed suit, the Abbot looked at the cards, nodded and passed them back.

'So how can I help you, my sons?'

'We are here at the special request of Father Sinclair who called to see you recently and left a small case containing an important religious relic for safe keeping,' replied Devaux.

The Abbot looked surprised and asked 'has anything untoward happened to our Brother Sinclair?'

'Oui, Monsieur it has, but he is safe now because we have him in our protective custody.'

'Oh dear God... what has happened to him?'

'Two violent men attacked him, tried to force him to reveal the whereabouts of the relic and kept him prisoner in chains before we released him from his terrible ordeal,' replied Devaux.

'May God Almighty have mercy upon us,' whispered the Abbot.

'It has been deeply shocking to us all, Monsieur.'

'I am sure it has my son... have the men who committed this terrible act been caught?'

'Not yet, Monsieur, but we have armed officers searching Crieff and the surrounding countryside as we speak, so it is only a matter of time before they are brought to justice,' replied Devaux.

'I'm relieved to hear it, but why does Brother Sinclair want to have his case back now? Surely it would be better for it to remain here until these violent men are apprehended?'

'Ah, it would make sense if only it was that simple, Monsieur, but Father Sinclair has said that after receiving orders from the Vatican he must take the relic to Rome as quickly as he can and we have been sent to guard him all the way,' said Devaux.

'All the way to Rome, Captain?'

'Oui, Monsieur, we have come to Scotland with direct orders from our Commissioner at the Palace du Justice in Paris to assist the Holy Father,' replied Devaux with a smile.

'Good heavens... but how did you know about all this?' whispered the Abbot.

'It is an involved and complicated story, Monsieur, but finally our Commissioner was informed by Cardinal Charnay in Toulouse that Father Sinclair had discovered this important holy relic and so we were sent immediately,' replied Devaux.

'Good gracious me.'

'And at the request of our Commissioner, the British Police have been kindly assisting us in this delicate and secret quest,' added Devaux.

'It is pleasing to hear of close co-operation in such an

important matter.'

'I agree, Monsieur Abbot, now if you would kindly give me the case we will be on our way to London and Rome with Father Sinclair,' said Devaux with a smile.

'Do you know what the relic is, my son?'

'Non Monsieur, I only know that it is very valuable and a treasure of the Catholic Church,' lied Devaux.

'So I believe,' said the Abbot.

'Do you not know what it is, Monsieur?'

'No, I have no idea, Captain but Brother Sinclair told me it was priceless.'

'It is no surprise then that we are armed and have been sent to guard it,' said Devaux.

'That is quite so, my son.'

'Très bien… and as we have a long journey ahead of us, Monsieur, I would be pleased if we could now be on our way.'

'Of course… please wait here whilst I fetch it, my son,' smiled the Abbot.

'Merci beaucoup, Monsieur.'

Devaux and Rousseau could hardly contain their excitement when the Abbot returned with a portmanteau and placed it on the table. Devaux's hand shook slightly with emotion when he stretched out and wrapped his fingers around the leather handles to pick it up.

'Merci, merci, beaucoup,' he whispered to the Abbot with a smile.

'You are welcome, my son, and I wish you and Brother Sinclair a safe journey to Rome.'

'Merci.'

'And ask him to write to me with all his good news from the Vatican,' said the Abbot.

'Indeed I will, Monsieur.'

Within minutes they had been shown out by the monk and stood for a moment in the sunshine breathing deeply before Devaux said to the driver 'we have to return to Stirling immediately!'

'Very good, sir.'

'After you have left us there, you can turn around and come back to Crieff to collect the Constables, they should have finished their inquiries by then.'

'Right you are, sir.'

Devaux resisted the temptation to force open the locked portmanteau in the coach and gaze upon the Holy Grail. He decided that would be done in his hotel bedroom and he informed Rousseau of his decision.

'Oui, mon Captain, I think it makes sense.'

They made plans for their arrival at the hotel and the journey back to France. The time seemed to pass quickly and soon the coach arrived in the outskirts of Stirling. Devaux instructed the driver to leave them at the Falkirk Hotel before returning to Crieff.

Once at the hotel they hurried up to Devaux's room where he locked the door before placing the portmanteau on the bed.

'Now let's look at our glittering prize,' he said to Rousseau.

'I am very frightened, mon Captain.'

'Why, mon ami?'

'Because it is so precious... I am just so excited and nervous,' whispered Rousseau.

'So am I, now give me your knife so I can force this lock.'

The lock was a small clasp affair at the top of the portmanteau and it soon clicked open when Devaux attacked it. Opening the case slowly he looked inside at a bundle of cloth, which he lifted out and laid on the bed. His hands trembled again as he started to uncover the Grail. Suddenly the gold, jewel encrusted cup came into view and they both gasped before Devaux picked it up and held it high.

'Mon Dieu... mon Dieu,' whispered Rousseau.

'As you say...mon Dieu... and to think that our Lord Jesus Christ used this to drink from at the last supper...'

'Oui, mon Captain.'

'I can barely hold it,' whispered Devaux, his voice trembling with emotion as tears began to stream down his cheeks.

'Oui, mon Captain... and we have done a wonderful thing for France.'

'We have, mon brave,' whispered Devaux before he placed the Grail back on the bed. They both stared at it for a while in silence then they embraced each other and Devaux said 'go and pack your bags, we must leave immediately!'

'Oui, mon Captain!'

When Devaux was alone he wrote a short note to Hadley on the hotel stationery and sealed it in an envelope.

Twenty minutes later they had paid their bill, left the note for Hadley, booked out of the hotel and taken a trap to the railway station, where they caught the three o'clock train to Edinburgh to connect with the five o'clock express to London.

Two hours later the express train had just pulled in at York when Talbot arrived at the Infirmary with Tyler's shattered remains, MacKay had returned with his men and Hadley began his interview with Major Fielding.

Hadley looked hard at Fielding across the table.

'Let me be rightly understood from the very start, Major...'

'I'm sure there will be no misunderstandings between us, Inspector,' interrupted Fielding with a sardonic smile and Hadley made no reply but just stared at him.

'I am charging you with incitement and complicity to murder, kidnap and perverting the course of justice...'

'This is all absolute nonsense and you bloody well know it!' interrupted Fielding angrily.

'Doyle has confessed to me that you employed Tyler and him to search for a holy relic and he also stated that Tyler murdered the Porter brothers, Sefton and Professor Pennington, all of which I suspect you ordered!' exclaimed Hadley.

'That isn't a confession... it's the wild, incoherent ramblings of a man who is near to his death,' said Fielding.

'You may think what you like but I can assure you that you will remain in custody and face trial on these charges!'

'And you, sir, should be aware that I refute absolutely these monstrous allegations and will defend myself with the greatest legal team of barristers that money can buy!'

'That is your privilege, sir.'

'After my acquittal I will ensure that you're charged with my false arrest, harassment and imprisonment, which should be the end of your Police career!'

'Others have tried and always failed miserably.'

'But I will be successful I assure you!' exclaimed Fielding.

'That remains to be seen... now tell me about this relic you were searching for.'

'I know nothing about any relic, I assure you, Inspector!'

'Doyle says that you employed him and Tyler to find it...'

'As I've already said... it's the confused ramblings of a dying man!' replied Fielding as MacKay entered the room.

'Inspector Hadley, Sergeant Talbot has just arrived and told me what happened at Drummond today,' said MacKay solemnly.

'Ah... then you're well briefed.'

'I am... and I'm sorry to hear that Cooper has been wounded.'

'Thank you... it is serious but the Doctor thinks he will recover quickly,' said Hadley with a smile.

'That's very good... so this is the man behind everything,' said MacKay as he glared at Fielding.

'He is indeed,' said Hadley.

'It's all lies...' began Fielding but he was interrupted by MacKay asking 'now you've got him will you be taking him to London, sir?'

'Indeed I will... along with Sinclair,' replied Hadley.

'That's excellent news... I will order armed officers to accompany you as prisoner escorts,' said MacKay, relieved that Hadley would be responsible for the two suspects and the entire investigation.

'Thank you, I propose to leave for London first thing tomorrow, Inspector.'

'I will organise everything for you, sir,' said MacKay.

'Thank you... I'll telegraph my Chief at the Yard with a report and request armed officers to meet us when we arrive,' said Hadley.

'Very good, sir.'

'Now Major, as I have no more questions for you at the moment you will remain in custody and accompany me to Scotland Yard tomorrow,' said Hadley.

'You are making a grave mistake, sir that will cost you your career... you'll end up a pauper begging on the streets!' exclaimed Fielding angrily.

'Only time will tell, Major,' said Hadley calmly.

After Fielding was removed by the Custody Sergeant and taken to a holding cell, Hadley said to MacKay 'I propose to leave Sergeant Talbot here with the French Officers to continue the search for this holy relic.'

'I think that's a good idea, sir and he can also see Cooper when he has the time.'

'Yes... now have the French Officers returned yet?'

'Oh ay, they're at the hotel and according to my driver he took them there this afternoon before returning to Crieff to collect the Constables,' replied MacKay and alarm bells rang loudly inside Hadley's head.

'I think I'll just check that they are still there,' said Hadley.

'Do you think that they may have gone off somewhere else, sir?'

'It's a distinct possibility.'

A Police coach hurried Hadley and Talbot to the Falkirk Hotel where the receptionist confirmed that the Frenchmen had left earlier and gave Hadley the note. It read *'Cher Jim, we have left for Paris on urgent business, au revoir, Marcel.'*

Hadley's jaw dropped and he said 'the hell they have!' as he handed the note to Talbot to read.

'Blimey, sir, they must have found it!'

'I fear that is so, Sergeant and as we have now accounted for all the murderous villains... we only have to catch the thieving French!'

CHAPTER 24

Immediately the detectives arrived back at the Police station Hadley advised MacKay of his fears and asked to interview the Constables and the driver.

'They've all gone off duty now, sir,' said MacKay.

'Then please send someone for them… it is imperative that I speak to them!' exclaimed Hadley.

'Very well, sir.'

Hadley composed a detailed telegraph message for Bell with all the day's events and hoped that he would read it tonight and take action. He suggested that Hanson and Mercer should wait at Kings Cross with armed officers for the arrival of trains from Edinburgh to apprehend the French and recover the relic. He also sent a message to his friend, Inspector Bagley at Dover, requesting him to hold Devaux and Rousseau in custody on theft charges and gave a description of the French Officers. Hadley hoped that the Frenchmen would be caught at Kings Cross but he could not be certain about the outcome of that and Dover was the last point at which they could be arrested.

After sending the messages, he and Talbot made their way to the Infirmary for a quick visit to see Cooper. The Sergeant was sitting up in bed and smiled when they approached.

'Evening sir… Bill,' said Cooper.

'Evening Sergeant, how are you feeling?'

'I've felt better in the past, sir, but mustn't grumble.'

'I'm sure.'

'The nurses have been very attentive and matron keeps a beady eye on them all, sir.'

'Quite right too… I've telegraphed the Chief and asked him to let your wife know what's happened and that you're in hospital but getting better.'

'Thank you, sir… I know she'll be worried.'

'Of course, it's only natural, but I'm sure you'll be out of here in a day or so.'

'Here's hoping, sir.'

'Indeed, now we're going back to London in the morning with Fielding and Sinclair…'

'But what about the relic, sir?' interrupted Cooper.

'I think the French have found it and are busy trying to make their escape to Paris,' replied Hadley.

'You must stop them, sir!'

'I intend to… so I've requested the Chief to send Hanson and Mercer to Kings Cross to wait for them and I've telegraphed Inspector Bagley at Dover in case all else fails,' said Hadley with a smile.

'We'll catch them, never fear, Bob,' said Talbot.

'I do hope so after all this blimmin' malarkey,' said Cooper.

'We will, Sergeant. You just concentrate on getting better and leave everything to us.'

'Yes, sir.'

'And I'll ask MacKay to let me know how you're progressing each day and pass the news to your wife.'

'Thank you, sir… so tell me, where was the relic hidden?'

'We don't know yet but I am hoping that the Constables accompanying them will be able to give us a clue,' replied Hadley.

Cooper shook his head and said 'I doubt if we can ever trust them again, sir.'

'I think you're probably right, Sergeant.'

After leaving Cooper, Hadley spoke to the duty Doctor and inquired after Doyle.

'He's stabilised, but still in a critical condition I'm afraid, Inspector.'

'I see… and how is Sergeant Melrose progressing?'

'Quite well I'm glad to say, he's a fit man and should make a full recovery in time,' replied the Doctor.

'And my Sergeant?'

'He should be discharged in a few days if all goes well and he continues to improve.'

'Thank you Doctor… that is a great relief to me,' said Hadley.

Leaving the Infirmary they hurried back to the Police station where Redman, Allan and the driver were waiting for Hadley in MacKay's office. They looked anxious and Hadley guessed that

MacKay had given them an initial dressing down so he smiled to put them at ease and said 'gentlemen, you're not in any trouble, I just need to know in detail what happened today.' They all looked relieved and Redman said 'thank you, sir.'

'So please tell me everything from the very beginning,' said Hadley. Redman gave a succinct account of the visit to Mr Burns' house, which Allan substantiated, before they were left in the town centre to carry out inquiries. The driver confirmed that he had been ordered to stop in the centre of Crieff to let the Constables off, then carry on to Inchaffray Priory.

'And what happened at the Priory?' asked Hadley.

'The officers went in and came out about half an hour later, sir.'

'Were they carrying anything?'

'Yes, sir, the Captain was carrying a leather portmanteau.'

'Did he open it?'

'Not to my knowledge, sir.'

'Then what happened?'

'He ordered me to take him back to Stirling then come back for the two Constables, sir, which I did.'

'I see… and you left the French officers at the hotel?'

'Yes, sir.'

'Thank you, gentlemen that will be all.'

'Thank you, sir,' they chorused and filed out of the office.

Hadley looked at MacKay for a moment and said 'well, Inspector, it seems that after speaking to Mr Burns they somehow knew the relic was at the Priory and concocted a believable story, told it to the Abbot and he must have given it to them,' said Hadley with a sigh.

. 'It would appear so, but I'm sure your colleagues will apprehend them in London, sir,' said MacKay.

'I do hope so because it's too late for me to catch up with them tonight.'

'Yes indeed… and you know sir, I never did trust the French.'

'And after this adventure, I must admit that I'm also beginning to change my mind about them,' said Hadley.

The detectives returned to the Falkirk Hotel, had a pint of stout at the bar and enjoyed a fulsome dinner of tender roast lamb. As they sat by the fire in the lounge Talbot said 'I'm glad it's all over up here, sir and we can get back to London now.'

'So am I, but we have to hope that the Chief has managed to organise a reception for our French colleagues at Kings Cross otherwise they'll be hell to pay if they get across to France with the relic.'

Hadley spent a restless night worrying about all aspects of the case and was glad when morning came. After breakfast he settled their bill and they left the hotel, arriving at the Police station at eight o'clock. The first thing Hadley did was to ask MacKay if any messages had come in overnight from Scotland Yard.

'I'm afraid not, sir.'

'I hope that they have not slipped the net,' said Hadley anxiously.

'I doubt it, sir, we know that they left Stirling in the late afternoon so they wouldn't have caught a train to London before five o'clock and you sent your message at about seven so I'm sure the Chief Inspector would have put officers in place to apprehend them at Kings Cross.'

'I only hope that you're right, Inspector,' said Hadley with a sigh.

MacKay had organised the prisoner escort which consisted of Sergeant Dundee, Constables Elgin, Redman and Allan.

Hadley thanked MacKay for all his help and he and Talbot said their 'goodbye's' to him in the yard as the two prisoners were brought from their cells and placed in a Police coach. The party caught the nine o'clock train to Edinburgh which connected to the eleven o'clock express to London.

They had to travel in the open carriage to Edinburgh with passengers looking suspiciously at them but they managed to find a compartment to themselves for the journey to Kings Cross. Sinclair and Fielding hardly glanced at each other and Hadley wondered if they knew about each other's escapades. Fielding read newspapers in an unconcerned manner whilst Sinclair just stared out of the window.

Little was said during the journey and Hadley kept looking at his fob watch, wondering if the French Officers had been apprehended. When the train stopped at Watford, Hadley felt a deep unease but he put it to the back of his mind. Talbot smiled as the train pulled away and said 'next stop is King Cross, sir, and we'll be there soon.'

Hadley smiled back, looked at his fob watch and replied 'yes and if all goes well we should arrive by six o'clock.'

Devaux was sure that the Police would be waiting for them at Kings Cross so he and Rousseau left the train at midnight when it arrived at Watford. They hired a trap to take them as far as Highgate where they hailed a Hansom cab to take them the rest of the way to Waterloo station. Arriving there at two in the morning, they bought tickets and checked the departure time of the next train to Dover before they stopped for tea and sandwiches at the all night kiosk on the concourse.

'At last we are nearly home with our wonderful and sacred prize, mon ami,' said Devaux as he sipped his tea.

'Oui, mon Captain, and I can hardly wait to be back in France.'

'Neither can I... and I never want to visit Scotland again!'

'After this I doubt whether we shall ever come back to England, mon Captain!'

'Oh, I'm sure we will, the English are very forgiving and Jim will always be our good friend,' replied Devaux with a smile.

They sat in the waiting room and half dozed for the next few hours before boarding the Dover train standing at platform six. Finding an empty compartment, Devaux placed the portmanteau above him on the luggage rack and sat down with a sigh.

After Rousseau had loaded the other cases and sat opposite, Devaux said 'I think we are safe once the train leaves London.'

'But Captain, surely Monsieur Hadley will telegraph the Dover Police when he finds out that we did not arrive at Kings Cross?'

'That's probable, so in case they are waiting at the station, we will get off the train at the last stop before Dover and travel to the Ferry by trap, mon ami,' replied Devaux with a smile.

'And what about getting on the Ferry, mon Captain?'

'They are looking for two men travelling together so we will buy our tickets and board separately, I will go first and you follow a few minutes later, mon ami,' replied Devaux.

'Très bien, I just hope that it works,' whispered Rousseau.

'It will,' replied Devaux with a smile as the guards whistles blew, doors slammed shut and the train pulled away from platform six in a cloud of steam. Devaux breathed a sigh of relief and looked at his fob watch knowing that they would be in Dover within two hours.

After stopping at Canterbury the train picked up speed and Devaux was becoming more excited as it neared Dover. There were two more stops before the train reached its final destination and when it pulled into Whitfield station they hurriedly disembarked and stood on the platform with their luggage. A porter carried their bags out to a waiting trap and Devaux instructed the driver to take them to the Ferry port. They relaxed as the horse clip clopped along the road in the early morning sunshine and the five mile journey to the Ferry port was soon over. After paying the driver and watching him go, they glanced around for any Policemen and were relieved when they saw none. Devaux made his way towards the ticket office, clutching the portmanteau, whilst Rousseau lit a cigarette and waited on the pavement with the rest of the luggage.

There were a large number of passengers milling about in front of the ticket office with a Constable standing some distance away by the gangplank onto the ship. When he noticed the Constable, Devaux whispered to himself 'courage, mon brave, courage.'

Joining the queue, he bought his ticket, glanced back at Rousseau, gave a nod and made his way towards the gangplank with his heart beating. He was within yards of it when he heard a man's voice behind him say 'hold up, mate, you've got my case there!' Devaux turned for an instant and saw a large, red faced man pointing at the portmanteau.

'Oh non, Monsieur, I think you're mistaken,' replied Devaux with a smile.

'I'm bloody well not my friend... I put my case down when I bought my ticket and you just picked it up!' shouted the man.

'I assure you, Monsieur you're mistaken!'

'You're a bloody thief! Give it back!'

'Non, Monsieur...'

'He sounds like a bloody foreigner to me, they're all thieves!' said a portly woman and a crowd began to gather.

'Give it back!' shouted another man. Devaux's heart was now

beating madly and it increased when he noticed the Constable moving slowly towards the gathering crowd.

'He's blimmin' French,' said another woman

'You can't trust any of them!' shouted the man.

'They're all liars!' shouted the portly woman as the Constable arrived.

'What's going on here?' he asked, glaring at Devaux.

'He's stolen my case! Arrest him Constable!' shouted the red faced man and he pointed at the portmanteau, which Devaux was now clutching tightly to his chest with both arms.

The Constable looked hard into Devaux's eyes and asked 'now is this case really yours sir?'

'Oui, Constable, it is,' replied Devaux and he wondered if he should identify himself but thought better of it.

'Tell him to open it then!' said the red faced man and Devaux's heart sank. Rousseau appeared at the back of the crowd as another Constable arrived and pushed his way through.

'Would you mind, sir?' asked the first Constable but before Devaux could reply, the red faced man said 'open it… that'll prove it's mine, because it's got my best white shirt in it, my silk pyjamas and my blue slippers!'

'Just open the case please, sir,' said the Constable calmly and there was a moment of silence while they all waited. Devaux thought quickly about his options and decided that he would bravely face the inevitable but would not allow the motley crowd of onlookers to see the Grail. He produced his warrant card and said 'I am Captain Marcel Devaux of the French Gendarmerie in Paris. I will only open this case at the Police station in front of senior officers!' There followed a stunned silence before the Constable exclaimed 'good gracious me!'

'Well whoever you are mate… I'm coming with you!' said the red-faced man.

'Why not, Monsieur?' asked Devaux with a smile. He felt sure that he could talk his way out of the situation until the first Constable said 'we've been on the lookout for you, sir and your Sergeant.'

'Oh, really? I'm sure there must be some mistake...'

'There's no mistake, sir, now please come with us and tell your Sergeant, wherever he is, to follow on,' replied the Constable as he

224

took Devaux's arm and led him through the crowd with the other officer. Devaux nodded at Rousseau, who sighed, shook his head and followed with the red-faced man. They had only walked a few yards when a woman hurried up and called out 'Bert... Bert, I saw some blimmin' girl pick up your case when you were buying our tickets!'

'Oh blimey!' said Bert.

'I did tell you but you didn't listen as usual... so I chased after her... but the little beggar thief got away... I'm so sorry, Bert,' said the woman.

'Oh Gawd, Mildred... I thought you'd gone off to the ladies!'

'No, Bert, I didn't need to... because I went before we left home.'

Devaux turned, glared at the hapless Bert and shouted angrily 'mon Dieu... you cretin! You bloody imbecile!'

Inspector Bagley had been waiting with Sergeant Milton at the railway station since the first train had arrived from London that morning and was pleasantly surprised when a Constable informed him that the French Officers had been apprehended at the Ferry port and were now in custody.

Bagley and Milton hurried back to the Police station where Devaux and Rousseau were waiting in the interview room with the Duty Sergeant.

'Good morning gentlemen, I'm Inspector Bagley and this is Sergeant Milton.'

'Bonjour Monsieur Inspector... Sergeant' replied Devaux in a disinterested tone.

The detectives sat at the table opposite the French Officers and Bagley said 'Captain, I received a telegraph message from Inspector Hadley last night...'

'Ah, mon ami, Jim,' said Devaux with a smile.

'... who requested I hold you on suspicion of the theft of a holy relic until he arrives.'

'And knowing Jim, that will not be long, Monsieur Inspector.'

'Probably not, Captain... I presume whatever you have stolen is in one of these cases?' said Bagley as he pointed at their luggage in the corner.

'Oui, it is.'

225

'May I ask what this relic is, Captain?'

'Oui, it is the Holy Grail… and belongs to France'

Bagley and Milton looked stunned and their jaws dropped.

'The Holy Grail?' stammered Bagley.

'Oui, Monsieur.'

'But how did you…'

'It's a long story so just open my portmanteau and look for yourselves,' interrupted Devaux.

Bagley nodded at Milton who got up, retrieved the case, placed it on the table and opened it, un-wrapped the gold cup and looked at it in amazement before placing it on the table.

'My God,' whispered Bagley as he reached out to touch the gleaming vessel.

'But it is not stolen, Monsieur Inspector, it rightfully belongs to France and we were ordered by our Commissioner to return it to Paris, Jim Hadley has made a great mistake in requesting our arrest, which could be very embarrassing for him,' said Devaux firmly.

'Goodness gracious me,' said Bagley in surprise as he glanced at the Grail.

'We have been travelling down from Scotland and have had very little sleep so I would be grateful if we could have some tea and rest until Hadley arrives and explains everything to you, Monsieur.'

'Yes, yes of course, Captain… Sergeant, arrange tea and some sandwiches for our guests and then find them somewhere to rest where they won't be disturbed,' said Bagley.

'Very good, sir.'

When Milton had left the room Devaux said with a smile 'thank you, Monsieur, I will see that my Commissioner in Paris knows of your kindness and I'm sure he will comment favourably to your Commissioner at Scotland Yard, who has been assisting us.'

'Thank you, Captain,' said Bagley suitably impressed by Devaux's story while wondering what trouble awaited Hadley.

'Now after tea all we have to do is rest and wait for mon ami, Inspector Jim Hadley,' said Devaux with a smile.

When the express from Edinburgh arrived at Kings Cross just after six, Hadley waited for all the other passengers to leave the train before disembarking. As they walked along the platform Hadley was pleased to see Hanson and Sergeant Wells at the ticket barrier with a number of Constables. After the prisoners had been handed over to the Scotland Yard officers, Hadley asked Hanson 'well... have you caught those bloody Frenchmen yet?'

'No Jim, we haven't seen them!'

'Oh dear God....'

'But Inspector Bagley at Dover has!'

'Do you mean...'

'Yes, they were caught at the Ferry Port... Bagley has got them and the relic!' interrupted Hanson with a smile.

'Oh thank God for that,' gasped Hadley as Talbot smiled and said 'well what a turn up for the book, sir!'

'You can say that again, Sergeant,' said Hadley.

'When the Chief got your message, Jim, he sent Mercer and me here straight away to meet every train from Edinburgh.'

'Well thanks for that, Bob, but I guessed that they may leave the train before it arrived here and that's why I sent a telegraph to Bagley, just in case they did,' said Hadley.

'Good job that you did, Jim... Bagley telegraphed the Chief with the news and he is delighted and by all accounts, so is the Commissioner,' said Hanson.

'Well that's a relief,' said Hadley with a grin.

'So all's well that ends well,' said Hanson.

'It's not over yet, Bob, we're off to Dover now to collect those thieving French and bring them back to the Yard!' said Hadley.

'But...' began Hanson.

'Off we go, Sergeant... let's finish the job!' said Hadley.

'Right you are sir!' replied Talbot.

Outside the station they hailed a Hansom to take them to Waterloo where on arrival they checked the time of the next train to Dover. They had twenty minutes before it departed which allowed Hadley time to send a telegraph to Bagley informing him that they were on their way and to meet them.

CHAPTER 25

Bagley and Milton joined the French Officers for tea and found they were happy to discuss their adventures in Scotland. Devaux did not tell them the truth about the discovery of the Grail and they were led to believe that the Abbot at Inchaffray Priory alerted the French authorities to its existence. After Devaux and Rousseau were escorted to a rest room to sleep, along with the portmanteau containing the Grail, Bagley sent a telegraph message to the Duty Officer at Scotland Yard informing him that, following Hadley's request, the French Officers had been apprehended with the relic.

Chief Inspector Bell was delighted when he was given the news and immediately informed the Commissioner, who beamed triumphantly.

'I'll see that Hadley and his young Sergeant receive commendations for this, Chief Inspector,' said the great one.

'Yes, thank you, sir, they do deserve it,' said Bell.

'And of course it reflects well on you, Chief Inspector.'

'Oh does it, sir? '

'Yes indeed.'

'Well I'm very pleased to hear it, sir.'

'So where are they now?'

'Hadley and Talbot are travelling back from Scotland with the suspects, sir.'

'Excellent… and what news of Cooper?'

'He'll be in hospital for a few more days then he'll be back, sir.'

'That's good to hear.'

'I'm relieved that his injury wasn't more serious, sir.'

'Quite so, Chief Inspector, we need more keen young officers like Cooper.'

'We do indeed, sir.'

'As well as Hanson and Mercer, you know they all played their part in this investigation under your leadership,' said the Commissioner.

'You are too kind, sir, we're only doing our duty.'

'Yes I know, but thanks to all their efforts we now have the Holy Grail and one murderer dead and the others in custody, what a splendid outcome!'

'It is very satisfactory, sir.'

'We can inform Lord Stillwell and the Archbishop of the good news then stand down the armed officers who are guarding them.'

'Very good, sir I'll see to it right away.'

'We'll put out a press statement saying that the danger has now passed and we have the prime suspects in custody... that should make acceptable reading for London society at tomorrow's breakfast table, Chief Inspector,' said the Commissioner with a smile.

'Quite so, sir,' beamed Bell.

'I think that after I've informed the Home Secretary of our success, I'll have a leisurely lunch at my club, Chief Inspector.'

'You richly deserve it, sir if I may say so.'

'You may.'

It was eight thirty that night when Hadley and Talbot eventually arrived at Dover station and were met by Bagley.

'Good to see you again, Jim,' said Bagley with a smile.

'You too, Tony... now tell me all about the Frenchmen's arrest.'

By the time they arrived at the Police station Hadley had been told everything in detail and he smiled when he heard about the red faced man's mistake. He knew that Devaux and Rousseau had almost succeeded in boarding the Ferry and it was only by the merest chance that they were apprehended.

When the detectives entered Bagley's office, Devaux was holding court and entertaining Rousseau, Milton and the Duty Sergeant with fanciful stories about his dalliances with the nurses at Stirling hospital.

'Ah, mon ami, Jim!' said Devaux with enthusiasm as he stood up to greet Hadley and he had to grin before saying 'so we've caught you at last, Marcel.'

'Non, non, mon ami, I am not caught but just staying here whilst we sort things out!'

'That'll be the day when we ever sort you buggers out!'

'Oh, Jim, I am like an open book to you,' said Devaux with a broad smile.

'Oh how I wish that was so... now show me this relic, Marcel.'

'Oui, mon ami, it is here in my case,' said Devaux as he picked up the portmanteau and placed it on Bagley's desk. Hadley was quite amazed when he saw the golden cup and he held it in awe whilst Talbot stood in stunned silence.

'My God, no wonder they were prepared to kill for this,' Hadley whispered.

'But of course, mon ami, any man would... and I am so happy that it belongs to France!'

'Only if her Majesty's Government say so, Marcel,' replied Hadley.

'There is no doubt of its rightful ownership, Jim.'

'Well, we'll soon find out as we are leaving first thing in the morning for the Yard,' said Hadley.

'Très bien... we will quickly sort out this silly misunderstanding in London and then we can leave for Paris.'

'All in good time, Marcel.'

'Of course mon ami... now where are you taking us for dinner?' asked Devaux and Hadley smiled then shook his head.

The next morning they caught the nine o'clock train to Waterloo and arrived at Scotland Yard as Big Ben struck twelve. Hadley immediately went up to report to Bell leaving the French Officers drinking tea and discussing their adventures with Hanson, Mercer and Talbot.

'I'm glad that you're back safely, Hadley,' said Bell as he waved him to sit.

'Thank you, sir, so am I... it's been a bit of an adventure to say the least.'

'Very true... pity about Cooper though.'

'Yes sir, but he should be back with us in a few days.'

'That's good... now the Commissioner has arranged a meeting this afternoon at three o'clock with Sir George West at the Home Office.'

'Right, sir.'

'Lord Stillwell and his Grace the Archbishop will also be present.'

'Very good, sir.'

'And I understand that two learned Professors will be there to examine the Grail.'

'Am I invited to this meeting, sir?'

'Yes you are, along with Devaux, but only on the strict understanding that you both remain absolutely silent unless actually spoken to,' replied Bell 'so try to convince Devaux to mind his manners on this occasion.'

'Yes I will, sir.'

'A difficult task at the best of times I fear,' said Bell with a sigh.

'I know what you mean, sir,' said Hadley with a grin.

'How we ever put up with these foreigners I'll never know, Hadley.'

'Neither will I, sir... now do you know if Devaux will be allowed to take the Grail back to Paris?'

'That's a decision for the Minister, which will only be reached after it has been authenticated. If it turns out to be worthless then I think the answer will be 'yes', but if it is genuine then it will almost certainly remain here,' replied Bell.

'That's understandable, sir.'

'Now just to let you know, Hadley, Sinclair is still in custody but Major Fielding has been released on Police bail after threatening to sue for wrongful arrest and unlawful imprisonment.'

'I'm not surprised, sir.'

'He will be back for interview tomorrow afternoon with his solicitor, so it gives you time to prepare your line of questioning.'

'Very good, sir.'

'What are the chances of getting him convicted of murder?'

'Well, it will be difficult, sir, as we only have the confession of Doyle to link Fielding to the killings.'

'And you said in your report that he is not expected to live.'

'No, sir.'

'What about Sinclair?'

'Again, this could be difficult, I suspect him of murdering Murphy but proving it will be almost impossible, sir.'

'Probably so... unless he confesses, Hadley.'

'I think that's highly unlikely, sir.'

'Well do your best to get him to admit to his crime when you interview him.'

'Of course, sir.'

'Now go and start to prepare a detailed written report for me and be back here at two thirty with Devaux,' said Bell.

'Very good, sir.'

'The Commissioner wants to see the Grail and have a few words with us before we leave for the Home Office.'

Over a lunch of cheese and ham sandwiches along with several cups of George's tea, the detectives discussed the events in Scotland before Hadley began writing his notes for George to type. Devaux was anxious to attend the meeting at three o'clock and proclaim the Grail belonged to France, although Hadley warned him not to say anything unless asked.

'But I discovered it, mon ami, so surely I have the right to tell them it belongs to France!'

'Listen to me, Marcel, I know how their minds work and you will only make things difficult for yourself if you dare utter one word!' said Hadley firmly and Devaux shrugged his shoulders and pouted.

Just before two thirty they arrived at Bell's office and after he gave Devaux a cursory, frosty greeting, led them up to the Commissioner's office.

The great one looked at them in turn and said 'gentlemen, as you are aware we have a meeting with very important dignitaries at the Home Office, so I will not tolerate any unsolicited and un-necessary comments from any of you.'

'That's quite understandable, sir,' said Bell.

'You are there as witnesses and only speak if asked, is that clear?'

'Of course, sir,' replied Bell and Hadley, while Devaux just smiled.

'I'm glad that's understood… now let me see this holy relic that has caused such mayhem, Captain.'

Devaux placed the portmanteau on the Commissioner's desk and produced the golden chalice from the cloth wrappings.

'My God… what a wonderful thing it is to behold,' whispered the Commissioner as Devaux handed the Grail to him. The great one remained in awestruck silence as he gazed at the chalice until Brackley entered and said 'it's time for you to go, sir.'

On arrival at the Home Office they were escorted up to Sir George

West's office where Lord Stillwell, the Archbishop of Canterbury and two elderly gentlemen were already seated at a long table. Sir George introduced the Commissioner and allowed him to present Bell, Hadley and Devaux before Sir George invited them to sit at the far end. The two gentlemen were introduced as Sir Crispin Fitzmaurice, curator of religious artefacts at the British Museum and Professor Hector Bullivant, head of medieval history at the Victoria and Albert Museum. When they were all settled, Devaux was asked by the Commissioner to produce the Grail and give it to the Archbishop. When he un-wrapped the chalice and placed it before his Grace, they all gasped at its beauty.

'This is a truly divine moment,' said the Archbishop as he picked up the chalice, held it high and gazed at it.

'Quite so, your Grace, it is indeed very moving,' whispered Lord Stillwell.

'Thank God that we have it in our possession now,' said the Archbishop and Hadley glanced at Devaux who looked as if he were about to burst with indignation.

'May I examine it now, your Grace?' asked Sir Crispin.

'Of course,' he replied and he passed it to the curator who produced an eye glass from his top pocket and began to peer at the chalice. After a few minutes of careful observation he handed it to Professor Bullivant sitting opposite and turned to Devaux asking 'where did you discover this cup, Captain?'

'It was being held for safekeeping at the Priory of Inchaffray near Crieff in Scotland, Monsieur.'

'I see... do you know if it had been at the Priory for a long time?' asked Sir Crispin.

'I am not sure, Monsieur,' lied Devaux.

'Hmm,' murmured Sir Crispin before he asked Bullivant 'what's your first impression, Professor?'

'Well at first glance I'd say that it is not more than seven hundred years old,' replied Bullivant and they all gasped.

Sir Crispin nodded and said 'I must agree with you... '

'What are you saying gentlemen?' interrupted the Archbishop anxiously.

'Your Grace, it is very similar to many medieval French Catholic artefacts that were made in the eleventh and twelfth centuries for display on the magnificent altars of their splendid

Cathedrals,' replied Sir Crispin.

'It is very beautiful and extremely well made… it truly reflects the superb craftsmanship of the French at that time,' added Bullivant and Devaux smiled.

'Are… are you both absolutely sure?' asked the Archbishop in shocked disbelief.

'I think we are agreed, your Grace, and subject to some minor tests to confirm it's actual date, I can say with some certainty that it is not more than seven hundred years old and therefore cannot be the Holy Grail,' said Sir Crispin.

There was a collective gasp from everyone followed by total momentary silence before Devaux asked 'so may I take it to Paris now, Messieurs?'

Sir George cleared his throat, glanced at the Archbishop who gave a slight nod and replied 'after the test to confirm it's date, Captain, you will be free to return to France with it, provided it is not stolen property.'

'Merci beaucoup, Monsieur.'

The Commissioner dismissed Bell, Hadley and Devaux while he remained to discuss the investigation with Sir George and the distinguished guests. As the detectives walked along Whitehall towards the Yard, Hadley said to Devaux 'you don't seem to be concerned that relic is not genuine, Marcel.'

'I'm not concerned, mon ami, because I think your experts are wrong,' replied Devaux with a smile and Bell scoffed then shook his head.

'You French are incorrigible!' said Hadley with a grin.

When they arrived back at the Yard, Bell asked Hadley to come to his office whilst Devaux hurried off to tell Rousseau the good news that they would be returning to Paris with the Grail.

Chief Inspector Bell slumped in his chair, sighed and looked hard at Hadley before he said 'now that this adventure with the relic and bloody French is over I must remind you that we have important work to do, Hadley!'

'I realise that, sir.'

'I hope you do, because we have on our hands five murders to investigate with two prime suspects, one of which is threatening to sue for wrongful arrest, two villains shot by Talbot, one dead and the other seriously wounded and Cooper in hospital!'

'I am aware of absolutely everything, sir and do not need to be reminded!' replied Hadley angrily.

'I'm very pleased to hear it!' said Bell angrily.

'Good, sir.'

'So I suggest that you get started on the paperwork right now and prepare to interview the suspects.'

'I will, sir.'

'You realise the Commissioner will not tolerate any dilly dallying delay now that the relic is proved to be just a French altar piece,' said Bell firmly.

'I'm sure he won't, sir.'

'Go to it then and let's have your detailed report before you leave tonight,' said Bell and Hadley nodded.

Whilst Hadley and Talbot continued writing up their report, the French Officers went for a relaxing walk along the Embankment in the late afternoon sunshine. While George was busy typing the report, Hadley and Talbot went down to Custody to question Sinclair. In the interview room the priest complained bitterly about his treatment before he went over the events leading up to his arrest. He stated that as God was his witness he had nothing to do with the murder of Murphy. He was more reticent about the Grail and when told that it was a twelfth century French altar chalice he looked positively shocked. The detectives left Sinclair to consider his situation overnight and returned to the office.

Big Ben was striking six o'clock when Hadley read the typed report, signed it and took it up to the Chief Inspector. As he placed the buff folder on his desk, Bell said with a smile 'a day of revelation I do believe, Hadley.'

'Indeed, sir.'

'Let's hope that tomorrow's interview with Fielding produces something significant that the Crown Prosecution can work with.'

'Yes, sir, but I think that in his case a conviction will be difficult,' said Hadley.

'Hmm... probably... but we must try.'

'Of course, sir.'

'What about Sinclair?'

235

'He denies murdering Murphy but he now has to think about his circumstances, he looked very shocked when I told him the relic was a twelfth century French chalice.'

'I'm sure he was... but that may be the surprising jolt of information that makes him crack, Hadley.'

'Let's hope so, sir.'

'I expect you're going home now for an early night... you look as if you need it.'

'Yes sir... but I plan to call on Mrs Cooper on my way and tell her what has happened to her husband.'

'Ah, that's very good of you, Hadley.'

'And with your permission, sir, I propose to send her up to Stirling to see him and bring him back safely when he's discharged from hospital.'

'Yes indeed, it's the least we can do.'

'Thank you, sir.'

Alice had tears of joy and relief in her eyes when Hadley arrived at their comfortable home that evening.

'Oh my dear husband, you look so tired,' she said, kissing him several times.

'I am my dear... I really am.'

CHAPTER 26

Hadley was at his desk by eight o'clock the next morning and Talbot arrived minutes later. George made tea and the detectives planned the day ahead whilst drinking the hot reviver. Hadley prepared his questions for Fielding and was just about to interview Sinclair again when a telegraph arrived from MacKay informing him that Cooper would be discharged in two days and Doyle was now out of danger and making a slow recovery.

'This is good news all round, Sergeant.'

'Indeed it is, sir, it'll be good to have Bob back.'

'Yes of course and if Doyle makes a full recovery then he might be persuaded to turn Queen's evidence and help us nail Fielding,' said Hadley.

'We can only hope, sir.'

'We must do our best to persuade him, Sergeant.'

'Yes, sir.'

Hadley sent a telegraph to MacKay asking him to book a comfortable room for Cooper and his wife at the Falkirk Hotel for the day he left hospital. Hadley planned that Mrs Cooper would travel up to Stirling the day her husband was to be discharged and stay overnight before travelling back the next morning. Hadley wrote a note to Mrs Cooper advising her of the good news and sent it by Police messenger to their home.

When Hadley had Sinclair brought from his cell for interview he was surprised by the priest's demeanour, he looked pale and totally forlorn. He slumped down on the chair across the table from the detectives and sighed pathetically.

'Are you un-well, Father?' asked Hadley and Sinclair just shook his head and gazed at his clasped hands. Hadley glanced at Talbot who raised his eyebrows.

'Would you like to see our Doctor?'

'No, my son, I am now beyond all earthly help,' replied Sinclair as tears began to course down his cheeks.

'Would you like some time to compose yourself?'

'There is no need for more time for anything, my son, as I have

237

sinned dreadfully and now will face my maker stained with the blood of another man on my hands... may God forgive me!' he wailed then sobbed.

'Compose yourself, Father.'

'I have prayed all night for God's guidance and know what I must do now.'

Hadley and Talbot were taken aback for a moment but quickly regained their presence of mind and Hadley asked 'then do you confess to the unlawful murder of Father Murphy?' The priest nodded as he sobbed and Hadley looked at Talbot who smiled triumphantly.

'Please tell us in your own time what happened, Father,' said Hadley calmly.

'I murdered this holy brother in a moment of madness, blind, dreadful madness... over a worthless relic that I believed was the Holy Grail,' said Sinclair and he sobbed again. Hadley realised that the priest was in no state to continue with the interview so he sent Talbot out for the Duty Doctor.

'I think it would be advisable for our Doctor to see you and perhaps give you something to help you to sleep and we will talk later when you have recovered,' said Hadley and Sinclair nodded. Within minutes Talbot returned and said 'the Doctor's on his way, sir.'

'Thank you, Sergeant, please escort Father Sinclair back to his cell.'

'Very good, sir.'

Hadley immediately went up to the Chief's office and reported to Bell that Sinclair had confessed to the murder of Murphy.

'That's excellent news, Hadley, now we can hang him without the palaver of a long and un-necessary trial!' exclaimed Bell with a triumphant smile.

'Yes, sir.'

'Only Fielding to go now, eh, Hadley?'

'Yes, sir.'

'And if we can get him to confess to his cruel misdeeds we can close the investigation and leave everything to the Crown Prosecution and the hangman.'

'Indeed we can, sir and I can also report that Inspector MacKay telegraphed me to say that Cooper will be discharged in two days time...'

'I'm pleased to hear it,' interrupted Bell.

'And that Doyle is recovering and I believe that we may be able to turn him to Queen's evidence, which would ensure Fielding's conviction.'

'It couldn't be better, Hadley... the Commissioner will be delighted with all this good news.'

'I'm sure he will be, sir.'

'He's been under a lot of strain over this case you know,' said Bell.

'We all have, sir.'

'Yes... and it has been made worse by the presence of the French and their worthless trinket... thank heavens they'll be leaving soon!'

'I'm sure they will be pleased to return to Paris, sir.'

'Yes... well get along now and prepare a full written report on everything, Hadley, we must have it all in writing, it's the backbone of good, modern policing and you can never have too much paperwork these days.'

'If you say so, sir.'

'I do say so... it makes us more efficient in these hard pressed financial times,' said Bell and Hadley nodded as he left the office.

Over a lunch of cheese sandwiches and tea with Talbot, Hadley put the final touches to his notes for the interview with Fielding and his solicitor. They were alone in the office as the French Officers had decided to go on a sightseeing tour of London whilst they waited for the dating tests to be carried out on the Grail by Sir Crispin and Professor Bullivant.

Big Ben was striking two o'clock when a messenger came up from reception and advised Hadley that Major Fielding had arrived with his solicitor and were now waiting in an interview room.

'Now let's see what he has to say for himself, Sergeant,' said Hadley.

'It'll be interesting, sir.'

'Indeed it will... George, please bring plenty of paper, pens and ink.'

'Right you are, sir.'

When Hadley entered the interview room with Talbot and George he instantly recognised Fielding's solicitor.

'Afternoon Inspector,' said Fielding in an abrupt tone.

'Good afternoon, Major.'

'May I present my solicitor, Mr Morton Barrymore of Olivier and Barrymore from Holborn?'

'Yes, Major… we have met before,' replied Hadley.

'Indeed we have Inspector,' said Barrymore with a smile.

After they were all seated and George was ready with his pen poised to record the interview, Barrymore said 'Inspector Hadley, let me state at the very outset that my client denies all the charges levelled against him and will be seeking formal apologies from the Commissioner in writing, a Press statement to that effect and a substantial financial payment from the Metropolitan Police for his distress, wrongful arrest and unlawful imprisonment caused by this whole fiasco!'

Hadley remained silent for a few moments for effect and then said calmly 'Major Fielding is facing serious charges that I intend to prove and he will be appearing in court at a date to be advised, Mr Barrymore.'

'This is all bloody nonsense, Hadley and you know it!' shouted Fielding.

'Please control your client, Mr Barrymore and instruct him to answer my questions,' said Hadley.

'Yes… yes, Inspector… Major, for your own good you must be composed and answer the questions calmly…'

'The hell I will, sir!' interrupted Fielding.

Barrymore glared at Fielding and said firmly 'if you persist with this belligerent attitude, Major, I will be forced to withdraw my professional assistance and leave you free to appoint another solicitor.' Hadley smiled whilst Fielding looked chastened and lowered his head before mumbling 'very well then… but do get on with it.'

Despite Hadley's intense questioning, Fielding denied all knowledge of the holy relic or employing Doyle and Tyler, insisting that he was on leave in Scotland with Sefton for deer hunting when Hadley found him at Drummond Castle. Fielding claimed that he was deeply shocked when he was informed of Sefton's murder and could only assume that either Tyler or Doyle had killed his brother officer. Hadley did not believe him for one moment and said so, much to Barrymore's consternation.

When Hadley said the interview was over Fielding looked relieved but paled when Hadley told him that he was going to question Doyle in hospital now that the villain had recovered sufficiently from his gunshot wound.

'Is that really necessary, Inspector? I mean the fellow is a murderous, deranged villain and was shot down by your Sergeant here whilst trying to escape… surely you can't believe anything a man like that says,' said Fielding.

'Major, we leave no stone unturned when investigating murder,' replied Hadley before adding 'we will be in touch for further interviews that you will be required to attend under your bail conditions… good afternoon.'

Returning to the office, Hadley made some notes whilst George began typing up the interview for the report that would go up to the Chief.

Big Ben was striking four o'clock when Mr Jenkins entered the office and said 'the Chief Inspector would like to see you, sir.'

'Very well, Mr Jenkins.'

When Hadley entered Bell's office the Chief was smiling broadly and waved him to sit.

'I've just come from the Commissioner and he is delighted with the news so far.'

'I'm pleased to hear it, sir.'

'So how did the interview with Fielding go? Have we got a confession from him yet?'

'I'm afraid not, sir, in fact quite the reverse, because he denies everything and claims that he is totally innocent,' replied Hadley.

'Well we know he's not!'

'Quite so, sir but proving it in court will be difficult and almost impossible if he retains a top barrister to defend him, as I'm sure he will.'

'We can't let him get away with his crimes… so what next,

Hadley?'

'I think it would be a very good idea for me to talk to Doyle and try to get him to turn Queen's evidence, sir.'

'That would mean another trip to Scotland, Hadley.'

'But worth it if Doyle's evidence convicts Fielding, sir,' said Hadley and Bell leaned back in his chair, gazing at the ceiling for inspiration.

'You could be right, Hadley… travel up as soon as possible.'

'Thank you, sir, I thought I might accompany Mrs Cooper…'

'But she is not going for a day or so!' interrupted Bell.

'I know that, sir, but it would give Doyle more time to recover… besides I have a lot of paperwork to do regarding Sinclair's confession,' said Hadley with a smile.

'Yes… yes, of course you do, so travel up with Mrs Cooper and make sure that Doyle turns Queen's evidence so we can hang Fielding after his trial,' said Bell firmly.

'I will do my best, sir.'

The French Officers had returned from their sightseeing trip and were drinking tea with Talbot when Hadley arrived in his office. They were buoyant as usual and only settled down when Hadley explained what had happened at the interviews with Sinclair and Fielding.

'Mon Dieu… you have got them both, mon ami!'

'Not quite, Marcel, but after I've been to see Doyle then perhaps we can get Fielding convicted,' said Hadley.

'Très bien, now we will wait until you return with Cooper so we can celebrate together with the ladies,' said Devaux.

'But don't you want to get back to Paris with the Grail, Marcel?'

'Of course, mon ami, but those two old fossils from the museums who are looking at it will be a few days yet, besides I have telegraphed my Commissioner and informed him that we found the Grail for France and it is safe,' replied Devaux and Hadley smiled as Talbot chuckled.

Hadley sent a telegraph to MacKay informing him that he would be accompanying Mrs Cooper and requesting he book a room at the Falkirk Hotel for him and also advising that he wished to interview Doyle in his presence. He sent a short note to Doris

Cooper telling her that he would now travel to Scotland with her.

The next day Sinclair had recovered sufficiently to be interviewed again and as he was resigned to his fate he told Hadley everything. George took the notes while the priest recounted all the events that led to the murder of Murphy. It started when Professor Pennington wrote to Sinclair requesting him to look through his church records for any mention of a holy relic being brought from France by Knight's Templar in medieval times and held at a Scottish castle. Sinclair discovered some obscure entries which led him to believe that the relic was the Holy Grail and hidden at one of three castles, Drummond, Culcreuch or Doune. He believed that Drummond was the most likely place, so he searched it first and discovered the chalice, which he hid in the crypt at Saint Mary's. He received a letter from Porter about the relic, which alarmed him and shortly afterwards Porter came to see him. Sinclair realised that Porter was only interested in a reward and so would be helpful in assisting him to transport the chalice to the Vatican. Sinclair became aware of a rumour that others were searching for the chalice and when Murphy arrived un-expectedly it confirmed his fears. When Murphy told him that he had been instructed by Cardinal Charnay at Toulouse to recover the chalice and take it to Rome, Sinclair had been incensed with jealous rage and during a violent argument he grabbed Murphy by the throat and accidentally strangled him. He panicked and removed all traces of identity from Murphy but carelessly dropped the list of castles by the body.

Doyle and Tyler arrived demanding to know where the relic was hidden and kidnapped him, proposing to exact its whereabouts by torture. Sinclair stated that he did not know whether Doyle and Tyler were acting alone or under orders from someone else. Hadley believed him and when the priest had finished his confession he looked quite relieved.

'Now I have told you everything, Inspector, I can face my maker with an untroubled and clear mind,' said Sinclair with a smile before he was returned to his cell.

After completing a long report Hadley went home and had a quiet evening with Alice and the children, followed by a restful night.

He was looking forward to the journey up to Stirling with Doris Cooper and hoped it would bring a good result. The next day he collected her in a Police coach and they were driven to Kings Cross to catch the nine o'clock express to Edinburgh. Doris was a petite, shy young woman but she soon relaxed with Hadley and was put at ease as he talked about his family and friends. The journey seemed to pass quite quickly and the train arrived on time at four o'clock in the afternoon. MacKay was waiting to meet them when they arrived at Stirling. The Police coach took them to the Infirmary where Mrs Cooper was re-united with her husband. Hadley was delighted to see his Sergeant looking so well after the trauma of being shot and following relieved smiles, kisses and tears from Doris, the happy couple left for the Hotel.

Hadley discussed the investigation with MacKay bringing him up to date with Sinclair's confession and Fielding's denial before they went into the side ward, guarded by two Constables, to speak to Doyle. The Duty Doctor informed them that the patient had made a speedy and quite remarkable recovery, was now sitting up and eating well.

Doyle looked anxious when the detectives entered the room but Hadley put the villain at ease when he said with a smile 'Mr Doyle, I think that we may be able to help one another.'

'Oh... how is that, guvnor?'

'Let me put a proposition to you that will undoubtedly save you from the gallows,' replied Hadley as he sat at Doyle's bedside.

'I'm listening, guvnor.'

'I would like you to consider turning Queen's evidence and telling me all that you know about Major Fielding's involvement in this violent murder conspiracy,' said Hadley as MacKay sat down beside him and took out a notebook.

'I dunno what that means, guvnor.'

'It means, Mr Doyle, that you will be absolutely free of any prosecution if you admit to your part in the conspiracy and give all the facts to the court.'

'So, if I do this I won't blimmin' hang?'

'No you won't,' replied Hadley with a smile.

'But how can I trust you?'

'Only you can decide that, Mr Doyle, but what I can tell you is that at the moment you are the prime suspect for the murders of the Porter brothers, Professor Pennington and Captain Sefton…'

'Tyler killed them not me!' interrupted Doyle.

'Tyler is now dead… so you are the only villain who is left to be hanged… and you certainly will be,' said Hadley.

'What about the Major?'

'He'll get off Scot free.'

'Why's that?'

'Because he has denied everything and claims that you and Tyler acted alone…'

'Well he's a blimmin' liar!'

'I'm sure he is, but without your help I doubt if I can prove it and whilst you hang he'll be free to carry on as usual.' Doyle thought for a moment, looked at Hadley and said 'right, guvnor, I'll trust you and do it!'

'I'm very pleased to hear it and when you are well enough to travel you will be brought to London and meet the Prosecution Barrister who will present the case to the court.'

'Will he ask me lots of questions, guvnor?'

'He will… but don't worry because I'll be there to help you.'

'That's good to know.'

'Now tell me everything so I can prepare a report.'

Once Doyle started telling his story, MacKay could hardly keep up writing his notes. It seemed as if the villain was now free of all constraints and the information just poured out.

Doyle met Tyler in The Ten Bells pub in Whitechapel a year ago when Tyler was on leave from the army. They got on quite well although Doyle saw that the man was prone to violence as he had several fights outside the pub when he was drunk. Two months ago, when Tyler was on leave, he met up with Doyle and told him that he needed someone he could trust to help him search for a relic in Scotland. Doyle said he was suspicious at first but when Tyler told him the sum of money he was prepared to pay for his services, he could not refuse, he was out of work and had a family to feed. Tyler never told him what the relic was but said that they had to find out from various people where this relic was hidden. It started with William Porter who Tyler knew from his service with the 4th Hussars. They had both been on deployment in Afghanistan under Major Fielding's command and Tyler admitted that the Major was behind the quest for the relic, along with Captain Sefton. Doyle said he was alarmed at Tyler's behaviour when they called at Porter's lodgings and tied him up.

'He was like some blimmin' madman, guvnor and told Billy that if he didn't tell him where it was hidden he'd skin him alive. Well, I could hardly believe what he was saying but as Gawd's my witness, he produced a skinning knife and started to cut Billy up… it was 'orrible and I had to go outside and wait until he'd finished.'

'Did you realise that Porter was dead?' asked Hadley.

'Oh yes, guvnor, there was no mistaking that, when Tyler called me to help him search Billy's room I could see that the poor fella was past it.'

'Go on.'

'After that we went to his brother's place in Whitechapel because Tyler thought he may have told him where his relic was hidden but the poor bugger didn't know and I think Tyler just cut him up because he enjoyed it… he told me that he learned how to do it from some bloody Afghan hill men.'

'Dear God,' whispered MacKay.

'Please continue,' said Hadley.

'One night we had to wait for the Major outside his house, so he could tell us what to do next, but Tyler spoke to him privately so I didn't know what was said.'

'Then what happened?'

'We called on Billy Porter's parents and took them to an old coal barge at Limehouse where we tied them up and Tyler threatened them if they didn't say where this blimmin' relic was, but they obviously didn't know, so we left them.'

'Tell me about your visit to Oxford.'

'We travelled up there and saw some Professor who Tyler said knew where this relic was but the old boy said he didn't, so after we tied him up Tyler skinned him while I waited outside in the coach, believe me guvnor, I couldn't stand seeing it and I was so blimmin' scared of Tyler, he was a bloody monster!'

'He was indeed.'

'Then we met Captain Sefton, he was a proper gent, he told Tyler to meet him in Scotland at some castle after calling on a priest who knew where this relic was hidden. So we did that, but the priest told us that he didn't know what we were talking about, so we took him with us and chained him up at the castle... and when your Bobbies arrived we were really scared... Tyler knew you were on to us and he wanted to kill them.'

'It was fortunate that you didn't.'

'Right... and I was blimmin' glad when we found out that they'd escaped.'

'Please continue.'

'Tyler shot the other Bobbie who was with you, sir,' said Doyle glancing at MacKay.

'Ay, I know that.'

'How is he?'

'Making good progress I'm pleased to say,' replied MacKay.

'Good... by then the Major had arrived and told Tyler to kill the Captain... I couldn't believe it when he did it...'

'Why did the Major want him dead?'

'I dunno guvnor, but I was there when he told Tyler to do it,' replied Doyle.

'Did anything significant happen after that?'

'Not really, we were having a meeting with the Major at the castle when you arrived and shot us... so here I am and the Doctor says I'm lucky to be alive!'

'Indeed you are, Mr Doyle,' said Hadley with a smile.

The detectives left the Infirmary and went back to the Police station where they discussed Doyle's statement and MacKay promised that he would have it typed up for Hadley by the morning. Hadley joined Cooper and his wife at the Falkirk Hotel and enjoyed a relaxed dinner with them before retiring to his room, quite content with the days' events.

CHAPTER 27

Two days after Hadley had arrived back from Scotland and Cooper had returned to the Yard for light duties, the Grail was brought back from the British Museum. The French Officers were delighted and the portmanteau containing the Grail was handed over to Devaux by the Home Secretary in the Commissioner's office.

'Now that you have the chalice I presume you'll be leaving for Paris today, Captain?' asked Sir George.

'Non, Monsieur, we will leave tomorrow, because tonight we have to celebrate with Inspector Hadley and his Sergeants,' replied Devaux with a smile. The Commissioner and Sir George exchanged glances and the Commissioner raised his eyebrows then shook his head despairingly.

Sir George cleared his throat and said 'well, Captain, on behalf of Her Majesty's Government, I wish you a pleasant evening and a safe return to Paris with your holy relic.'

'Merci beaucoup, Monsieur.'

After Devaux had left the Commissioner's office, Sir George said 'I've had the report from Sir Crispin and Professor Bullivant... they both agree that the chalice was made in the twelfth century probably for the Cathedral at Chartres where apparently there is a record of a similar altar piece.'

'Then despite their fanciful claims, the report confirms that our French friends do not have the Holy Grail,' said the Commissioner with a smile.

'Precisely, Commissioner, I'm afraid they are deluding themselves!'

'Ah... the predictable weakness of the French.'

The Kings Head was as busy as ever when the Officers arrived and pushed their way to the bar. Vera smiled, tidied her scraggly hair and said to Hadley 'it's good to see you back, guvnor.'

'It's good to be back, Vera.'

'It certainly is,' added Cooper.

'I thought you'd all gone off and left us,' she said as she began to pull the first pint of stout.

'We'd never do that,' replied Hadley.

'Never!' said Talbot.

'And where we would go for a meal at night?' asked Cooper with a smile.

'I dunno... but I see you've brought the 'andsome French fellas back again,' said Vera with a coy smile as she placed the foaming pint on the wet counter.

'We have come all the way from Paris just to see you again, Madame,' said Devaux with a smile and Hadley laughed while his Sergeants grinned.

'Oh, have you now?' asked Vera with a smirk.

'Oui, Madame, and I must ask you... are you still married?'

'I'm afraid so, my love.''

'Ah... such a pity,' said Devaux with a shake of his head.

'Why's that?'

'I was hoping to tempt you away to Paris with me... but only if you were free, Madame.'

'Well I will be after closing time tonight, deary,' Vera replied with a smile as she placed another pint on the counter.

'Mon Dieu! What about your husband?'

'He can stay here and look after the blimmin' pub,' replied Vera.

'Good for him because someone's got to!' said Hadley as Devaux's face paled.

Vera grinned and said 'that's what I say... now, gents... before I'm rushed off to Paris, what's it to be to eat tonight?'

'What's tasty and hot?' asked Hadley.

'Well after me, guvnor, there's steak and kidney pie with mash and thick gravy or shepherd's pie... what d'you fancy?'

While they decided, Vera finished pulling the pints of stout before she took their order and disappeared out to the kitchen.

'Well here's to you, Marcel ... Michel,' said Hadley as he raised his glass to them.

'Merci beaucoup, mon amis... mes amis,' replied Devaux nodding at the Sergeants.

They had just placed their glasses down on the counter when Agnes and Florrie arrived. As soon as the women spotted the detectives at the bar they pushed through the crowd of drinkers and Agnes flung her arms round Hadley whilst Florrie did the same to Cooper.

'Oh, Jim... we were so worried about you both,' said Agnes before she kissed him.

'We survived and what's more... we're here to prove it,' said Hadley with a smile.

'But we read in the papers that our Bobby blue eyes was shot,' said Agnes, glancing at Cooper.

'I was, but it wasn't too serious,' said Cooper.

'Well thank Gawd for that!' said Florrie before she kissed him.

'I was wounded in my ankle... so do I get a kiss, Mademoiselle?' asked Devaux.

'Of course...' began Agnes but Vera interrupted saying 'leave him alone, Agnes Cartwright... he's all mine!' The detectives laughed whilst Agnes looked confused then Vera added with a grin 'he's taking me off to Paris after he's had his shepherd's pie!'

Agnes and Florrie were invited to join them in the back room for dinner and were very happy to do so. They listened to the events in Scotland with open mouths and Devaux exaggerated the part he played in the adventure whilst Hadley smiled and his Sergeants grinned. The detectives relaxed and enjoyed the celebrations that night and were more than a little drunk when they left the Kings Head at midnight to make their way home.

The next morning, after being revived by several cups of George's strong, sweet tea, the detectives accompanied the French Officers to Waterloo station where, after fond farewells, they boarded the ten o'clock train to Dover with Devaux clutching the portmanteau tightly.

A week later, Doyle was discharged from the Stirling Infirmary and brought under guard to Scotland Yard, where he remained in protective custody. The Barrister for the prosecution of Major Fielding was none other than Sir Rupert Fitz-Simmons of Middle Temple, who interviewed Doyle at length in the presence of Hubert Berkeley, the Yard's Duty solicitor and Hadley.

Major Fielding had retained Sir Digby Frobisher, London's leading Barrister, as his defence advocate at his trial.

The Press were in a frenzy of anticipation regarding the impending legal battle calling it 'the trial of the century', which did not please the Commissioner who wanted to see a guilty verdict after a short trial, with far less Press speculation.

During this short intervening period, Hanson and Mercer tracked down the Wang brothers and arrested them along with several Malays. After intense questioning, it transpired that the old coal barge, used by Tyler and Doyle to question the Porter's, had been used as an opium store by the brothers and Tyler knew about it. He had been trading with the Wang brothers and arranging regular shipments of opium from connections that he made when serving in Afghanistan. Doyle denied all knowledge of Tyler's involvement in the opium trade and he was believed. The Wang brothers were charged and brought to court where they were found guilty of opium smuggling, supplying drugs and the attempted murder of Police Officers. They were each imprisoned for ten years whilst the Malays were sentenced to various terms after which they were all ordered to be deported.

Hadley received a welcome telegraph from MacKay informing him that the missing Police coach and a large stage coach had been discovered in a disused barn at Balloch. According to the farmer, two men had rented the barn for a month and paid cash in advance.

Hadley was pleased to learn that Sergeant Melrose had recovered well from his injury, had been discharged from the Infirmary and was back on light duties.

At Major Fielding's trial he pleaded not guilty to all charges against him and then Sir Rupert began his prosecution. To commence the proceedings, Hadley gave the court an accurate and incisive account of the whole investigation. There were gasps of disbelief from the jury at various moments of danger, culminating in the shooting of Cooper and the response of Talbot to the violent killers at Drummond Castle. The Sergeants were called and gave accounts of their part in the investigation. Doyle was then summoned to the witness box and answered truthfully all the questions put to him by Sir Rupert, which incriminated Fielding as the instigator of the whole affair. The Barrister concluded by saying to the jury that Fielding was guilty as charged and should suffer the consequences of his premeditated actions.

For the defence, Sir Digby questioned all of the prosecution witnesses with relentless vigour and reduced Doyle to a stammering, nervous wreck, so much so that he had to be helped from the court at the end of the interrogation. Sir Digby addressed the jury and stated that there was not one shred of evidence against his client only a tissue of lies from a murderous villain trying to implicate his client in a web of deceit. The Barrister stated that Fielding was a respected army officer who came from a long line of military gentlemen who had served the country well and with gallantry. The Major, under cross examination, said that he knew nothing about the holy relic that Doyle alluded to in his statement. Fielding did admit that there were rumours circulating within the Hussars that at the time of the peninsular war in Spain, French speaking officers under Wellington's command were deployed as spies and sent across the Pyrenees to infiltrate the south of France to discover Napoleon's intentions. The rumour was that a holy relic of some significance had been brought from the Holy Land by the Knight Templar's to the south of France and one of Wellington's officers had discovered that it had been taken to Scotland. Fielding suggested that this rumour had prompted Tyler to seek an accomplice and commit terrible murder to discover the whereabouts of this mysterious relic.

At the end of the gruelling trial Sir Digby Frobisher demanded a verdict of not guilty to be returned and the release of his client without a stain on his character.

The impassive Old Bailey judge, Lord Manningham, instructed the jury as to the salient points of the case and told them to disregard the wild Press speculation surrounding the trial before they retired to consider their verdict

Chief Inspector Bell was with Hadley and his Sergeants when the jury returned a day later. They had deliberated and found Major Fielding not guilty of the charges of conspiracy to murder and kidnap but guilty of perverting of the course of justice because he had sought to mislead the Police investigation. The Major was stunned and looked appealingly at Sir Digby who shook his head.

Lord Manningham then sentenced Fielding to five years imprisonment, which was greeted by gasps from the public gallery.

The Major shouted out 'I am innocent! Innocent I tell you!' before he was led down to the cells. Bell looked at Hadley and said 'I'm not surprised that he got off so lightly... he is a man with money and the right connections.'

'Indeed he is, sir.'

Immediately after the trial Doyle was freed, he thanked Hadley and Cooper for all their help and forgave Talbot for shooting him. He told them that he had decided to take his family to Canada, where his brother had a small timber business and start a new life working for him, far away from the dreadful past. The detectives were pleased to hear that he wanted to make amends and wished him good luck in the future.

The trial of Andrew Sinclair was an open and shut affair and despite pleading mitigating circumstances by his Barrister, Oswald Dingle-Smith, the judge had no alternative but to sentence the priest to death by hanging after he readily confessed his guilt to the murder of Father Murphy. The sentence was carried out two weeks later at Pentonville Prison and his body was buried within the boundary of the Prison.

Hadley, Cooper and Talbot were awarded commendations for their bravery and the Commissioner was all smiles at the presentation. Chief Inspector Bell was delighted as it reflected positively on him while Hanson and Mercer were pleased to have been praised highly by the Commissioner for their part in the complex investigation.

After the ceremony the detectives returned to the office where George had a fresh pot of tea waiting for them. When he came in with the tray he said to Hadley 'sir, on my way in this morning I took the liberty of buying some dainties from my local bakery as a little celebration for all that you've achieved.'

'Why thank you, George, that is very kind of you,' said Hadley with a smile.

'It's my pleasure, sir.'

Hadley nodded, looked at his Sergeants and said 'well thank heavens it's all over, gentlemen, and we can now enjoy a spot of well earned leave.'

'It's a relief and no mistake, sir,' said Cooper.

'It blimmin' well is,' added Talbot.

'Yes indeed... but I shall be sorry to lose you Sergeant.'

'Thank you, sir, it's been something extraordinary working with you again,' replied Talbot with a grin.

'I'm sure there will be other occasions in the future when I need some heavy artillery!' replied Hadley with a smile.

'I will always be ready and look forward to it, sir.'

'Good... now I think I'll have one of George's dainties... the pink one looks very tasty!'

Follow Hadley and Cooper in the mysterious case of

THE DIPLOMAT MURDERS

Lightning Source UK Ltd.
Milton Keynes UK
176318UK00002B/1/P